Stasia Black

HUNTER
A STUD RANCH ROMANCE

STASIA BLACK

ISBN: [--]
ISBN 13: [---]

HUNTER

Stasia Black

Note to Readers about Name Change:

Please note that I've changed Tom Dawkins' name to Hunter Dawkins in this novel. I've since gone back and changed it in newer versions of The Virgin and the Beast, but if you read one the original, I wanted to explain so you aren't confused!

It was only after I finished and hit 'publish' on The Virgin and the Beast that I realized there might be more to the story than had fit in one book. Tom, the veterinarian for example. What happened to him in his unhappy marriage? The more I thought and daydreamed about these characters, the more I realized there was a whole universe to explore. And lots of brooding, sexy men with stories to tell :) Since each book is loosely structured around a particular fairytale, though, I wanted to change Tom's name to Hunter.

Mirror mirror on the wall, who's the fairest of them all?

Chapter 1
ISOBEL

VANESSA TO JASON: *Did you break up with her yet?*

VANESSA TO JASON: *I know her dad just died but thats not yr fault. We deserve to be :)*

Jason's cum was still inside Isobel when she read the messages on his phone. He was showering after they'd had sex.

They'd been dating for three years. Long distance for the past year since Isobel had come back to the city to be close to her dad after he got the diagnosis. Pancreatic cancer. The doctor gave him six months to live. He made it eleven, only passing away early last week.

Jason had come for the funeral. They hadn't been intimate for almost two months before that, but Isobel had wanted the comfort of being in his arms tonight. After everything with her father, and God, her stepmom, it had all been just too much.

So Isobel went to the guest bedroom and slipped into Jason's bed without turning on the lights. It seemed like the one thing that might make her feel like a whole, sane person again.

Jason had been hesitant to touch her at first. Which only stoked all her worst fears. She'd gotten fat. She knew she had. He wasn't attracted to her anymore.

So she'd redoubled her efforts. Touching him the way she remembered he liked best. Going down on him until he was hard and thrusting in her throat. Then crawling up the bed and going on her hands and knees so he could push into her from behind. He liked to grab her hips and pump her hard. She also suspected he liked to watch his big cock disappear between her ass cheeks.

But she wouldn't let him turn on the light when he tried. She could only handle so much. He had no idea what bravery it took for her to let him touch her naked body at all. With no clothes to obscure her problem areas, he could feel all her flaws if he brushed down her thigh, or even worse, if he moved his hands up from her hips to her waist.

In the end, though, it barely mattered. It was over so quickly. And the part she'd been looking forward to the most—the cuddling afterwards—was nonexistent. Almost the second he grunted and spilled in her, he started muttering about needing to get cleaned up. Then he was climbing off the bed and heading for the shower.

His cum was still dripping down the inside of her leg when the ensuite bathroom door closed and his phone on the nightstand buzzed with an incoming text.

Which was when she read Vanessa's words.

Vanessa, her best friend back at Cornell.

Vanessa.

With Jason.

Vanessa and Jason.

Isobel blinked in the dark. Her mind tried to reject the idea even as the evidence glowed on the screen right in front of her.

The screen went dark but then buzzed in her hand again, lighting up with another text alert.

VANESSA TO JASON: *to get you thru the lonely nite til you come home*

The phone buzzed again with a shirtless selfie of Vanessa squeezing one of her bared breasts and making a sexy face at the camera.

Isobel didn't look at Vanessa's breast, though. She just saw Vanessa's tiny, flat waist below it.

Of course Jason was banging her skinnier, prettier best friend. Isobel threw his phone against the wall, only feeling marginally better when she heard the screen crack.

And then she yanked the bedsheet around her and stormed into the bathroom. Because *enough*. She'd had enough. Hadn't life thrown enough shit-bombs her way lately?

"You cheating bastard!" She jerked the shower curtain back, revealing a startled Jason, foamy shampoo thick in his hair.

"Baby," he looked at her, his hands going up in a defensive posture. "What are you—"

Baby? Fury like she'd never felt before lit her up inside.

"Get out!" She leaned down and slammed the shower knob, shutting off the water. God, she couldn't even stand looking at him.

9

He'd just had sex with her and all she could think about was how he must have been comparing her to Vanessa the whole time. It made her want to scream. So she did. "Get out. Now!"

"Stop. Isobel, I don't even know what you're talking ab—"

"What, you tripped and your dick just accidently fell into Vanessa? I saw your fucking texts, asshole."

Jason pulled back, finally dropping silent.

"Get the *fuck* out of my *fucking* house!" she screamed right in his face.

"Okay, okay," he said. He reached for the shower knob. "Just let me finish washing my hair and I'll be—"

"Did you not hear me? I said get the fuck out *now*!" She grabbed his bicep and jerked him toward the tub's edge.

He slipped and fell, landing hard on his ass.

"Christ! What the fuck, Iz?" he cried as he scrambled to his feet, slipping one more time before he finally managed to get out of the tub, his hands moving to cover his crotch. Was he afraid she'd want to get a kick in? Not a bad idea.

But he was already backing out of the bathroom and hurrying toward his suitcase. He dressed faster than she would have thought possible. When he sat on the bed to put on his tennis shoes, she just shouted, "Out!" again. He obviously got the picture because he grabbed the shoes, his suitcase, and his phone from the floor and then he ran out of the room.

In another few seconds, she heard the front door slam. Good fucking riddance. She hoped more than just his screen was broken so he couldn't call an Uber.

She walked back to her bedroom, almost in a daze.

But after several more seconds, everything that had just happened sank in.

Jason had cheated on her.

Jason didn't love her anymore.

Dad was gone.

She was all alone.

Right as the gut-wrenching realization hit, she happened to look over and catch sight of herself in her full-length mirror.

She dropped the sheet she'd been carrying around, just to torture herself.

Fat.

Ugly.

Failure.

She squeezed her eyes shut. *Body dysmorphic disorder.* When she looked in mirrors, she never saw what was really there. Even if she weighed only ninety-five pounds, she still saw a fat pig. She *had* weighed ninety-five pounds—very briefly—right before she'd gone into the treatment facility at sixteen, surrounded by a ton of other skeletal girls all convinced they were fat too.

For a while when she'd been away at college, she thought she could change things—that she could change herself. Just like she'd thought she could finally fix her relationship with Dad by coming home and spending time with him before the end.

But if the last week had taught her anything, it was that things never changed. Dad died believing her stepmother's side of the story. And she was always going to be ugly, screwed up Isobel. She was so far from ninety-five pounds it wasn't even funny. She avoided scales like she tried to avoid mirrors, but barely any of the pants she'd brought home from Cornell fit anymore.

Without the anger that had been animating her for the past ten minutes, she felt completely empty. She wanted to drop to the floor right there and just...*stop*. It was all too hard. She couldn't do this anymore.

Instead, her feet started moving.

First to her dresser. She put on her underwear and pajamas mechanically. The bedrooms were on the third floor of the Upper East Side brownstone and she clutched the banister as she hurried downstairs. She knew where she was going even as she hated herself for it. Nothing ever changed—so why fight fate?

Like a magnet, she was drawn quickly toward the kitchen. It was a pristine room with white marble countertops and dark espresso colored cabinets. Isobel pulled out the ice cream from the double refrigerator. She never bought it but it was always here. She shook her head, knowing it was her stepmother trying to sabotage her and hating that she was giving in. But seriously, what was the fucking point,

11

anyway? She was a sucker for ice cream. Sugary, addictive, with a high calorie count? Sign her up.

She grabbed a wooden stirring spoon and ate the chocolate chip cookie dough straight out of the container.

She finished one pint and was halfway through another before disgust with herself sent her running to the trash can underneath the sink. Opening the cabinet, she yanked out the can. She knelt on the dark hardwood floor and then her finger was down the back of her throat before she could even think all the way through what she was doing. She retched and retched into the trashcan until all the ice cream came back up. Then she sat back against the cabinet, shoving the trashcan away in disgust, wiping her mouth with her forearm.

"Goddammit!" she screamed in frustration, furious at herself. She hadn't binged and purged for four years before coming home to be with her dad. And now this was the second time this week since the funeral.

She pulled her knees to her chest, tears streaming down her cheeks.

She was about to give into a good sob fest—not unusual for her lately, she would go on random crying jags what felt like every half hour, even before her dad died—when she saw something strange.

The cabinet door under the sink was still open from when she'd grabbed the trashcan. And tucked in the back of the cabinet behind the Ajax, Windex, and dish soap was a tall container of... was that...?

Isobel blinked back her tears and leaned in, pushing aside the other cleaners to better see the big plastic bottle.

What the—?

Why was there a container of *protein powder* hidden at the back of the sink?

Isobel stared at the bottle in bewilderment. Was it Dad's from before he got sick? But why on earth...? It wasn't like Dad was into pumping iron. He'd go jogging occasionally, but she thought this kind of stuff was usually for guys trying to build up huge muscles.

She tugged out the bottle and unscrewed the cap. It was more than half empty.

She glanced back inside the cabinet and froze. Right beside where the protein powder had been was a bottle of the special cognac her stepmother drank—the shit cost six hundred bucks a bottle and Catrina was always paranoid and accusing Isobel of drinking it when she wasn't looking.

The truth was Isobel had tried it once but then never again because it tasted like donkey piss.

But looking back and forth between the cognac and the protein powder, she froze, her teeth grinding.

That *bitch*.

"So he cheated on you."

Speak of the devil.

Isobel's back went stiff at her stepmother's voice. She got to her feet, not wanting Catrina to have her at a disadvantage by towering over her.

"Why am I not surprised?" Catrina sounded almost bored as she stood in the kitchen doorway. It was ten o'clock at night but Catrina was still perfectly made up, her thin former model's frame standing erect, elegant and dignified in a pale green silk robe. Even in her early fifties, Catrina was still an undeniably beautiful woman. A fact that she'd never let Isobel forget ever since she'd married her father. Isobel had only been ten at the time.

"You've become such a fat pig lately. Did you really think he'd stick around?"

Isobel's jaw locked and she looked back down at the open container of protein powder.

"You've gained, what, thirty pounds since you came home to be with your father?" Catrina asked, voice needling. "He was worried about you, you know. He talked about you so much at the end. All he wanted was his beautiful little girl back." Catrina let out an incredulous little huff and Isobel's hands balled into fists. She would *not* be goaded into reacting.

"Of course a father is blind to his daughter's flaws. You were a little porky pie back then too, weren't you? But even he couldn't deny what was in front of his face when you visited him every day. Who will love my Isobel when I'm gone, he'd ask me, looking like she does?"

"Shut up!" Isobel glared at her stepmother and then she reached down and grabbed the protein powder container. "You've been adding this to my morning smoothies, haven't you?"

13

Upset at the unexplained weight gain, Isobel had gone back to her old habits of counting her calories religiously. She hadn't struggled with her eating disorder for years. Being away at college, out of this toxic environment, it had been so much easier to establish healthy eating and exercise habits.

But as soon as she got back here and Catrina's constant verbal digs started up again, along with the unexplained weight gain, plus the emotional stress of everything with Dad, the old obsessions had started coming back.

She *hated* that she could still be so weak. She'd assumed that she'd overcome all this shit for good when she kicked it the first time.

So as a part of trying to get it all under control again, she made a green veggie and fruit smoothie each night so she could just grab it and go the next morning on her way to the hospital.

But if Catrina had been adding protein powder to her smoothies, that would explain the weight gain.

Catrina's eyes widened at seeing the container in Isobel's hands, but then her features settled back into a calm mask of superiority. "I have no idea what you're talking about. Sounds to me like you're looking to blame everyone else for your lack of self-control, just like always. Then again, you always were just looking for attention. What was it Dr. Rubenstein used to say? Poor little Isobel acts out and tells elaborate lies so people will notice her because she got addicted to the attention people paid her after her mommy killed herself. Though," she sighed, "by the end, even he admitted crazy might just be in your DNA. But still, isn't part of your therapy program taking responsibility for your own problems?"

How dare she— To bring up Dr. *fucking* Rubenstein—

Isobel screamed and threw the container to the ground, ignoring the powder that flew out of it as it fell.

It wasn't enough, though. Not nearly enough.

She wanted to grab the pots that hung from hooks on the ceiling and fling them at the walls. She wanted to smash the coffee maker to the tile floor. Break it all. Tear it all fucking down—

Catrina tutted, then shook her head at Isobel. "Oh darling, I promised Richard I'd take care of you after he was gone. He worried you might slip back into your…" she leaned in and whispered, "*old habits.*"

She mimed sticking her finger down her throat and Isobel's hands squeezed into fists so tight her nails cut into her palms. She needed to leave. To get the hell out of here before she did something she regretted. She turned to go but Catrina's voice echoed across the kitchen.

"Is poor Isobel going to run away now? You think you can just escape your problems like that? By running?" Catrina made a tutting noise. "That's a coward's way of coping. Then again, your mom took the easy way out too. Hanging herself from the ceiling fan like she did." She shook her head. "And she was what, thirty years old?"

"You're almost twenty-five now, aren't you? Everyone always said you're so much like her. It's cute you try to fight it but eventually you're going to have to give into the inevitable. Frankly, I think Richard was glad to go before he had to see you institutionalized again."

"Shut the fuck up!" Isobel spun back around and flew at her stepmother. Her hands wrapped around Catrina's throat. She slammed the older woman down against the counter. "Shut up, shut up!" Rage like she'd never known burned so hot, Isobel could barely breathe.

Poison. The woman was poison.

Every day her insults chipped away at Isobel. First when she was just a little girl. All throughout adolescence. Even when her father was *dying*. Still every single day, Catrina never let up. And now to find out she was actively undermining her recovery, *trying* to trigger her old demons—!

Isobel screamed and squeezed harder.

Catrina smiled at her at first, even while she was choking. Like she was laughing at Isobel, even in this.

But as Isobel kept squeezing, finally fear came into Catrina's eyes. Catrina's hands flailed, trying to latch onto Isobel's wrists and pull her off.

Isobel was stronger, though. She felt fucking triumphant. Catrina would never torment her again.

But then she blinked.

What was she—

She looked down in horror at her hands.

Her hands that were around another person's throat.

Choking the life out of her.

Isobel let go of Catrina and stumbled backwards.

Catrina fell to the floor, hoarsely gasping in huge gulps of air between coughing fits.

Holy Jesus, what had she just done?

Isobel looked at her hands in disbelief. Had she really almost just... Oh God. Oh God oh God *oh God.*

"They'll put you away for this," Catrina gasped, still clutching her throat.

Isobel turned and ran out of the kitchen.

Run.

She had to get out of here.

Run.

Right now.

Catrina would call the police any minute. *They'll put you away.* Catrina hated her. And Isobel had just given her stepmother the perfect opportunity to get rid of her for good.

An attempted murder charge.

Isobel felt sick as she fled upstairs to get her purse and car keys.

She was about to pick up her phone to toss it in her purse when she stopped at the last second. It was easy for people to track phones, right?

Shit, was she really thinking like that? Like a fugitive?

She looked toward the ceiling. How had everything gotten fucked sideways so quickly? She shook her head and took a quick breath in, trying to steady herself. There was no time. No time for thinking. No time for anything.

She jammed some clothes and shoes in a bag, grabbed her keys, and was almost out her door when she stopped.

"Shit."

She turned around and ran back into the bathroom. She'd almost forgotten her anti-depressants. She grabbed the pill bottle from the medicine cabinet. Had she even taken them today? With as fucked up as her moods had been lately, the last thing she needed was to be screwing with her medication.

She unscrewed the lid and poured one of the small pills into her hand. Not that it was helping much. She'd been so stable for *years* and then for it to all go down the shitter so drastically—

She reached for a glass of water and as she did, she knocked the bottle of pills over, spilling them out on the counter.

"Fuck!" She did *not* have time for this. Had Catrina already called the cops?

But as she started scooping the little pills back into the bottle, she paused. Some of them didn't look right.

A bunch of the tablets had a little line down the middle where you could split them in half if you needed to. But about half of them didn't have the line.

"What the hell?"

She reached down and flipped one of the non-lined pills over, thinking maybe they were just lined on one side.

But nope, the lined ones were lined on both sides and others were smooth on both sides.

Isobel's eyes flipped back and forth between the two pills, nothing making sense for a long moment.

But like downstairs, it eventually dawned on her and she swung in the direction of her door. The same killing fury as earlier made her fists shake all over again.

"Bitch!" she screamed.

It would have served Catrina right if Isobel hadn't stopped earlier. She'd been fucking with Isobel's medication in addition to adding the protein powder to her smoothies?

Isobel's hand shook as she swept all the pills back into the bottle. Had Catrina switched out half her meds with sugar pills so she'd only be taking half her regular dosage? Or were they something worse? Something meant to make her moods more volatile?

What the fuck? *Why?*

Was Catrina just a fucking psychopath who got off on tormenting people and Isobel had always been the closest, convenient target? Isobel's adolescence had been hell. It started almost as soon as Catrina moved in after the wedding. The snide comments about Isobel's looks just got more and more nasty as time went on. But only when no one was around.

17

Isobel cried and ran to her dad about it in the beginning. Catrina of course denied everything. They sent Isobel to Dr. Rubenstein and he didn't believe her either. He told her father it was normal for kids to 'act out' when significant changes were introduced in a household.

Dad grew less and less tolerant of Isobel's complaints and by the end of Catrina's first year with them, Isobel knew it was useless to say anything. Which just made Catrina more vicious since she knew she could get away with it. Dad traveled a lot for his import/export business. He always told Isobel how all he wanted was for her and Catrina to get along. That was one of the reasons he had wanted to remarry in the first place. He wanted Isobel to have a female role model to look up to since Mom was gone.

Too bad Catrina was a vicious hell-whore.

Isobel stared at the pill bottle.

It was evidence.

For once she had evidence. It wasn't just Catrina's word against hers.

Then she started laughing hysterically.

Because no, that wasn't true. This wasn't any different than it had ever been. What did Isobel have? A bottle of some unknown pills? With her luck, Catrina would get her booked on assault *and* possession for whatever the hell was in this bottle. After all, there was nothing tying the pills to Catrina. Did Isobel think she'd find Catrina's fingerprints on the bottle or something?

Even if she did, that was hardly a smoking gun. Catrina could just say that she'd picked up the bottle from the pharmacy for her stepdaughter, so of course her fingerprints were on it.

Isobel was well and truly fucked. She hiccupped, something between a laugh and a sob. Her hands shook as she pushed her hair out of her face.

Back to the original plan. Get the hell out of here.

And go where, exactly?

Fuck knew. She'd figure that part out later.

She ran to the other room and picked up the bag she'd haphazardly stuffed full of clothes and her purse. On a whim, she also grabbed her riding boots from her closet since the time she'd been happiest in her life was when she'd worked in the stables near their house in New

18

Hampshire. She clutched it all to her chest as she ran down the stairs and out the back door.

Catrina hadn't been anywhere in sight, thank God.

Isobel ran toward her little Toyota parked in their narrow garage. Her hands were trembling so badly, it took her three tries to get her key in the lock. She finally managed. She jumped in the car. A few seconds later, she had it in reverse and was peeling out onto the street.

"Okay," she whispered to herself as she wove through Manhattan's night traffic. "Okay, you're okay. You're okay."

So what if she had no clue where she was going? Starting from the shit show she'd just left behind, things could only be looking up from here, right?

Right?

Chapter 2
HUNTER

"It's good to see you out and about, Hunter," Bubba said, looking Hunter over as he sat his beer in front of him.

Hunter just nodded without comment. He hated coming out to town for just this reason—that look of pity on everyone's faces when they talked to him. Even after more than a year. Drinking at home alone was even more depressing, though, so here he was.

Last week was the one year anniversary of Janine leaving him. What was the quote from that movie he loved—*get busy living or get busy dying?* It was from the Shawshank Redemption, a movie about being in prison. Which was what his house had felt like lately. He'd had enough of holing up there by himself. He was sick of the silence. He used to find the quiet of country living calming. Peaceful.

But for the past year all he heard was the absence of her voice. Man, she'd always been complaining about something. The hot water ran out too quickly. She hated the mosquitos in the spring. The gravel driveway meant her car was perpetually dirty. Not that she had anywhere to go where a nice car would be noticed.

It was funny how the things that drove you nuts about a person ended up being the things you missed most.

Or maybe he was just a damn fool. Sentimental. Nostalgic.

What he probably really missed was her body warm beside his in the bed at night. The way he could roll over and kiss the nape of her neck, and, no matter how ornery she'd been that day, her body would go all soft. How she'd open her legs and grasp his ass and pull him into her.

Even when they were both furious with each other, they could still communicate that way. By the end, it seemed like the only thing they had left. Stony silences all evening would give way to furious lovemaking at night. Biting and clawing as she brought him to the brink. Clinging to him for the briefest moment of their mutual climax like there was some hope, some future for them.

And then pulling away the second it was done, sometimes going to sleep on the couch like she couldn't stand his touch a second longer.

He'd never understood her. But he hadn't been able to ask her why she did it—why she kept coming to bed each night only to wrench herself away right afterwards. At first he thought it was because she loved him. But eventually he realized it was to punish him. Yet another reminder that he might have his ring on her finger but she'd never truly be his.

Hunter's phone buzzed in his pocket and he pulled it out to check who was calling. There was never a night off when you were the only large animal veterinarian within two counties.

Mom flashed across the screen. Hunter's face soured. Jesus, if there was anyone worse than people in town staring at him with pity it was Mom with her cheer-Hunter-up routine. She meant well. He knew she did. But he could only handle so much enforced cheer a week and he'd already spent most of Sunday at her and Pops' house. He let the call ring out since she'd know being sent to voicemail after a couple rings meant he'd rejected her call.

When it finally stopped buzzing, he shook his head. Jesus, coming out tonight wasn't helping anything. He'd still been fixating on Janine as much as he ever did at home. And these bar stools were damn uncomfortable.

He set his beer back on the bar and turned sideways on his stool so he could reach into his back pocket to grab his wallet when he saw the door to the bar open.

And in walked the most stunning woman. She had long black hair that was pulled back in a slick ponytail. Her face was flawless. Porcelain skin, big blue eyes. Heart-shaped face, pink lips.

Unlike most of the women in the bar, she wasn't dressed like she was looking to get noticed. She was wearing a dark t-shirt and jeans—not too tight but just enough to show she had curves in all the right places. Also unlike everyone else in the bar, Hunter didn't recognize her. Unusual in a town the size of Hawthorne, which was barely a blip on the map.

Apparently everyone else found her just as interesting because half the bar had turned to stare at her.

Shit. Hunter knew that feeling. Hunter hated that feeling.

He turned back to the bar and took another sip of his abandoned beer. He was just about to reach for his wallet again when the woman sat down on the barstool beside him.

He froze, hands on his mug of beer. Had she seen him and come down to sit by *him* specifically or had she just randomly chosen an empty seat at the bar?

He watched her out of his periphery and she didn't so much as glance his way. Yeah, wishful thinking, jackass.

Still, he didn't go for his wallet again.

The woman glanced up and down the bar. Bubba was bartending tonight, along with Jeff. Jeff was at the other end of the bar, making an ass of himself like usual while Cherry and Lacey hung on his every word. Cherry was leaned half over the bar top, her cleavage so low he bet Jeff could see her belly button.

The newcomer smiled and shook her head a little at the scene, like it amused her in some way. Bubba finally finished mixing drinks and handing them off to Mary who was waitressing tonight and then came over to the woman.

Bubba was as much an institution as his bar. A big man with a belly to match, he had a long gray beard and a ride or die tattoo on his knuckles that pretty much said it all.

The woman didn't look intimidated by him though. She just smiled back at him when he turned to her and asked, "What can I get you, beautiful?"

She hesitated a moment, like she was about to order something but then reconsidered. She tilted her head sideways, showing off the long curve of her neck. "What do you have on tap?"

Bubba listed off several beers and she chose a dark IPA.

Hunter sipped at his beer and pretended to be minding his own business while Bubba served her up a big glass of dark beer. She took a long sip, licking the foam off her lips at the end.

Hunter swallowed hard and averted his eyes.

"Ah, that hits the spot," she said after another long sip. "Is the kitchen still open?"

"Till ten," Bubba answered. "What can I get for ya?"

She was quiet a moment, then blurted, "I'd kill for a burger," like it was a confession she was admitting to a priest.

"My kind of lady. Beer and burgers. Coming right up." Bubba turned and walked to the end of the bar where it connected to the kitchen to put in her order. Hunter couldn't help his eyes seeking her out again as she sank back on her stool, taking another long sip from her beer.

But then his vision was blocked by Larry leaning on the bar between Hunter and the woman. Larry was in his late forties and had been a teacher at the high school before he got fired for showing up to school drunk.

"I agree with Bubba," Larry slurred, obviously drunk. He smelled like a damn brewery. "It's sexy seeing a woman who knows how she likes her beer. With plenty of head."

Son of a—

"I'm Lawrence."

There was no response from the woman. Hunter imagined her giving Larry a cold, "fuck off, I'm not interested" face.

"So you're new in town," Larry persisted, shouldering between us even more.

"This is a small town. Everyone knows everyone. So when a bombshell like you walks in…" Larry paused, "…well, it's hard not to notice. Hard being the operative word, if you get what I mean."

All right, that was enough.

But the woman seemed fully capable of standing up for herself.

"Whoa whoa whoa," Hunter heard her say. He still couldn't see because of Larry blocking his vision, but from the way Larry was leaning in, he had to be crowding the woman.

Her firm voice was clear. "I'm not interested. You need to back up. Now."

Larry's body moved sharply like she might have shoved him, but he had a firm grip on the bar top and he barely budged.

"What?" Larry said, a nasty tone entering his voice. "I'm just being friendly, don't be a—"

Hunter had had it.

"She said she's not interested." Hunter yanked the back of Larry's collar, choking him and knocking him off balance until he stumbled backward and landed on his ass.

23

Hunter was already on his feet, standing between the red-faced Larry and the woman still sitting on the stool behind him.

"Get the hell out of here before I call Marie," Hunter threatened.

Larry blanched and struggled to get to his feet.

"And call a cab or I'll call her anyway."

Larry nodded and stumbled off toward his table.

Larry was mostly harmless but there was nothing Hunter hated more than men who disrespected women.

He turned around to apologize to the woman and her eyes jerked up almost guiltily. Had she been checking out his ass? Hunter bit back a smile.

"Sorry about him."

She just waved a hand and took a long pull of her beer. Too big a swig, it turned out, because she was immediately choking and spraying beer all over the bar top.

Hunter jumped forward and pounded her back several times. "Are you okay?"

She coughed again but nodded, grabbing a napkin to wipe her mouth and then, discretely, the bar top.

"I'm fine," she gasped when she could finally breathe through her windpipe again. She took another sip of beer to soothe the last of her coughing fit. Then she winced. "I don't suppose you could ignore the part where I was just the bar's own personal beer geyser? I haven't been let out in polite society for a while and apparently I'm rusty at it." She smiled self-deprecatingly and Hunter couldn't think of the last time he'd seen anyone more charming or lovely.

"So," she said when the silence had gone on long enough to be awkward. Shit. Talking. He was supposed to be talking here. He should say something witty. Engaging.

He had nothing.

"Is Marie his wife?" she asked.

It took him a second to realize what she was asking and he finally shook his head with a smirk. "Larry wishes. No, she's the sheriff."

"Oh." She looked a little surprised. "I take it Lawrence has had a few run ins with the law?"

Hunter gave an eye roll. "I think he spent more nights in the drunk tank last year than he did at home. Marie got so tired of hauling his ass

24

in she started playing death metal all night on full blast at the station, which, from what I understand, is hell when you've got a hangover." He smiled. "Most nights Larry gets himself home now before getting too sloppy."

"I'm Hunter, by the way. Hunter Dawkins." He held out his hand but then pulled it back at the last second. "Shit, I don't want you to think I'm just another asshole at the bar trying to hit on you. Sorry," he pointed a thumb over his shoulder. "I can just leave you to your beer."

He started to grab his drink, ready to get up and leave.

"No," she put a hand on his forearm briefly before jerking it away again. His arm tingled where she'd touched him. When was the last time a woman had touched him? He'd thought about trying for a fling a few times since Janine, but in such a small town, it hadn't seemed worth the effort. Hawthorne wasn't exactly the kind of place you could pull off an anonymous one night stand.

"It's fine," she smiled. "I don't mind the company. With someone who knows how to respect personal space, that is," she clarified with a smile. "I'm Isobel."

"You want another, Hunter?" Bubba asked, pointing to Hunter's now mostly empty beer mug.

"I'll just have a Coke this time. Thanks, Bubba." He had to drive home.

Hunter looked at Isobel quizzically. "So what does bring you to our little town? It's true we don't get too many new faces around here."

"I'll be working at Mel's Horse Rescue for the summer."

Of course. "I should have guessed," Hunter nodded. "The few new faces we do get around here are usually the ones who cycle through there. You should have a good time. Mel and Xavier are great people."

"You know them?" Her interest was obviously piqued. Then she shook her head, "I guess everyone knows everyone around here."

"True enough," Hunter chuckled in agreement. "But I'm actually godfather to their second son. He's two and a half."

"Really? Wow, that's awesome. So you *know them*, know them."

Hunter nodded. Mel and Xavier had been nothing but supportive, both when he and Janine were together and… after. He tried to get out

25

to the ranch to hang out with them whenever he could. It was impossible to be too sad with two rambunctious little boys running around, asking you questions a mile a minute.

"They're good people," he repeated.

Isobel propped her elbows on the bar top, her head tipped slightly sideways as she watched him. Her blue eyes were bright but there were slight shadows underneath them.

What was her story, he wondered? She'd done nothing but smile since he'd been talking to her, but it was like he could sense a sadness layered just underneath the surface. It was hard to describe, but it made her even prettier. She was obviously a strong woman not afraid to stand up for herself, but there was a fragile quality to her at the same time.

"It's amazing work they do," she said. "I heard about their horse rescue from a horse trainer I know back in New Hampshire. He couldn't stop singing their praises. Is it true they've got twenty-five horses at the ranch that they've rescued now?"

"More than that," Hunter said. "Some of the horses they're able to rehab and get adopted but there are usually a steady stable of at least thirty horses out there now."

Her eyes were wide with admiration.

"So that's how you heard about the rescue," Hunter asked. "From your trainer friend?"

"Yeah. He told me about it a while ago. I always thought working out here sounded like an amazing opportunity, just something I'd never have time for." Her eyes clouded over for a moment and she looked down before pasting on a bright smile and shrugging. "Well, I finally have some time and it seemed like a perfect fit."

Hunter's eyes narrowed, wondering what was going on in that lovely head of hers. "New Hampshire, you said? Is that where you're from?"

But before she could answer, Jake came up and interrupted, beer in hand. "Hey Hunter," he gestured toward the pool table. "Connor's leaving if you want in on the next round."

"Oh." Hunter shot a quick glance at Isobel, then looked back at Jake, trying to communicate telepathically. *Come on, Jake, move the fuck on.* Hunter wanted to smack the guy upside the head. Couldn't he see he was talking to a beautiful woman?

But Jake just kept standing there so Hunter finally said, "I'm good. You guys can keep playing."

"Ohhhhh," Jake said, looking over at Isobel like he finally understood. And was being totally fucking obvious about it.

Hunter felt the back of his neck heat up as Jake winked at him and turned around, finally walking off. But when he looked back at Isobel, she was just smiling into her beer.

"Here ya are, darlin.' Char-grilled just like the good Lord intended." Bubba set down Isobel's burger in front of her.

She thanked Bubba and picked up her burger but then paused, looking over at Hunter. "Sorry, is it rude if I just dig in right in front of you?"

Hunter waved his hand. "By all means. I already ate."

"Oh thank God, I'm starving."

He laughed and she took a huge bite of the juicy burger. Apparently it tasted good because her head fell back in bliss as she chewed.

Annnnnnnd now his jeans were tight because, *fuck.* That was the hottest thing he'd seen in a long while.

Her eyes had dropped closed, she was so lost in the sensual experience of eating the burger. Hunter watched the delicate column of her throat as she chewed and swallowed. His eyes traced down her throat, past the collar of her t-shirt, down to the round swells of her—

Shit.

He jerked his eyes back to her face, only to find her watching him ogle her. Well, fuck.

He felt his neck heat and he looked away, back behind the bar. Only to see Isobel's reflection in the mirror, two spots of color high on her cheeks as she watched him surreptitiously over the top of her burger like she was amused by his embarrassment.

Everything he was feeling right now—God, he hadn't felt it in so long he barely recognized it. Attraction. This was what attraction felt like. He almost couldn't believe he was actually sitting here, talking and flirting with this beautiful woman.

She finished swallowing her bite. "So this bar is like Cheers. Where everybody knows your name?" She took another bite and Hunter couldn't help smiling sheepishly.

"Yeah. Well. Small towns." He couldn't help his thoughts turning back to Janine. "You either love 'em or you hate 'em."

"I've always liked them," Isobel said, leaning in like she'd detected his suddenly soured mood and was trying to jostle him back into the moment with her. "My best memories are of the small town where I lived in New Hampshire."

Right.

Because she wasn't Janine. This girl grew up in a small town in New Hampshire, not an expensive neighborhood in Manhattan. Janine used to brag about being from Soho like it was an exotic foreign country. Hunter shook himself and loosened back up.

They chatted easily as she ate her burger. He learned she loved working with horses and all about the personalities of the horses at the stable where she'd worked in New Hampshire. She was so animated as she talked about each one, Hunter couldn't take his eyes off her. She mentioned she was taking some time off from college but she'd gotten a far away look in her eye and seemed uncomfortable so he hadn't pressed anymore.

"I feel like I've been talking non-stop," she said, taking a sip of her beer. She'd only drunk about half of it, and eaten a little more than half her burger before setting it down on the plate and ignoring it. "Tell me about you."

Hunter shrugged, feeling embarrassed. What could he say? He was the town vet who spent his days armpit deep up the back end of cows and horses, struggling every month to pay his bills and keep the lights on? He knew all too well exactly how unimpressive he was.

Besides, really, what was the point? It wasn't like he could have a relationship with this woman, even if she was as perfect as she seemed. He wasn't sure he was ready, if he would ever be. And she was only going to be here for the summer. The last thing he needed was to get involved with another woman who couldn't wait to be rid of him.

28

But at the same time, the thought of saying goodbye to her and going back to his empty house… The thought of spending another night alone in his cold, empty bed…

God, it felt like it might kill him, especially after spending the evening talking with this bright, lovely creature and remembering what it felt like to be a real, live man.

And just as he was thinking all this, he realized Isobel's eyes were locked on his lips. Like she was thinking about what it would be like to kiss him. His blood heated at the very thought.

Fuck it. He threw caution and rational thought to the wind. "Isobel?"

"Hmm?" She jerked her gaze away from his lips.

Her eyes were heated when he met them.

Here went nothing. Either she'd slap him in the face and tell him to go to hell. Or not. But nothing ventured, nothing gained, right?

Hunter leaned in and dropped his voice to a whisper. "Look, I don't usually do this and feel free to tell me to take a hike…" His hand went to the back of his neck and he trailed off, wincing. "Jesus, that sounds like such a line." Maybe he couldn't go through with it after all.

But just then, Isobel's hand reached out to his thigh. "No, keep talking."

Her intense blue eyes met his again, and the spark in them gave him the confidence to say the rest quickly. "I'm lonely. And you're gorgeous and funny and perfect and I'd like to take you home tonight."

Her breath hitched at his words. Dammit, he'd fucked up. No doubt here came the hand lashing out toward his face—nothing less than he deserved—in three, two, one—

"Okay." It was barely a breath, and then her hand on his thigh gave a quick squeeze.

He blinked. Wait, what? Really?

He searched back and forth in her bright blue eyes but she wasn't flinching away from his gaze. He sat frozen for another short moment before finally pulling his foot out of his ass and jumping into action. He stood up and yanked out his wallet, dropping a couple twenties on the table. "My treat."

When Isobel tried to protest that she could pay for her own meal, he just grabbed her hand and pulled her behind him out of the bar.

She laughed. "Okay, okay, so the caveman act is a little bit sexy. But I can walk on my own." She wiggled out of his grasp.

But then she froze and planted her feet. When Hunter looked back to see what was the matter, she grabbed his left hand and jerked it up between them.

What was she—

She pointed at his fourth finger where there was a clear wedding ring tan line. "Did you accidently forget dropping your wedding ring in your glove box on the way into the bar?"

Hunter jerked backwards and all the people sitting at the table closest to them immediately stopped talking.

Shit. He hadn't thought how that would look. He'd only just recently taken it off, but he was used to everyone already knowing his business.

"She left me last year."

Now it felt like the entire bar had gone silent. Everyone staring at them. At Hunter. Giving him *that face*. Jesus, he could feel their pity like a heavy blanket suffocating him.

"Shit." Isobel's hand jerked to her mouth. "I'm sorry." He took a step back at seeing the pity on her face too.

She winced at his reaction. "I'm sorry," she repeated. "It's just my last boyfriend and my..." She looked down, took a deep breath, then pasted on a bright smile. "Forget about it. It was nice meeting you."

Then she pushed past Hunter out the door.

Wait, what? No, he hadn't meant—

"What are you still standin' there for?" Bubba called. "Go after her, you dumbass."

Right. Hunter rushed out the door to run after Isobel.

The night air was chilly as he stood on the street looking for her. She was nowhere to be seen. "Shit," he swore, jogging around to the back parking lot.

He breathed out in relief when he saw her leaning over the car door of a Toyota Carola, banging her head on the window and whispering, "Stupid. Stupid, stupid, stupid."

"Isobel?"

She screeched a little as she swung around to look at him. "Jesus Christ, you scared me."

"Sorry." He held his hands up. "I'm the one that's sorry. Of course that was a logical assumption for you to make back there." He hiked a thumb behind him toward the bar. "You don't know me from Adam."

"No, I'm sorry," she said. "I shouldn't have assumed—"

"Stop apologizing," he said. And then, because he couldn't stand another second not touching her, he leaned over, caging her in with his hands on both sides of the car, and kissed her.

HUNTER

Chapter 3
ISOBEL

God, he was a good kisser. Isobel's toes immediately curled at the soft pressure of his lips on hers. And when his tongue teased at the seam of her lips, she couldn't help groaning and immediately opening to him.

That was all the invitation he needed, apparently, because he deepened the kiss and then started to absolutely devour her. One of his hands dropped, curving down the line of her back to her waist, and then around to her ass.

Before she could obsess or wonder if he thought her butt was too big, he grabbed a handful and squeezed, kissing her even more furiously.

And all of it felt amazing. She moaned so loudly that she was immediately embarrassed. But God, she couldn't remember the last time she'd felt so turned on. Things with Jason certainly hadn't been like that for a long time. Sex was more of a chore than anything else, even before they were long distance. Jason had been a football star in high school and he had a big dick. Those two things combined had convinced him that he was a sex god.

All it really meant was that he had absolutely zero clue about getting women off. Isobel had tried to work with him on it but he just wasn't that interested. He pointed out that Isobel got off a lot of the time.

And while at first, yes, that was true—in the initial blush of their relationship, sex had been exciting. If Isobel worked and angled herself just right on that big dick of his, she could get friction on her clit. But by the end she'd gotten so pissed that he didn't even want to try she didn't bother. Then she'd gone home to be with Dad and with them being long distance... well, apparently Jason had found other places to stick that big dick of his.

"Jesus, sorry, I got carried away there," Hunter pulled back and leaned his forehead against hers. "We should move this party some place more private."

He was panting heavily and one of his hands fisted in the bottom of her shirt like he was barely holding himself back from ravaging her again.

Isobel was breathing heavily too. All of this was so reckless. So *not* like her. But hadn't that been the point of tonight?

Everything in her life had fallen apart. All the worst case scenarios she could have imagined had actually *happened.*

Her father had died.

Jason cheated.

Her eating disorder had relapsed.

Her step-mother's manipulation had driven her to violence.

Isobel had seen the absolute worst in herself.

She spent the first day driving out west wallowing in all of it. But then, somewhere around the Mississippi River, she just started laughing. Because what the fuck did she have to lose at this point?

Nothing. She had nothing to lose. The worst had happened.

And she was still here.

She was free.

Free to start over.

Free to be anyone she wanted to be.

With no past history or future expectations.

She could just *be.*

That realization made her chest feel so full, so sun-burstingly bright that she felt almost light-headed as she walked into Bubba's Bar, the only place open in the tiny town of Hawthorne, Wyoming at 9:00 at night on a Wednesday.

And didn't they say the best way to get over someone was to get under someone else? It hadn't been her intention heading into the bar, but Hunter was so sweet and handsome and when he'd made his indecent proposition, she'd wanted to drag him out to her car and jump him right there.

"You want to ride with me or take your own car?" Hunter asked, pulling back after another long kiss. It looked like it took effort to yank himself away.

He was such a good-looking guy. He had a square jaw with a few days growth of beard that gave him a rugged, sexy look. His brown hair was thick and curly and he was obviously overdue for a cut. It was the kind of hair that made you want to dig your fingers in. Add to that a strong brow line over blue eyes that were bright with lust. For *her.*

"I'll follow." Isobel felt equally breathless. She was reasonably certain Hunter was an okay guy since everyone in the bar seemed to know him, but she didn't want to be without her car.

"Okay," he said. But instead of going to his car, he leaned down and kissed her again. His body pinned her to her car and almost unconsciously, her leg lifted to wrap around his hip.

Which was when she felt just how hard he was. It didn't scare her, though. With the freedom of her new lease on life still loosening her inhibitions, she let out a desperate breathy moan and rubbed her core against his hardness.

He ground into her several times before swearing and pulling away. His nostrils flared as he looked down at her. With only the light of the lamplight, his brow shadowed his eyes, making him look dark and dangerous. And sexy as fuck when he leaned over and growled in her ear, "I might break a few traffic laws to get to my house because I need that sexy as hell body wrapped around me this second."

Isobel's sex clenched at his words but then he was already turning and striding away with purposeful steps.

"I'm parked out front but I'll pull around so you can follow me," he called over his shoulder.

She opened her car and slid into the front seat, closing her eyes and pressing her forehead to the steering wheel.

"Holy shit." She drummed her feet against the floorboard in a spastic little happy dance and then she turned on the engine and watched out for Hunter's car.

She didn't have to wait long. It only took a minute before he pulled up beside her in a rugged blue truck that looked like it had seen better days. At the same time, the masculine vehicle perfectly fit the man. She backed up and then headed out down the main street and into the dark roads, always keeping Hunter's rear truck lights in view.

In spite of his 'break traffic laws' comment, he actually kept to the speed limit and drove very responsibly. Which both impressed and annoyed Isobel because the pulsing between her legs only got worse with every passing mile.

It was fifteen minutes before they finally turned into a long gravel drive. Isobel bit her lip, apprehension snaking in when she realized just how remote Hunter's place was. Any other time, she would have said that following a strange man back to his house in the middle of nowhere was a really *stupid* idea. But everyone in town knew this guy. And they saw them leave together.

Then again, if he was the town's darling, he'd be the last one they would suspect of being a serial killer. What if his nice guy act was just how he lured women in? Then if anybody asked, he could just say Isobel had been passing through if she didn't turn up tomorrow. It's not like anyone at the horse rescue was actually expecting her. There hadn't been a way to call ahead since she'd left her phone behind. Plus, the way Rick—the stablemaster where she kept her horse Buttons at their summer house in New Hampshire—had described the rescue, they were always short on help. It was in a remote location and the pay wasn't much more than room and board. She was planning to apply for the job in person tomorrow.

And hadn't she just been thinking about how the worst-case scenarios always seemed to happen to her? It would just be her luck if the nice guy from the bar was actually a psychopath with a penchant for chopping up dark-haired girls into little itty-bitty pieces and—

The porch light turned on and she could see Hunter standing by the front door to his house, the door slightly ajar. He was obviously waiting for her, but it was like he could tell she was second guessing her decision in coming out here. And he wasn't pressing the issue. He just stood there waiting. Letting her choose to come in or back out and drive away.

She took a deep breath. Okay, maybe her paranoid brain was getting a little imaginative.

She grabbed her purse and got out of the car, then walked toward his house.

"Just so you know," she said when she got closer, "I called a girlfriend and told her your address and to call the cops if I don't check in with her tomorrow morning." No need for him to know she was bluffing.

Hunter inclined his head. "That's good. I want you to be as comfortable as possible."

35

He gestured toward the front door and after she passed, his hand came to the small of her back. He followed her into the house. As soon as he closed the door behind them, he nuzzled his nose into the back of her neck where her hair touched her shoulders. Goosebumps immediately shot up and down her arms.

"You have a lovely house," she barely managed to say, her breath hitching as he slowly pushed her hair away and began dropping light kisses across the base of her neck. He was being so gentle, his lips so achingly soft that they barely made any contact at all.

She wasn't just saying it about the house, either. It was a large cabin with an open living room and kitchen. The ceiling was tall with a pitched A-line roof and there was a second floor loft where she assumed the bedrooms were. It was a simple but classic space that, like his truck, seemed well-suited to its owner.

Speaking of whom... Hunter withdrew his lips and had moved on to massaging her with those big, glorious hands of his. She sank back against him as he released knots in her shoulders she hadn't even realized she was carrying around.

"God, that feels amazing," she groaned.

"I need to touch your skin."

A shudder wracked her body at his whisper.

She started moving toward the staircase at the other side of the cabin—they'd come in the back door and the staircase was by the front entryway—but Hunter's hands on her shoulders stopped her.

"Lift." He urged her arms over her head. Like he meant to take her shirt off right here in the middle of the brightly lit living room.

She clutched her arms to her sides.

"The bedroom," she said, trying to move that direction again. Where she would make sure the lights were *off*.

But he just shook his head and lifted the bottom of her cotton T-shirt. She expected him to jerk it off quickly. His kiss had been so urgent back at the bar by her car.

But he only lifted her shirt slowly, his fingers tracing her stomach inch by treacherous inch as he glided her shirt up. By the time he reached her breasts, her breaths were coming in panting gasps.

Her mind was a mess of conflicting thoughts: did he feel how soft and squishy her stomach was? And: oh God, that felt *so* good, oh, oh, *yes*—

"Slowly," he whispered in her ear from behind. "Slow down your breathing. I want to wring every ounce of pleasure possible from your body tonight." His thumbs brushed the tips of her nipples through her bra and her breath hitched.

"Ah ah ah," he chastised. "Deep breath in," he demonstrated at her back, her shirt still just barely lifted over her breasts. She licked her lips and tried to humor him, though, because his every touch told her that this man knew what he was doing.

She took a deep breath in and tried to shut out all worries about her body. He obviously liked what he was touching if the hardness against her ass was any indication.

That's only because he hasn't gotten a good look at you. He's standing behind you right now. If he saw how ugly and bloated your stomach was from eating that burger, he'd run—

No. She shut down the voice in her head that sounded so much like her stepmother's. She wasn't that Isobel anymore. She'd left *that* Isobel behind in New York.

"Good, and now breathe out."

Her breath rushed out before he'd finished the words. He instructed her through several more rounds of breathing and then, once she had the hang of it, he ever so slowly pulled her shirt up and over her head.

When he gently lifted her shirt off her arms, she didn't resist this time. His thumbs caressed up and down her forearms as he drew her arms back down, her shirt falling to the floor. No one had ever paid so much attention to every detail of her body.

"Your skin," he whispered reverently, his thumb rubbing the inner pulse point on her wrist. "It's so soft."

God, he was driving her insane. She couldn't take it anymore. She turned in his arms so that they were chest to chest. It felt dangerous doing it—he could actually *see* her now—but she needed to look into his eyes.

She could tell she'd startled him but his quick smile let her know it wasn't unwelcome. She threw her arms around his neck and drew herself up on tiptoe to kiss him.

Strong arms encircled her waist and he lifted her up even as their mouths met. His tongue tangled with hers. Unlike at the car, though, he delved in only slightly. When the very tip of his tongue connected with the tip of hers, she'd swear it was like a thousand volts of electricity shot straight to her sex.

He must have felt it too because the next thing Isobel knew, he had her slammed against a wall. She felt all of him—his strong arms wrapped around her, his seeking tongue, his hardness pressing into her through his blue jeans.

She moaned into his mouth and lifted first one leg up and around his waist, then the other, until she was all but riding him. He dropped an arm underneath her thigh, hiking her up even further.

She locked her ankles around his back and moved her pelvis back and forth against his hardness. He thrust up and into her as she moved on him.

She broke their kiss and threw her head back because oh God, *yes*. Right there. Holy shit. She rubbed herself back and forth even more shamelessly.

Hunter's mouth latched on to her neck, lavishing open mouthed kisses all over. She couldn't even care if he was giving her a hickie because he was taking her so high, it was so good—

His hands had been holding her under her thighs but as he leaned in to pin her against the wall with his body, his rock hard cock thrusting against the place where she needed it most, he reached and grabbed a handful of her ass.

Oh shit, that was so hot. Especially considering how he buried his face in her chest, his teeth nipping at her already hardened nipples. But he couldn't get very good access to them and it must have frustrated him because the next thing she knew, he pulled her away from the wall.

Then he was carrying her. She let out a squeak of surprise, her pleasure popping like a bubble as she clutched onto him. He must feel *exactly* how heavy she was.

"Let me down, I can walk."

He ignored her and carried her to the center of the living room. Finally her feet touched the floor and he immediately pulled her down to the soft rug with him.

Hunter pushed her backward so that she was lying down and he started peeling off her jeans. She covered her face with her hands. Like a little kid, if she couldn't see him, then he wouldn't be able to see her. Or her cellulite.

She couldn't help her whole body going tense as he finished pulling her jeans off her legs. Oh God, this was a bad idea.

She wasn't a new Isobel.

She was the old Isobel. She always would be. Miserable and insecure and fat and—

"Hey, you okay up here?" Hunter's big hand gently peeled one of hers away from her face. His handsome features were creased in concern.

"Fine," she squeaked.

Oh God, the super-hot guy was seeing exactly what a disastrous freak she was. Not that he knew the *half* of it. There was probably an arrest warrant out for her in New York at this very moment.

"We can stop." His hand cradled her cheek. "There's no pressure here. We can do whatever you want."

His eyebrows had dropped low in concern. "Do you want to stop?"

He moved to withdraw his hand but she grabbed it and held it to her face, turning her head and dropping a kiss on his palm. This was the first thing that had felt good, that had felt *right*, in months. "I don't want to stop."

It only came out as a whisper. That was all she could manage at the moment. But she didn't want to stop. She didn't *want* to be the old Isobel.

She lifted up from the ground and pulled his face down to hers. As soon as his lips touched down she felt the spark that had been doused by her obsessions fire back to life. She closed her eyes and lost herself in the kiss.

"Christ, you're beautiful," he whispered in between kissing her lips and up her neck to her ear. "So fucking beautiful."

Isobel automatically frowned. He sounded earnest. For a moment, though—just a *moment*—she could almost believe him. His words were perfect. *He* was perfect.

Her eyes still closed, she took his other hand and pushed it past her belly and down to her sex. As soon as his fingers made contact, immediately circling and teasing her clit through the thin fabric of her panties, she gasped and arched into his touch.

After just a few moments, he pulled away. Isobel dared to open her eyes and was rewarded by seeing Hunter pull his own shirt off over his head. Her breath hitched. He was muscular in a normal-guy way, not like he hit the gym for hours a day. Like those were the kind he got by doing regular hard work. Isobel imagined him lifting bales of hay and carrying heavy equipment around all day.

She didn't have long to just stop and stare, though, because almost immediately, he dropped and his mouth was back at work kissing his way down her stomach from just underneath her bra all the way to— Her breath hitched when he got to the top of her panties.

Oh God, he wasn't going to…?

"Wait," she squeaked, pulling her legs together and to the side when his tongue darted out along the top seam of her underwear. "You don't have to do that."

But when Hunter looked up at her, there was a devilish grin on his face. "I want to." He leaned in and buried his nose in her crotch. "Fuck, do you know how good you smell?"

Isobel felt her cheeks flood with heat. Did he *really* think— Was he serious or just trying to—

He pushed her legs open wide and lowered his head between them. She was about to object again, but then that wicked tongue of his was back at work, right where her thigh met her sex. She squirmed and her legs started to draw back together but he easily pushed them apart again.

One of his fingers teased underneath the seam of her underwear, running along her swollen vulva and dipping ever so slightly inside her. She cried out at the sensation.

Somewhere in the back of her head she imagined herself like a beached whale, flopped out in the middle of Hunter's living room floor like this, her flabby legs spread so wantonly. But every other part of her brain was consumed with firing neurons of pleasure.

He pushed aside her underwear and his tongue teased along the path his finger had just traced. But then he pulled back again. He was driving her so freaking insane. She didn't recognize her voice as she reached down and buried her hands in his dark brown curls. "Hunter, please," she begged. "*Please*."

"Please, what?" he asked, and she could feel the warmth of his breath through her damp panties. As close as his face was, he had to be drenched in the smell of her arousal.

"Touch me." She couldn't help the whining quality to her voice. But she couldn't stand any more teasing either.

His hands grabbed her inner thighs just above her knees and he started massaging up toward where his tongue continued its torture. "I am touching you," he said.

Her hands fisted in his thick hair. "Touch my…" She swallowed. God, was he really going to make her say it? "Touch my cunt. Lick my cunt."

His hands squeezed her thighs and he buried his face in her sex at her words, breathing her in and biting at her pussy.

She cried out, almost coming on the spot at the contact after so much teasing. He dragged her underwear down over her hips. She lifted her butt off the ground to help him and he had her panties halfway down her thighs the next moment.

And then, oh God finally, he was diving face first into her most intimate area. He ate with abandon, like he wanted his mouth everywhere at once. He was licking between her folds and sucking on her clit one moment, then thrusting his tongue deep into her passage the next, then just burying his face as deep as he could in her cunt like he couldn't get enough of her.

She couldn't help the unintelligible high-pitched squeaking noises that came out of her throat. She'd never— Jason had never— He always said it wasn't hygienic. That she smelled like fish down there. She'd been paranoid about it when she was with him, using all kinds of products to make sure she smelled fresh and clean whenever she knew they'd be spending the night together.

But she hadn't showered in a couple days and here Hunter was lapping at her like he'd never tasted anything as sweet. And having his mouth there, his tongue, doing such—

She cried out and shamelessly thrust her pelvis up and into his face. "Oh God, yes," she cried. "Eat me out. Eat me out so fucking good!"

She'd never in her life been so vocal during sex, but she'd also never had sex in a cabin in the middle of the woods before. It was freeing to shout her dirtiest desires at the top of her lungs. She slammed her hands to the soft rug underneath them, clawing into the carpet fibers as the pleasure ramped higher and higher. White spots burst as— Oh God, how could it feel *so*—

"It's coming, it's coming!"

He pulled away from his meal only long enough to say, "let me hear it," before wrapping his arms underneath her ass and pulling her even more roughly into his face.

Her breasts arched into the air and she did. She let him hear every moment of her increasing pleasure as she got closer and closer to the edge.

"Oh God, oh God, oh God—"

But it wasn't until she felt one of his fingers pressing at her back entrance that she really went wild. No one had ever touched her there. The pressure felt so forbidden and wrong and— oh!

"Hunter," she screamed his name, as his finger made it past the ring of muscles and slid into her ass. He fucked her with his tongue at the same time, right before licking up and latching onto her clit, sucking for all he was worth. She grabbed his head and shoved his face in her pussy as she came so hard she thought she might black out.

Ohhhhhhhhhhh, fuck, it just kept going and going and—

She thrust her pelvis into Hunter's face over and over and—

Oh shit, could he breathe? She let go of his hair and dropped back to the floor, completely mortified. She expected him to pull away gasping and pissed, but he just followed her down, still sucking mercilessly at her pulsing clit.

Aftershocks spasmed down her legs and she cried out again. When he finally pulled away and wiped his mouth on his forearm, his eyes were heated as he looked her up and down. Any other time a man perusing her naked like that would have sent her insecurities into overdrive, but after that orgasm, God, she could only watch Hunter with a lazy, distracted pleasure.

And damn, was he something to watch. Especially since he was busy pulling off his jeans and boxer briefs, revealing a truly beautiful cock. It was a little shorter than Jason's, but thicker. Her sex clenched in anticipation just by looking.

She wanted to touch it.

She wanted to lick it.

She lifted up, reaching for it but Hunter moved out of her grasp, groaning. "Don't move." He looked at her and held out a finger while he got to his feet. "I'm serious. Don't move that gorgeous ass one inch."

"What are—"

"I'll be right back. Not one inch." His eyes dropped down her body and he shook his head and let out a low whistle like he couldn't believe he was lucky enough to have her there with him.

Which was ridiculous.

But then he jogged to the other side of the room toward the stairs, his tight ass providing an excellent view as he went. He disappeared around the corner up the stairs.

Isobel flopped back against the rug, her whole body limp. The next second, though, her thighs were rubbing together. She wanted more. Which was insane. She barely knew Hunter and God knew she was the last person on earth she would have thought of as sex-starved. But damn, that was the best orgasm she'd had in a *long* time. But her sex clenched, feeling empty.

When she heard Hunter's feet pounding on the stairs as he came back down, she went up on her elbows and bit her lip in anticipation. Especially when she saw that he was holding not just one condom packet, but a whole strip of them.

Her mouth broke into a wide grin. Both because of how many he'd brought and the fact that he hadn't just pulled one out of his wallet, like he'd gone to the bar intending to score. She arched an eyebrow. "Somebody's feeling ambitious."

"Not at all," he grinned. "Just inspired.

He was also holding a plush dark blue blanket. Isobel snatched it from him when he got close enough, quickly draping it over her nakedness. She'd been brave, not flinching the whole time he walked back toward her while she was completely exposed. But she felt immediately better having the cover.

Hunter just looked at her with his brows furrowed. "Are you cold?" He flashed a crooked smile. "Because I'm happy to warm you up." He dropped down beside her and immediately captured her mouth in a deep kiss.

He reached beneath the blanket and lifted her by her waist like she weighed nothing. She yelped as he settled her on his thighs, her legs straddling his waist. His thick cock lay erect and hard between them. She couldn't take her eyes off it and Hunter flexed it so that it jumped.

She bit her lip and looked up into his eyes as she reached down with her right hand to stroke him up and down.

He hissed out the second she made contact and his whole body went tense as her small hand wrapped around him.

"Jesus, Isobel," he bent over and nipped at her shoulder. "I want to be inside you. Can I be inside you?"

When he looked up at her, his cock still in her hand, he looked so vulnerable it made her heart stutter. Like he was asking for more than to just have sex with her.

She didn't trust her voice so she just nodded. He didn't break her gaze as he reached beside him for the condoms. She ran her thumb over the bulbous head of his cock and his neck tensed, the vein straining. A drop of pre-cum dripped out and she rubbed it all around his cock. His hands fumbled as he ripped a condom packet open and then he had it at his cock.

Isobel bit her lip as she took it from his hands and rolled it down over his length. Then before she could second-guess herself, she shifted up his thighs and positioned him at her entrance.

His hands went to her waist, guiding her as she sank onto his cock. He held her from going too quickly. Instead, she dropped by increments, the head of his shaft pressing through her folds. He moved so slow she was aware of every sensation as he spread her open and stretched her.

She gasped a sharp inhale at his size. She'd been right—he was thicker than Jason. But the feeling was such a delicious fullness. She adjusted her legs so she was spread even wider to accommodate him.

He groaned low as his cock slid along her inner walls. But then he paused. "Isobel, open your eyes."

Her eyes popped open. She hadn't even realized she'd closed them.

She wasn't prepared for the sight of him, his mouth slightly dropped open, nostrils flared, his eyes dark with lust. And all his focus zeroed in on her at the same time he plunged *inside* her.

"Eyes on me," he breathed out.

It was so intense she couldn't handle it after a few seconds and her eyes dropped. She dipped to kiss his neck but he ducked out of the way and, with his hand, he directed her chin back up.

"Look at me," he repeated, thrusting up at the same time pulling her down by her waist. His face strained with pleasure as he fully seated himself inside her.

He stilled again, wrapping one hand around her waist and the other up underneath her shoulder, pulling his chest to her breasts until there was no space at all between them. Isobel had literally never been this close to another person in her life. Jason never held her so close when they'd made love. God, even when she breathed in, Hunter's chest moved with her.

His eyes were so bright. Cornflower blue. They searched back and forth as he watched her. His face was so earnest, brows slightly scrunched, like he was trying to figure her out.

She kept waiting for him to start moving. Then again, she was on top so maybe that was her job? She'd never had sex sitting up like this, but just because he'd been directing her so far didn't mean he should be expected to do all the work. When she tried to lift up off his shaft, though, his grip on her waist only got tighter to hold her in place.

She cocked her head sideways in confusion but he just said, "Shhh. Just keep looking at me."

She looked at him.

And it was awkward.

45

When did people just sit around and stare into each other's eyes for more than five seconds? Apart from when she was a kid and they played that game where you tried not to blink. Speaking of, when did she last blink?

She blinked. And then blinked again. Shit, now all she could think about was blinking.

Okay, this was getting really awkward.

In fact, being naked with this stranger's cock up inside her and just *staring* at each other—without the frantic kissing and tugging and touching and imminent orgasm to distract her... God, how long had they just been staring at each other now? A minute? Five?

Was her body being so close like this making him sweat? Did she smell? She'd given herself a sponge bath at a gas station in Colorado but that was earlier this morning.

What was he thinking while he looked at her? Was *he* thinking about blinking?

She started watching for him to blink.

But he just seemed to blink at regular intervals. Like a normal person. Because he wasn't a weird freakazoid who obsessed about how often they blinked while screwing someone.

As the seconds dragged on, and he just kept looking at her, she'd never felt more naked in her life—even though it was just her eyes he was staring into. Somehow that was even more scary than him seeing her cellulite. Because there was nowhere to hide. It felt as intimate or more than his cock penetrating her body.

They said the eyes were the window to the soul. If that was true, could he tell what a fucking mess she was?

"It's been so long since..." She almost jumped when he finally spoke even though his voice was soft. And then he was quiet so long she thought he might not continue. Finally, he did, still never breaking eye contact. "I've missed being intimate with another person. You go through life alone long enough and part of you just starts to feel dead inside. Without this kind of connection..."

His cock stirred inside her but he also lifted their hands, palm to palm, interweaving their fingers. He shook his head. "...it's like being thirsty and there's nothing to drink. Months and months and maybe years, you can be surrounded by people, you can walk around all day long, but you're dead. The spark's gone out."

"So then you need some good sex to recharge your battery?"

His cock jumped at her words and he chuckled, his eyes lighting with his smile. "Something like that."

She was glad she could make him smile. He was a little intense. But she liked it. What he was saying—it did feel amazing to truly connect to another person. Not just in a bullshit way. But to experience true intimacy… God, she couldn't remember the last time she felt that.

Things with Jason were never really… They just weren't— They hadn't been like that. There were so many red flags that she'd refused to see for what they were. And Dad— She swallowed hard. They'd been close when she was little, but ever since Catrina moved in, Catrina had forced him to choose sides.

And he'd never chosen Isobel's. He'd never believed her when she told him the horrible things Catrina said to her. She was just a child and no one ever took what kids said seriously—that was what she told herself over the years so she could forgive him and have any sort of relationship at all with him. But God, it still hurt. She was his *daughter*. His flesh and blood.

Before she even realized what was happening, a tear slipped down her cheek. She only became aware of it when Hunter reached out with his thumb and wiped it away. And then she was horrified because his cock was inside her and they were—

Her cheeks heated and she turned her head, trying to pull off of his lap. But his arms held her tighter than ever.

"Don't. You don't have to be afraid of anything you feel here," he murmured, pulling her so close that they were cemented, torso to chest, their noses only inches away from each other. When he breathed out, she inhaled it.

"What are you—?"

"Let it happen." His eyes searched hers. "It's okay. To feel sad. To feel happy. Everything is okay here. Christ, do you know how long I wished there was just one place I could be fucking honest? Where I could feel something *real*?" Then he started to kiss her again, light feathery kisses on the side of her face, on her temple, up to the crown of her forehead.

And then finally, finally, his lips came to hers. They weren't soft or explorative this time. No, he kissed her deeply, wrapping his arms around her and pulling her into him like he was desperate for her. If they were sharing one breath earlier, now it was like they were trying to share one body.

His tongue tangled with hers, thrusting and demanding. She felt it now—that thirst he was talking about. He was drinking from her like he was demanding to be quenched.

Her legs wrapped around the small of his back and he hiked her up by her ass so that she was better positioned in his lap. Then he guided her up and down his hard cock. Once. Twice.

She groaned into his mouth. His hands grasped at her waist before sliding up her ribcage and to her breasts and then down again. She couldn't help crying out at the briefest graze of his thumbs on her nipples, arching toward him and throwing her head back.

God, oh God, that felt—

Before she could even finish the thought, his hands were behind her back, unfastening her bra. She helped pull it off and his mouth immediately latched on her left breast, his tongue flicking back and forth over the hardened nipple. She couldn't help the high-pitched squeal that came out of her throat—because if she thought it felt good a second ago with the barest touch of his thumbs, God, she had no idea—

She ground down on him restlessly as he switched to the other breast. She needed him to move again.

He wanted real?

Well, what she really wanted was for him to fuck her. To fuck her rough and hard.

She bent over his head buried at her breast and gripped his hair. "Fuck me, Hunter," she growled in his ear. "I need you to fuck me. Fuck me dirty."

His teeth bit down on her nipple in response. She cried out and arched into him. Oh God, yes. He reacted every time she told him the things she wanted him to do to her. He was driving her absolutely crazy. Time to see if she could do the same to him.

"Stop teasing. Don't you feel how slick I am around your cock? I need you to fuck me." She had no idea where the confidence was coming from to demand these things out loud. But the more she said them, the bolder she got. "I need it hard, Hunter. Fuck me hard, please—"

With a roar, Hunter flipped them so that her back was on the soft rug. His cock had slipped out while he moved them, but he quickly realigned and then shoved back home, hitting a spot so good, oh God, it was sooooo good.

He was inside her. Inside. Oh God, *yes*.

"Look at me." His demand was growled as he pulled out and then thrust back in again, so hard he speared her to the floor.

"Oh God. Hunter. *Yes*. Harder."

His nostrils flared and he pulled his pelvis back and then slammed in again. Every time hitting that place inside her that— She'd never— She didn't know it could feel—

"More!"

He gave her more, fucking her rough and dirty, his balls slapping with every thrust. Their bodies grew slick with sweat and her moans echoed off the cabin walls. She clenched as hard as she could around him. Clenched. Released. Clenched.

He swore, his rhythm getting faster and more frenzied. With every thrust, his groin rubbed against her clit, his cock also hitting that place deep up inside her with each plunge. Pleasure lit up every nerve below her waist and she squeezed hard around his cock as her cries came out higher and higher pitched.

She howled as the orgasm ripped through her.

He dropped to his elbow so he could wrap both arms around her. He clutched her to him and thrust into her more deeply than ever. She was still riding her high when he roared through gritted teeth and shoved himself to the hilt inside her.

She reached down and grabbed his flexed buttocks, not wanting to miss a moment of the shared experience. He jerked back and then thrust in again, his face knotted with agonized pleasure.

For a precious second, they peaked together.

And then his body went slack over hers. Where his entire body had been strung taut as a bow only moments before, now he crumpled almost completely limp, sliding out of her and rolling to her side. He didn't let go of her, though. He just dragged her with him so that she was captured against his chest, her body cemented to his side.

She didn't mind. She was glad, in fact. After such an intense experience—holy shit, that was just—

"Wow," she whispered.

He squeezed her close and laughed. She could hear it rumbling through his chest where her head was propped.

"Yeah, you can say that again." He sounded just as in awe as she was.

Her own body relaxed at his words. She'd thought maybe this was how sex always was for him. All his moves were so smooth, she couldn't help wondering if he was just some sex god who took home a different woman every other night to quench his 'thirst.' Women probably a lot prettier and skinnier than her.

Then she clenched her eyes shut. God, she did *not* need to be worrying about that. She could just enjoy this for what it was without analyzing it to death.

All she'd wanted was one night to let go.

To celebrate her new freedom. Her new life.

Besides, she was far from ready to dive into another relationship right after ending things with Jason. As if a one-night stand would lead to a relationship anyway. She internally rolled her eyes and sank against Hunter's warm, muscled chest. She wrapped her arm around his broad body. After the year she'd had, she deserved tonight and enjoying the little slice of heaven that was Hunter Dawkins.

They laid there in silence. She would have thought he'd fallen asleep except for his hand tracing patterns up and down her back. He seemed content to simply lie there, snuggled against her.

Like the intense sex they'd just had, his tenderness threatened to crack the determination she'd just come to that this was just a casual one-night stand.

And she couldn't have that. She was all too aware of how fragile she was at the moment.

Before leaving New York, she'd stopped at the pharmacy and gotten a refill of her prescription—pills she could trust to be her real medication and a ninety day supply so she wouldn't have to worry for awhile—and already she'd been feeling more evened out over the past few days. But still. It usually took a couple weeks to a month whenever she had a medication change and who knew what the hell Catrina had been dosing her with that she still had to get out of her system?

All of which meant she couldn't trust any of her emotions right now—no matter how intensely she might be feeling for the man she was currently snuggled against.

So, determined to keep it light, she turned into him and nipped at his chest, grinning up at him when he jerked in surprise and looked down at her.

She arched an eyebrow. "Don't tell me you're done with me already." She nodded toward the rest of the condoms he'd brought. "You came so prepared, after all. It'd be a shame to put it to waste."

His nostrils flared and his mouth hitched up on one side. "I was an Eagle Scout."

"Ooo. Impressive."

"I live to impress." He was all out grinning now.

She sat up and pulled back from him, drawing the blanket up with her, leaving him bare. She put her fist underneath her chin and looked him up and down, evaluating him in an overexaggerated fashion. "Well, Eagle Scout Hunter, I give you a ten for presentation and let's say a…" She pursed her lips, "…an eight point five for performance."

His eyebrows shot to his hairline. "Only an eight point five?"

She smiled at him. "There's always room for improvement." Then she added magnanimously, "The judge is open to another demonstration if you'd like to try upping your score."

"Oh she would, would she?" He crawled toward her like a stalking predator. She jumped to her feet, shrieking, and running for the stairs. She didn't make it two steps before his arms wrapped around her from behind. He lifted her up off her feet. She squealed and giggled as he carried her over to the couch.

But her laughter quickly died down as he got down to the business of showing her just how skilled he was in the performance department.

Chapter 4

ISOBEL

Every limb was sore as she climbed out of bed the next morning. Yes, they finally made it up to Hunter's bed—just before dawn, on round number four. She never knew a man could have that much stamina. But then again, she'd never met Hunter Dawkins before.

She smiled, clutching the spare blanket she had wrapped around her body to her chest. For only having one night with him, he definitely made sure it was one hell of an experience.

But it was over now.

The smile dropped from her face as she watched Hunter sleeping peacefully, the morning light streaming in on his gorgeous face and exposed back. The sheet was pulled up to the bottom of his spine, but the tantalizing curve of his ass was visible right at the top of the fabric's fold.

She bit her lip. He'd had a couple hours of sleep. Maybe they could fit in just *one more*—

No. She cut the thought off at the root.

It was daylight. The clock had more than struck midnight. It was time to go back to the real world.

There was no way she was going to tarnish the perfection of last night with awkward morning after BS and false promises that they'd call one another—or worse, him *not* even asking for her number. No, she'd just quietly exit stage left before he even woke up.

With effort, she pulled her eyes away from the gorgeous specimen on the bed and turned toward the stairs. She winced at the loud creak of the second stair as she started heading down. Whipping around to see if the noise woke Hunter, she saw that other than him shifting slightly, he didn't stir.

She let out a deep breath and then tested each step before putting weight on it. It seemed to take forever, but she finally got to the bottom of the stairs. She gathered her clothes from where they'd been tossed off the night before and dressed in record time.

Then she grabbed her purse and was out the door, biting her lip as she closed it gingerly behind her.

She ran to her car and pulled away from Hunter's house with only a quick wistful glance in her rearview mirror. The cabin looked like something out of a fairytale, a cabin in the woods with trees shading it.

She shook her head like she could clear it from the spell of sex and pheromones that she'd been lost in for the last fourteen hours.

Hunter's gravel driveway was longer than she remembered it. It wound through the woods almost like a little road. Isobel glanced down at her rumpled clothes and then pulled over just long enough to change into a summer dress she'd thrown in her bag at the last minute. First impressions could be everything. The dress gave the message that she was friendly and approachable.

She got going again as soon as she could though, glancing over her shoulder every few seconds. But Hunter's truck never appeared and in another minute she finally pulled out onto the paved county road. With a press on the screen, she pulled up the directions she'd already input into her GPS for Mel's Horse Rescue.

It was half an hour away and she scanned radio stations to distract herself from thoughts of Hunter while she drove. Unfortunately, the only station that wasn't full of static was a modern pop country station blaring crap she couldn't stand. After a few minutes, she gave up and turned off the radio all together.

And in the silence that followed, she couldn't help her thoughts turning to the man she'd left back in bed.

What would he think when he woke up and found her gone? Would he just be glad she'd left with no awkward fuss? Or did last night end up meaning more than just a one-night stand after all…

Her hands tightened around the steering wheel and she shook her head. No. She wasn't a stupid girl.

But try as she might, she couldn't get the sexy man with his gorgeous body and intense eyes out of her head. Suffice it to say, it was a *long* thirty minutes.

When she finally saw the sign for Mel's Horse Rescue, she was more than relieved. She couldn't believe after all the shit she was running away from it was thoughts of a *man* that had her so distracted.

Maybe it was just easier to focus on Hunter than her real problems. Either that, she sighed, or Hunter was just a man worthy of distraction.

She drove past the gate into a gravel driveway leading to the ranch. As she pulled up, she saw a large three-story building in the distance.

It was time to move on. Several vehicles were parked in a small parking area off to the left of the main building. A few trucks of various sizes. One dirt-spattered SUV. Isobel's little Toyota was dwarfed by the others when she pulled in and parked beside a huge Dodge 4x4. That wasn't intimidating or anything.

She took a deep breath and then stepped out of her car.

No more thoughts of the past.

No more thoughts about Hunter or last night.

Time to *really* start this new chapter of her life.

She squared her shoulders and walked up to the front porch. The outside of the large building and wraparound porch were bright white, like they'd been freshly painted. Several rocking chairs were set up, along with a porch swing, looking out on the gently rolling hills that surrounded the property. It was so idyllic and different from the chic brownstone where she'd grown up in Manhattan that it almost felt like a different planet. But she'd done it. She was really here.

She looked around, trying to take everything in as she rang the doorbell.

Then the front door jerked open and a tall, tan, good-looking guy in his twenties stood there. He was wearing a linen shirt and pants, his dirty blond hair in dread-locks that were then pulled up in a man-bun.

She paused. Um. Maybe it was cliché, but this guy looked more like he belonged at a hippie commune than a horse ranch.

And you're standing here and staring, Isobel. Not awkward at all.

"Hi," she blurted, about to hold out her hand and introduce herself.

"Whatever you're selling, we don't want any." Hippie Guy crossed large muscled arms over his chest, a dour look on his face.

"Oh. No, I—" She stumbled over her words. Shit. She'd already made a bad impression and she'd only been here thirty seconds. "That's not what I— I'm here for—"

"Stop being an arsehole, Reece," a man's voice with an Irish accent called out. Then a second guy clapped the first on the back and dragged him away from the door.

But not before Hippie Guy—Reece, did the other one say his name was?—broke into a wide smile and winked at Isobel.

God, he was just joking? She'd about had a hard attack over making a bad first impression.

"What can we do you for, lovely lady?" asked the man with the accent, equally as handsome as Reece, though his hair was dark and his skin pale instead of tan.

He held out his hand and smiled at Isobel, a dimple appearing. "I'm Liam. Ignore my arsehole friend. With only the horses and other blokes except for Mel for company, we all start going a bit feral."

"I was just kidding with her," Reece said, shoving his friend out of the way and taking up the whole frame with his body again. He flashed Isobel a bright, dazzling smile. "Everybody needs to loosen up around here."

Liam pulled the door open wider so she could see both of them. "I'll show you loose." He grabbed Reece in a headlock.

"Doorbell! Doorbell!" screeched a little kid voice. Except the child must be small and not good with pronouncing his 'r's yet, because it came out sounding more like, "Dow bewl, dow bewl!'

Then a toddler ran full speed into Reece's legs, asking. "Who at da dow, Wyeece?"

Liam let Reece go and the little boy almost bounced off Reece's legs due to his momentum. Reece leaned down just in time and swooped the boy off his feet and up into the air. This made the little boy squeal in delight and kick his feet. Isobel didn't know much about little kids but guessed he was between two and three years old.

Reece settled the kid on his hip and it was bar none the cutest damn thing Isobel had ever seen. Her heart did a little *squish* in her chest.

"Ah hell, I've lost her afore I even had a chance," Liam shook his head. "They all go gooey when they see him with the baby."

"Swing," demanded the child, grabbing fistfuls of Reece's linen shirt. "Awound. Awound!"

Reece rolled his eyes like it was a chore and he was completely put out by the child's demands—it was similar to the face he'd made when he first greeted Isobel so rudely at the door. But then his eyebrows jumped up and he shouted, "Boo!" right before turning left,

55

then right, swinging the now-giggling little boy around and around with him.

"Swing!" the boy cried when Reece stopped.

"What?" Reece said, his face going sober again. He leaned down and looked the little boy in the eye. "Do you think I'm your personal swinging jungle gym or something?"

"Yes!" the boy said ecstatically.

Reece shrugged. "Fair enough." Then he swung the boy around even faster.

"I'll go get Mel and tell her she's got a visitor." Liam said, shaking his head as Reece spun even faster with the boy.

"Don't say I didn't warn you when you end up with his breakfast all over you."

Reece ignored him. Or maybe not. He got too dizzy—or at least pretended to—and collapsed on the floor, the little boy landing on his chest. Then he pretended to play dead while the toddler poked at his face and called out for him to wake up. It was obviously a game they'd played before.

Reece pretended to rouse a little bit but then his head fell back and he started to snore loudly, eliciting a fresh round of giggles from the boy. Isobel couldn't help smiling at their antics.

"Brenton Samuel Kent, what are you doing to poor Reece now?"

"Mommy!" the toddler abandoned Reece on the floor and ran to the very pregnant woman walking into the wide entry area. He flung himself with as much energy into her legs as he had into Reece's.

"Oof," she said, reaching for the wall to keep her balance in spite of the bundle of energy that just barreled into her. She was a beautiful woman who didn't look more than thirty, if that, with long brown hair. She smiled, bemused, down at her little boy. Brenton. Isobel repeated it to herself, trying to keep track of all the names. Brenton and Liam and Reece. Brenton was busy tugging on the leg of his mom's jeans. "Come, Mommy, we haf to wake up Wyeece."

For his part, Reece stayed completely still, splayed out on the floor without moving.

The woman pried her son's hand from her jeans. "I'll let you do the honors, Brent honey. I need to talk to this nice lady."

Brent looked up at Isobel like it was the first time he'd realized there was someone else in the room. And then he ran around behind his mom's legs like he was suddenly shy.

Only then did Reece jump to his feet. "Hey bud, it's about time for lunch. Why don't we see if we can go find your brother and rustle up some peanut butter and jelly sandwiches?"

"Can we have gwape jewy?" The boy's head peeked around his mom's legs.

"You bet." Reece reached down and scooped Brent up. Then they headed off into the big room that the entryway opened to on the left.

"Hi," Isobel jumped forward to introduce herself to the pregnant woman. Liam said he was getting Mel. Was this her? As in, Mel of Mel's Horse Ranch and Rescue? "I'm Isobel Snow. So nice to meet you."

She smiled at Isobel warmly. "Hi. Melanie Kent. You can call me Mel. Everybody does. How can we help you?" Her other hand rested on her large belly.

Now that Isobel was standing here in front of her, nerves assaulted her. "I stable my horse with Rick at Northingham Stables in New Hampshire."

Isobel's summers riding Buttons and training with Rick had been a rare bright spot in her teenage years. The summer after her senior year she even spent the summer with him and his family working at the stables in an unofficial internship.

That was when everything had first started getting better. She'd already been accepted into Cornell, but it was during her summer at Northingham that she decided to focus her studies in biology with an emphasis in veterinary sciences so she could continue on to get her doctorate of veterinary medicine degree. Nothing helped her get her mind and focus off of herself and her problems like working with animals, especially horses.

Mel nodded at Rick's name—obviously she knew him; Rick had told her as much.

"Well, Rick told me that every summer you look for helpers for your rescue. He said that you never have enough." Isobel smiled and held up her hands, feeling more than a little awkward. "So here I am."

But Mel wasn't smiling anymore. Her face had fallen, in fact, her features scrunching in remorse. "Oh no, I'm so sorry. I wish you would have called ahead. You didn't come all this way just for this, did you? From the East Coast?"

Isobel's stomach dropped to the floor. "Um…" Rick made it sound like such a sure thing. Granted, it had been a while ago. Maybe a year. Or two? But he said they were always looking for help. Isobel daydreamed about spending the summer here, never thinking in a million years she'd actually do it.

Until she had suddenly needed a place off the map to disappear to where no one in the world would think to look for her.

"Usually it's completely true that we don't have enough help." Mel's face was apologetic. "But this summer we have more horses than ever since my husband's taking in and training several wild horses. And with another baby coming—" She put a hand to her stomach. "So we advertised for the positions and actually have more than enough help for a change. I'm sorry." She reached out and put a hand on Isobel's forearm.

"Oh don't be," Isobel said, trying to speak through her suddenly strangled throat. "It's my fault for not calling."

Now that she thought about it, it was completely ridiculous how much faith she'd put on the fact that this place would be waiting for her—the position didn't pay much but it provided room and board. And it had been her safe harbor. A place to hide. To stop running and find herself, if there was a *her* to find that wasn't the fucked-up girl she'd been.

And now?

Now there was nothing.

Her father was dead. She had nothing but her car and the few clothes she'd grabbed. She didn't dare use her credit or debit cards after she left New York. She'd withdrawn the maximum three hundred bucks allowed from an ATM at the pharmacy where she'd picked up her meds, and she'd already spent over a hundred of it on gas and the toiletries she'd forgotten to grab from home. She'd have to stay on the run except now she had no idea where to run *to*. She couldn't just keep sleeping in her car forever.

Calm down, Isobel. Think.

58

She could go to a public library and look online at jobsites, then surf Craigslist for roommates—but she'd need a paycheck to be coming in first for a deposit on any apartment—and what, sleep out of her car for two months while she waited for all that? No. God. There had to be a way to make this work. There just *had* to be.

"Maybe you have all the stable hands you need, but you're a rescue farm, right?" Isobel asked. *Please God don't let her hear the desperation in my voice.* Panic made blood rush in Isobel's ears. "I'm three years into my Doctor of Veterinary Medicine degree from Cornell in New York—they're the top veterinary school in the country—and my focus is actually on rehabbing injured horses. I could—"

Mel's eyes brightened. "Veterinary degree?" she cut into Isobel's rush of words. "Oh my gosh, that's perfect."

"It is?" Isobel's heart was in her throat.

"We don't have work here, but I know someone who *is* looking for help. He was just complaining about being too busy to handle things all on his own. And we'd be happy to provide room and board for the summer if it works out. We've done that in the past for his interns."

Isobel's heart leapt even as she told herself not to be stupid and get her hopes back up. "Who? What do you mean?"

The front door was still open and Mel grinned, her eyes looking beyond Isobel. She gestured out the door. "Look, there he is now. This is total kismet. Our local vet has been looking for an intern—the one he had lined up for the summer just fell through. I bet he'd be ecstatic to have someone from Cornell. Come on, let's go work out everything right now."

Isobel pivoted to see where Mel was pointing and her stomach, so recently pulled off the floor by the hope of everything working out after all, plunged right back to the ground.

Because the man stepping out of the dusty truck parked beside her little Toyota was none other than Hunter Dawkins.

Chapter 5
HUNTER

She was gone when Hunter woke up.

For the first time in a year, the first thing he felt when he opened his eyes wasn't the crushing weight of loss. He was actually smiling when he turned over in bed and reached for Isobel.

But she was gone.

Just like Janine.

That wasn't fair, he tried to tell himself as he sat up and swung his legs over the side of the bed, rubbing his hands brusquely over his face.

Isobel hadn't made any commitment to him. They barely knew each other.

Except… last night, when he'd been so deep inside her, when she'd cried out his name like he was the only god in her world—

But all thought was put on hold when he'd looked at the clock and saw that it was already ten. He was due at the Kent's ranch for a round of vaccinations and he was already late. He was never late.

He couldn't believe he'd slept through Isobel waking up and leaving, actually. Usually he was a light sleeper. That woman had woven a spell around him, that was for damn sure. From the moment she'd stepped into that bar, swaying those luscious hips.

And the possibility that he might see her again at the Kent's? Well yeah, he couldn't say that wasn't part of what lit a fire under his ass to shower and burn rubber to get out to the Kent's ranch as fast as humanly possible.

Now here he was. And there she was. As soon as he'd pulled his truck in beside her petite little Toyota, his heart had started beating double time.

Like he was back in high school and it was the first time he'd had a crush on a girl. Fucking pathetic.

It got even worse when he saw her standing in the doorway behind Mel. Mel was waddling down the porch to greet him, broad smile on her face like always, but Isobel stood frozen, her wide eyes locked on him.

Shit. He'd just wanted to hurry to get here. But he hadn't thought through what he'd actually say when he ran into her again.

Hi there. So, last night's multi-orgasmic marathon…that was pretty great, yeah? Wanna go for pizza and a movie sometime? Or let me fuck your brains out some more in the back of my truck?

But Jesus, last night had been about more than just the sex. Sure, it had started out that way. At the bar, he hadn't been thinking beyond the moment and the urge to have a woman again. That on its own had been a novel and refreshing impulse after a year of feeling pretty dead as a man, apart from the occasional mindless stress relief session with his hand in the shower.

But then she'd come so alive under his touch. She was so responsive. And then he couldn't bear for it to be like it had been with Janine—impersonal sessions where they'd just used each other until it was only the pretense of a connection between them.

No, he'd wanted Isobel to see him. To really *see* him. To know who it was she was having sex with.

When he and Janine had been going through their roughest patch yet, Hunter had researched techniques and ways to make the one thing that seemed to be still working for them—sex—more meaningful.

He read books and learned everything he could. But then when he'd approached Janine about trying out some of what he'd learned, she'd taken it as an insult. She thought he was implying she was bad in bed and who was he to think he could teach her anything and—

The whole thing had been a disaster. It blew up into a huge fight. That was when she'd started sleeping on the couch after sex. Using it as a weapon and never talking to him when all he'd been trying to do in the first place was just open the lines of communication. But she just wouldn't—

He breathed out heavily, stopping his thoughts in their tracks. Going over and over all the things that had been broken in his relationship with Janine wouldn't do anyone any good.

But then last night, when he'd tried out some of the same techniques with Isobel, she'd been so open to it. In some traditions, you used sex as a way to worship God.

The other person became your church. If you opened yourself up to them, you could connect in a way so much deeper than just at the physical level. Both to the other person and to the divine.

And it had worked. Isobel had felt it too, even if she didn't know why he was doing everything he was doing. He could see it on her face—he watched barrier after barrier come down until she'd bared herself to him. While he was hard, deep *inside* her.

It was one of the most raw, intense, and spiritual moments of his life.

And then they'd just let loose—no holds barred. They'd fucked like animals. Or at least like two people with no inhibitions, who were truly naked and vulnerable to each other. He'd always heard the phrase 'two become one' but had never felt it so deeply until that moment. Not even with his wife. And with this virtual stranger. He knew he'd feel guilty about it later but in that second he hadn't cared.

When he came inside her that first time, her body squeezed around him like a vice and his seed had shot from him like a geyser. Goddammit, he'd almost passed out or touched heaven or some kind of crazy shit because he'd never come so fucking hard in his entire life.

"Hunter," Mel called, jerking his thoughts back from last night—just in time too because his jeans were starting to get tight and that was the last thing he needed in front of his best friend's pregnant wife. "Good to see you." She leaned in for a hug.

"You too, Mel." He could barely get his arms around her with her giant stomach between them.

"Whoa." He looked down. "I think I felt junior there knee me in the ribs. I don't think he likes anyone but Xavier near Mom. Is it going to be another boy?"

Melanie's hands went to her stomach even as her eyes looked heavenward. "Only if God hates me. And you don't, do you, God? Please not another ten pounder?"

"You guys didn't want to find out ahead of time?" Hunter asked, doing everything in his power to focus on Mel and not look behind her to see where Isobel was. Would she come out and talk to him? Or did she want to avoid him for some reason? Had last night not affected her like it did him?

Christ, listen to him. Carrying on like he was a school girl biting her nails while a note was passed to the boy she liked, *does he like me, check yes or no*. He shook his head at himself.

"Oh we tried, are you kidding?" Mel said. "I hate surprises. But the kid got all shy when we did the ultrasound so the ultrasound tech couldn't tell."

Oh right. The baby. Hunter forgot what he'd asked her for a second.

Mel shook her head. "I've never been religious but I've taken to saying hail Marys every night that it's going to be a six-pound girl." She patted her belly. "You hear that, Penelope? You're going to be a petite little baby girl for mommy, aren't you?"

Then Mel looked sharply up at Hunter. "Of course if it's a boy, his name will be Peter, and we never had this conversation." She arched an eyebrow in warning and Hunter held his hands up.

"Conversation? What conversation?"

Mel patted him on the shoulder. "Good. Oh," she looked over her shoulder and Hunter finally permitted himself to look too. And there was Isobel. She'd changed into a little cotton dress that hugged her curves and perfectly showcased her round breasts and shapely hips. Her dark hair flew all around her in the wind. One of their sessions last night had been in the shower and he'd luxuriated in burying his hands in all that hair while he shampooed it. And then held fistfuls of it when she dropped to her knees and swallowed him deep—

"I'm being so rude," Mel laughed. "I forgot why I ran out here in the first place. Hunter, this is Isobel, from New York."

"New York?" Hunter echoed. And it was like a bucket of ice water was just dumped on his head. Isobel said she was from New Hampshire, he was certain. A *small town* in New Hampshire. She sure as hell hadn't mentioned New York.

"And this is Hunter Dawkins." Melanie beamed, missing the sudden chill in Hunter's tone. "Hunter, Isobel is getting her veterinary degree from Cornell. Isn't that impressive?"

She was studying to be a vet? How had it not come up last night that she was studying the same thing as he did for his job? This was too much shit coming at him at once. Hunter stared at her. "So do you just go to school in New York or do you live there too?"

Isobel swallowed, looking suddenly nervous. "Well, I just took a semester off from school and have been at home in the city for a little while."

"New York City?" he clarified.

She nodded, quickly glancing away from him.

So she'd been lying to him last night.

There hadn't been anything real between them at all.

No soul-searing connection.

Her leaving this morning with no goodbye should have been enough of a red flag.

But Jesus, he was such a fucking cliché. As if the first woman he slept with since Janine was going to be his soul mate or some bullshit. He was such a goddamn sap. Come to think about it, didn't he think he'd fallen for Janine after a few nights together too?

He had a bad habit of letting his dick do all his thinking when it came to relationships. Look where that had gotten him last time.

He clenched his teeth and extended his hand toward Isobel, but only because it was what Mel seemed to expect. If he never saw the woman again it wouldn't be soon enough.

"Nice to meet you." He didn't bother making it sound sincere. As quickly as he took her hand to shake it, he dropped it.

"You too," she said. Was it just him, or did she sound sort of breathless? Jesus, was he still at it? He wanted to sock himself upside the head.

He just needed to make his excuses and then get the hell out of here. Go to work. Vaccinations were monotonous but he'd take anything over the torture of standing here trying not to look at Isobel. Even her scent was getting to him. Which was ridiculous because she'd showered with *his* soap and shampoo, yet he'd still swear there was a scent that was distinctly *her*.

Was she aroused? Was that what he smelled? Did seeing him after their sizzling night together have her soaking her panties? Everything else might have been a lie, but she hadn't faked those orgasms. Hunter had felt them around his cock when she came. He lost count of how many times.

"Hunter," Mel went on, completely ignorant of the growing tension between him and Isobel, "I was just telling Isobel about how you were looking for a summer intern."

Hunter's attention jerked back to Mel at the words. *No.* If she was going where he thought she was going—hell no.

"She was hoping for a position on the ranch but we're all full up on workers at the moment," Mel went on. "But I thought maybe we could do an arrangement like we did with Murray last year and Carlos a few years back. She could board here and drive out to the clinic—"

Hunter shook his head vigorously. "I doubt that's how she'd want to spend her summer." He looked at Isobel finally. She had a deer caught in headlights look. "Giving cows and pigs vaccines hardly has the glamour of feeding and riding horses all day long."

"Did you forget about the mucking out stalls part?" Mel scoffed. "Your job is easy compared to shoveling shit two to three hours every day. Plus, she's in school for veterinary medicine. Interning with you would be far more interesting."

Hunter crossed his arms over his chest. "I run a very small-town practice. I'm sure she's used to a much faster pace of life. And Cornell is one of the top veterinary programs in the country. She could get an internship wherever she wanted. So if she's got another option, she should go—"

"*She*," Isobel broke in, eyes flashing like something Hunter said had pissed her off, "would be happy for any work, no matter how hard, if it comes with room and board."

She stepped right in front of Hunter and his spine became even more rigid. Fuck but she was sexy when she was angry. Her blue eyes flashed, her cheeks went pink against the rest of her pale, smooth skin, and her full lips went all pouty. And it pissed Hunter off that he was noticing any of it.

He took a deep breath as he regained his senses. He had to put a stop to this idea before it got a foothold. He loved Mel but apart from Janine, he'd never met a more stubborn female.

"Interning with me means long, irregular hours. Sometimes ranchers will call in the middle of the night with an emergency and my interns are on call with me. Seven days a week. Twenty-four hours a day. That's what it means to be a rural, small-town vet. You don't get a pristine little office somewhere with people bringing in their pets who have breathing problems because they're overweight. These animals have real troubles. And I spend half my day with my arm up their back ends."

Isobel crossed her arms over her chest and her lips pursed. Thank God, maybe he was getting through.

He continued piling higher and deeper. "Not to mention the mess of record keeping and office work that needs to be sorted. My last intern made a total jumble out of everything and it will probably take weeks to get it all organized again."

Then Isobel dropped her arms and gave Hunter a saccharine smile. "That does all sound challenging."

He nodded. Good. His shoulders relaxed. "So you're going to head back east, then? That's probably for the b—"

"I love a challenge," she cut him off. "I'm not afraid of hard work. I'll be happy to get all your records back in order and I've been needing more field training. On *all* kinds of animals. Not just *pets*." She still had that oh so sweet smile on her face.

Hunter could only stand and stare at her. She wasn't meeting his gaze. No, her eyes seemed locked further south, somewhere in the vicinity of his mouth. Or rather, his lips. When he licked them to get some moisture, her eyes flared slightly. Which made his pants start to get tight again.

Like she had some internal sensor about his arousal, her eyes finally flicked up. Their gazes locked. And for a second, just the merest moment, Hunter felt the same electric connection he had the night before.

Guess she was pulling out all the stops to get this job. Hunter jerked his eyes away.

"Wonderful," Melanie broke in. "So that's settled. Right, Hunter?"

Well fuck. Way to back him into a corner, Mel.

He offered Isobel his most insincere smile. "Of course. If she wants the job, it's hers."

"I want the job," Isobel said quickly. Too quickly. What was her deal? He wasn't joking about a student from Cornell having their pick of internships. Why the hell was she out here anyway?

Melanie smiled wide but Hunter just kept looking at Isobel suspiciously. His only solace was that whatever she was here for, she wouldn't stay long. That was for damn sure. City princesses like her never did. And anything he could do to shorten the trip, well, he'd be happy to do his part.

"Welcome aboard," he said, smiling for the first time since Mel brought up the ridiculous idea.

"When do I start?" Isobel asked, a smile that was wide but slightly frantic on her face.

Hunter looked to Melanie. "Are all the horses ready?"

Mel nodded. "The guys spent the morning prepping them. They're washed down and in the stable."

Hunter's attention turned back to Isobel. "No time like the present. If you're up for it, that is." He looked her up and down. He stared probably a tad longer than was appropriate but damn, she looked good in that dress. He finally pulled his eyes back up to her face. "If you've got a change of clothes." He nodded down at the strappy sandals on her feet. "I don't think those will do too well for dirty stable work."

The bright pink blush that rose on the apples of her cheeks only made her prettier. "Of course I have work clothes. And riding boots."

"Not work boots?" he questioned.

Hunter didn't think her blush could get any redder but she proved him wrong. She squared her jaw and glared at him. "I thought I'd be working here with the horses."

He waved a hand. "Better than sandals. I'll grab the vaccination kit. You change. But hurry up about it. I have several other calls I need to make today."

He started walking around the house toward the stables without another look back.

He could handle her working for him. She'd be no different than any other intern. He could keep entirely professional about this. Clinical even.

And he'd finally learned his lesson. Maybe the one Janine had been trying to teach him all along. Sex was just that—sex. Biological impulses seeking release. He'd been deluding himself trying to find some deeper, spiritual meaning in it.

By no means would he make the mistake of letting Isobel or any other woman anywhere near his heart again.

Chapter 6
ISOBEL

Isobel ran to the trunk of her car and popped it, grabbing some leggings and a t-shirt as quickly as she could, along with her riding boots.

God. Riding boots. She knew she'd look ridiculous wearing riding boots all day doing veterinary work. But she'd been in such a rush when she left New York, it was a miracle she'd even grabbed the boots.

She flinched, thinking of how Hunter had sneered at what she was wearing. The entire encounter had been cringeworthy.

Yeah, sneaking out this morning had been a coward move, but she hadn't expected… God, Hunter had been so nice last night. Turned out in the light of day he was a real asshole.

Ugh, she didn't have time to think about it. She had to get her butt in gear. She grabbed her toiletries bag with her deodorant and toothbrush and then hurried back toward the house where Mel was waiting for her on the porch. She directed Isobel upstairs to a room at the end of a long hallway.

"Once upon a time, aka, about fifteen years ago, this place was a resort," Mel said. "Sort of a dude ranch where tourist could come stay and pretend to be cowboys. Good for us because it means every room is already set up." She opened the door and gestured for Isobel to go first.

She immediately saw what Mel meant. It was like a hotel room, complete with its own attached bathroom. Though at the moment it looked more like a storage space.

"I'll have one of the guys get this stuff cleared out and sheets on the bed before tonight." Mel gestured toward the cardboard boxes stacked up along one wall and the bare mattress.

"Oh, don't go to any trouble," Isobel said. "I'm happy to do it. Just leave the sheets on the bed and I can—"

"Don't be silly," Mel waved her away. "I'll let you get changed."

Mel closed the door behind her as she left. Isobel only took one more moment to look around the little room. Hardwood floors. Wooden paneling that went up half the wall, painted a soft eggshell that matched the rest of the wall. Otherwise, the walls were bare.

She glanced at the mountain of boxes. She hated to inconvenience them, but she was too happy to have a place to stay to balk too much.

Speaking of—her having a place to stay depended on her working for Hunter, so she better get her butt in gear. She hurried over to the restroom and set her bag of toiletries down on the counter. She brushed her teeth and changed clothes in record time and then jogged back downstairs.

In her rush, she almost collided with Mel at the bottom of the stairs.

"Oh," Isobel exclaimed, stopping just short of plowing into her. "Sorry!"

"Common hazard of living here with so many people coming and going. Come on," Mel waved Isobel to follow her. "It's easiest to get to the stables from the back door."

She led Isobel through a big common area that had a couple of long tables, a few leather couches, a fireplace, and a huge flatscreen TV. The lodge was all wood and decorated very simply with a few large oil paintings of landscapes and a huge antler chandelier overhead.

At the end of the room were double pocket doors that led into a restaurant-style kitchen. A couple of men sat at a table set up in a small dining area off to the side beside a large bay window.

"Nicholas. Mack," Melanie said. "I'm glad we caught you. This is Isobel, she's going to be staying here while she's Hunter's intern for the summer."

One of the men stood up when Mel and Isobel entered. He was a huge guy with a barrel chest and shoulders so large he looked like he could bench press an ox. "Nice to meet you, ma'am." He had kind eyes and light brown skin. "I'm Nicholas."

"They raise them right in Alabama," Melanie said, grinning at him. He looked embarrassed at her praise and sat down, even as Mel's eyes narrowed at the other man. "You hear that, Mack? It's called manners."

70

Mack was wearing a Black Sabbath T-Shirt and had tattoos covering his arms, all the way down to his hands and fingers. He was muscular too but in a smaller, more compact way. Then again, anyone would look small next to Nicholas. Though if the way Mack was scarfing down his sandwich was any indication, the man was starved.

"Yeah, yeah," Mack mumbled with his mouth full of sandwich, not even looking their direction.

Mel scoffed. "Are you even going to say hi to our newest arrival?"

After shoving the last bit of sandwich in his mouth, Mack grabbed a full glass of orange juice and started chugging it. His Adam's apple bobbed as he swallowed. And swallowed. And swallowed some more. He finished the whole glass before wiping his mouth with his forearm and standing up.

He finally looked at Mel and his eyes briefly flicked in Isobel's direction. They paused and he looked her up and down, not even trying to hide the fact that he was checking her out. "Hey." The single word came out in a low, grumbling bass.

Damn. This one had bad boy written all over him.

If Isobel hadn't met Hunter last night, she might have been tempted to try rebounding with this guy instead.

As it was, she just said, "Hey," back and fought a shy smile even as Mel shook her head.

"He's hopeless."

Mack didn't respond. He'd already moved on from the conversation anyway. He was out the door, grabbing a baseball cap from a hanging rack right before slamming it behind him.

Isobel jumped from the loud noise.

Mel breathed out in a huff. "Well someone's in a mood today."

"More like every day," Nicholas said, gathering both his and Mack's plates. He carried them to the sink.

Mel's eyes softened as she watched Nicholas. "Don't worry about the dishes. I'll get those later."

"It's no trouble, ma'am," he said, rinsing the plates and grabbing the sponge.

Mel watched on like a proud mama. She leaned in to Isobel and whispered. "The woman who gets that man will be a lucky lady."

71

Then she linked her arm in Isobel's. "Now let's get you to your first day on the job." Her smile was infectious.

Isobel wondered what kind of man was lucky enough to win *her* heart because she seemed like a pretty awesome chick.

They exited out the same door Mack had slammed earlier and passed by a fenced in area with a chicken coop and several chickens walking around.

Mel saw Isobel looking at it. "I like fresh eggs. It used to be a dog kennel but it's hard to keep dogs around the place because of the horses, so we repurposed it." She ran her hand along the chain link fence and smiled like she was laughing about some inside joke.

Beyond the chicken coop were big fenced off pastures with a few horses in them. It wasn't until they rounded the side of the house that Isobel's breath caught, though.

It was a real horse ranch.

There were two big stables and beyond them, fenced off horse paddocks as far as the eye could see. They were mostly empty at the moment, except for one in the near distance where a man was standing in the center, running a horse in a circle with a lunge line. Even from this distance, Isobel could tell the man was huge—similar in size to Nicholas.

A boy stood outside the paddock, leaning with his arms on the fence. Mel's other son?

Isobel looked back to the man guiding the horse. "Wow, is there something in the water here that makes the men come in extra large?"

Mel laughed at that. "But Nicholas is from Bama, remember? That's my husband, Xavier. The little one is our son, Dean." She pointed at the boy on the fence. "And I thought shopping for groceries was bad when it was just me, Xavier, and the boys. Ever since we expanded the rescue and brought in the guys last year, I have to buy everything in bulk and I still go shopping once a week!"

Isobel laughed. "I can imagine."

"Come on, the rest of the horses are stabled in preparation for getting vaccinated." She gestured toward the closest stable.

Isobel was immediately hit by the familiar smells of hay and horses as they entered through the wide double doors. It wasn't an exaggeration to say the summer she'd spent with Rick and his family working at Northingham stables had saved her life. Seeing a functional family, feeling accepted for who she was—whatever her shape or size—and working every day with the animals had given her stability and sanity at a time when she was barely hanging on by a thread.

She hadn't been in a proper stable in almost a year and the scent memories were so strong, it was like she was that sixteen-year-old girl again. The sense of *at homeness* that washed over her was almost dizzying after being so desperate for a lifeline. For a ridiculous moment, she had to swallow against tears.

"Isobel?" Mel questioned when she saw Isobel had stopped.

Isobel blinked and hurried to join Mel's side.

Hunter was set up in the center of the stable with Reece, who held the reins of a brown mare. Reece rubbed down the horse's nose, murmuring to her while Hunter leaned over and opened up a tool box. Instead of tools, though, there were medical supplies inside.

Isobel's eyes were stuck on Reece, though. In the short time since she'd last seen him, he'd changed clothes. He'd exchanged his linen hippie duds for jeans, a sleeveless shirt, and cowboy boots. And wait—his hair. She did a double take. Hadn't he had dread locks? Now his blond hair was cropped close to his head.

"Who's this?" Reece asked Mel as she and Isobel arrived at the men's side.

"Um," Isobel laughed a little, confused. "It's me, Isobel. You met me up at the house just a little bit ago?"

Mack walked by carrying a water bucket. "Didn't your last girlfriend have trouble telling you two apart, too?"

Oh. Duh, now it made sense. "Twins."

"Reece will tell you he's the better half, but it's all lies. I'm Jeremiah." He dipped his head in a nod. He couldn't exactly shake her hand since he was holding the horse's reins.

"If you're done with pleasantries, I've got a job to do," Hunter interrupted.

Jeremiah's eyebrows went up as he looked Hunter's way, but he didn't say anything else.

"I'll be upstairs in the office if you need anything." Mel squeezed Isobel's hand. "I'll probably see you later but in case I don't, I'll leave a set of keys and the wifi password by your bedside."

"Thanks so much. For everything." Isobel flashed her a warm smile that she returned before turning to go.

Leaving Isobel with the surly vet. At least Jeremiah was still here. He seemed as nice as his brother.

"How can I help?" Isobel asked.

Hunter didn't look her way, he just opened a sealed syringe packet. "You're familiar with giving equine vaccinations?"

His brusque manner was such a one-eighty from the man she'd met in the bar she would have thought *this* was the man with a twin, but nope. Apparently this was all him.

"Yes. I've done it before." Once. She'd done it once before, at least on a horse, when she was at Rick's stables. Her only other experience was the semester she'd volunteered at a veterinary clinic near Cornell, but it had been a strictly small animal operation. She'd given tons of vaccinations to dogs, cats, and several guinea pigs. Since she'd been in her first year, the doctor hadn't let her get much more hands on than that.

She'd been more of a glorified animal wrangler, holding disgruntled cats and dogs down while the vet looked them over. But she'd die before admitting that to Hunter, especially after his intimidation tactics earlier when he'd been trying to talk her out of taking the position.

He seemed to sense her hesitation anyway. "You'll humor me if I want to keep up on my teaching skills?"

He didn't sound like he was being an ass about it. Isobel got the feeling that apart from whatever feelings he might have about her, when it came to his work, his first priority was for the animals in his care.

"The best place to give a horse an injection is this triangular area on the neck." He indicated the upper area of the horse's neck and explained how there were bones above and major vessels below the area he indicated. She nodded along. It was nothing she hadn't learned, but she appreciated the refresher.

"Then before you inject, you pinch the horse's skin, like this," he pinched a small flap of the horse's skin, "so they know you're coming and aren't startled."

He went on to demonstrate giving the injection safely, making sure to hit muscle and not a blood vessel.

"Is there a place I can wash up?" Isobel looked around and saw a deep sink at the back of the stable right as Jeremiah pointed it out. She went and scrubbed her hands with soap, trying not to let her nerves get the better of her at the thought of Hunter watching her. Was he looking at her right now?

Just think about the horses.

They could sense unease and it was important to be as calm as possible when dealing with the intuitive animals. She took a deep breath in and then let it out again—trying *not* to think about how Hunter had instructed her to do the very same thing last night while he was buried deep inside—

She twirled on her heel and walked back to where Jeremiah was leading another horse out of its stall. In the distance, she saw Mack leading the gelding who had just gotten his shot out of the stables. She knew it was important to let a horse move and exercise lightly after getting their shots to ease any achiness in the muscles.

Jeremiah brought a dark brown mare toward them. The horse's mane was glossy but she walked hesitantly. A clear indicator that she was in pain. Isobel's brows furrowed as Jeremiah brought the mare to a halt.

This place was a rescue. When Rick had first mentioned it, he told her some of the horses' stories. How they were abandoned racehorses that were considered useless after they were no longer in their prime. Or how other horses came here after it was discovered they were mistreated by their owners. If Isobel thought about it too much she'd want to break something. Not exactly the attitude she needed to have when dealing with this big, beautiful creature.

"Good morning, gorgeous." Isobel held out her hand to the horse's nose. Then, with her other hand she began to gently stroke along her wither, the equivalent of a horse's shoulder.

The mare turned her head toward Isobel, blowing out a puff of air through her nose, investigating her.

"What's her name?" Isobel asked, smiling and continuing to pat the horse.

"This is Bright Beauty," Jeremiah said.

"Bright Beauty. You *are* a beautiful girl, aren't you?" She leaned a little closer and blew lightly into the mare's nose to let her start getting acquainted with her scent. It was how horses in the wild introduced themselves to one another. Made offers of friendship, as it were.

Bright Beauty knickered in response and nudged Isobel's face, blowing back. Friendship accepted.

Isobel laughed and leaned her forehead against the horse. "I'm going to take real good care of you, Beauty. We've got to give you some medicine. It might sting for a second, but it will keep you healthy." Isobel patted down her neck, stroking along the grain of her coat.

"How's the rehab with her going?" Hunter asked Jeremiah, running his hand along Beauty's flank and down to her back leg.

Isobel stepped back to watch. The horse shifted and her head dropped. More indicators that she was in pain.

Isobel winced, her heart squeezing at the thought of the beautiful mare hurting. "What's wrong with her?"

"She was a show horse. Barrel jumping," Jeremiah said. "She got hurt and her owner didn't give her enough time to heal before jumping her again and reinjuring her even worse."

"Tore her suspensory ligaments in her hind legs," Hunter said, feeling along the horse's leg. "It takes between eight to twelve months for an injury like that to fully heal."

Jeremiah nodded. "The owners were real bastards. They were just going to put her down, but a friend of Mr. Kent's let him and Mel know about it. Mr. Kent drove two days straight to pick her up and bring her home."

"How long has she been here?"

"Just a little over a month."

A show horse. Isobel shook her head at the thought of her owners pushing her to the limit for their own selfish desires, even at the risk of her health.

Do you want to be pretty or do you want to be a fat hog everybody makes fun of? Your appearance reflects on your father. Who's going to trust a man with their business when his own daughter can't show any self-control? Do you know how embarrassing it would be for your father if I have to take you to the plus size section to shop for you?

76

Everyone would laugh at him. And to think, the name Isobel means beautiful.

Isobel swallowed hard. God, would she ever be free of that woman's voice in her head?

Hunter finished his inspection of Beauty's hind legs and stood back up. "The swelling has gone down some. Keep her on stall rest. Just ten minutes of walking a day to work out any soreness."

"Will do," Jeremiah said.

"What a beautiful, brave horse you are," Isobel murmured, stroking down her mane. Then she turned sharply to Jeremiah. "She won't go back to those people, will she? Even if she gets better?"

It was Hunter who shook his head. "Once you meet Xavier, you'll understand. He's not a man who puts up with cruelty to horses."

"From what I hear, it was a good thing Mel was with him," Jeremiah said. "Xavier was ready to pound that guy into the ground."

The more I heard about him, the more I liked Mel's husband.

"All right, everything looks good."

Hunter pulled open the package of another syringe. "Do you want to jump right in or would you like another demonstration?"

For a second, her gaze connected with Hunter's light blue eyes and she felt a flash of the...*whatever* it was that was so strong and overpowering last night. She didn't even have words to describe it.

He looked away almost instantly, though, and she swallowed against the disappointment.

Not what you need right now.

There. Those were some words to describe it.

She squared her shoulders. "I'm ready."

Hunter nodded and held out the syringe.

"Here we go, girl," Isobel said, pinching the skin below her withers. Isobel administered the shot without a hitch. "There we go. That wasn't so bad."

Hunter pointed to a small plastic sharps bucket he'd also brought and she deposited the used syringe.

"Beauty's ready for you, Mack," Jeremiah called.

Mack came over and, without a word to any of them, took Beauty's reins.

77

"Remember no more than ten minutes letting her walk around," Hunter said. "Then she's back on stall rest."

Mack nodded, his face never changing expression. At least until he took ahold of Beauty's reins. Isobel saw him sneak her a sugar cube and whisper something in the mare's ear right before they left the barn.

They continued vaccinating the horses in assembly line fashion, Jeremiah bringing the horses out, her preparing the syringe, Hunter looking over the general health of the horse, then Mack taking them out to pasture after the shot was administered. After another few horses, Nicholas joined them in the stable and started the arduous task of mucking out stalls of the horses who had already had their turn.

With so many horses, one of whom had an abscess that needed to be drained, it took several hours before they were finished. While Jeremiah and Hunter had bantered back and forth, Hunter hadn't spoken to her directly again the entire time. Jeremiah tried to include her in their conversation and he'd occasionally direct a question her way, but Hunter would just move around the horse and pretend she didn't exist.

After they finished with the last of the horses and Hunter had packed up and was heading for his truck, she went after him. She waited until they were around the front of the house almost to their vehicles before jogging up to him and grabbing his arm. "Hey."

His nostrils flared as he looked down at her hand on his forearm. She yanked her hand back. Just the feel of his skin seemed so intimate after everything they'd shared last night.

He stared down at her stone-faced. "Was there something you needed?"

Her mouth dropped open. "So that's it? We're just not going to say anything about what happened last night? Look, I'm sorry for how I left this morning." She lifted her hands and shrugged. "I figured you were a guy and you know, I was doing you a favor by leaving without any big morning after scene."

His whole body went tense at her words and he let out a short huff of air through his nose. "Consider last night forgotten." His words were clipped. "I'm just your boss and you're just my intern. Nothing more. Nothing less."

78

He reached in his pocket and pulled out his keys and his wallet. Opening his wallet, he slipped out a white business card that was slightly worn around the edges. It read *Natrona County Veterinary* and then had Hunter's name, phone number, and the clinic's address.

"Come to think of it, the office really does need tidying up," he said. "I can handle the rest of today's calls by myself. Why don't you head in, do some cleaning, and see if you can make heads or tails of the filing system."

"I should be done with Mr. Guzman's steer in a few hours." He searched along his jangling key ring. "Here's a key. There's filing to be done if you run out of things to do."

Isobel nodded and took the key after he unclipped a small carabiner with an attached key ring from the larger set. Their fingers touched for the briefest moment as he passed the key and it was like a spark of static electricity lit between them.

Isobel's breath hitched as she looked up at him. But if he felt it, he gave no indication.

"All right." Isobel's voice came out a little higher pitched than she would have liked. She swallowed and then finished. "I'll see you there."

Hunter nodded and then he opened the door to his truck. He paused before getting in, though, and turned back toward her. His eyes were focused past her and his jaw was still hard.

"And Isobel?"

"Yes?"

"In the future, don't do me any favors."

He flicked his eyes ever so briefly in her direction before he hauled himself into his seat and slammed his truck door behind him.

Chapter 7
HUNTER

The sun was low near the horizon by the time Hunter pulled open the clinic door. The stop at the Guzman ranch was supposed to just be a pregnancy check. But one of the heifers was calving early and there were complications.

Hunter ended up having to extract a dead calf. Never a nice scene, but at least he was able to save the mother. And before he left, he double checked two other pregnant heifers. Everything looked to be going great with them.

But now he was tired, he stank of cow, and the last thing he wanted to deal with was a certain black-haired beauty on the other side of that door. He should have just told her they'd start tomorrow but he thought he'd make one last attempt to discourage her from staying.

Surely anyone seeing the state of the clinic reception area would be put off the job. He knew it was a disgrace. He and Dr. Roberts—the aging veterinarian he shared the practice with—were strict about keeping the exam rooms clean and disinfected. But their regular cleaning lady had had to take time off to have a baby and they'd had difficulty finding a reliable replacement. Even a couple weeks without a good scrub-down and the waiting room full of animal patients started to stink to high heaven.

But when Hunter stepped into the lobby, instead of the normal sour smell of cat piss, he was hit with the strong scent of lemon and bleach. The lobby was also bright for once—the flickering fluorescent light that he kept *meaning* to get around to had been replaced.

And best of all, Hunter was greeted with the sight of Isobel's wiggling backside as she leaned over and scrubbed at the baseboard with a big sponge, a bucket of soapy water beside her. Her ass swung back and forth like she was bobbing to music Hunter couldn't hear. That was when he noticed she had earbuds in.

For a second, he could only stare in appreciation at her delectable ass in those tight little leggings.

All he wanted to do was drop his bag of instruments, walk over to her, grab her waist with one hand and yank down those leggings. He'd bite that sweet ass of hers and then—

Isobel pulled back to dip the sponge in the soapy water and shrieked, obviously just then noticing him. She almost knocked the bucket over in her surprise.

Hunter took a step back, quickly averting his eyes from her backside.

"Crap, you scared me." She jerked her earbuds out and wiped her hands down her thighs, standing up.

Hunter grunted in response. Shit. What the hell was he doing? Staring at her ass? Last night was bad enough. He didn't need to add idiocy on top of stupidity.

"I need to be getting home." He strode toward the lobby desk. "Let me show you how the system works so you can get familiar with it and start on the records tomorrow."

"I already figured it out," Isobel said as Hunter was shaking the mouse to bring the computer to life.

"What?" Hunter turned around, looking at her in spite of himself. Her long black hair was pulled up in a ponytail but wisps escaped all around her face. Jesus, he swore every time he saw her she got prettier. Creamy skin, vibrant blue eyes, cherubic cheeks flushed so prettily—he wasn't sure if it was because of the work she was doing or because he made her nervous. Why did he stupidly hope it was the latter?

He shook his head in disgust at himself as he looked down at the computer screen. It was already open to the advanced record keeping program that neither Dr. Roberts nor he could ever figure out.

"I saw you have the VAP system installed. I'm familiar with it—they used it at a clinic where I volunteered during my first year in vet school. But then I saw that you've just been keeping your records in Excel files." Isobel leaned over and took the mouse from Hunter, clicking to a patient roster tab. "So I organized the columns to match the input parameters and then batch uploaded the records into the VAP database."

"Oh," was all Hunter could manage. Damn, she smelled good. Like flowers or some shit. Which only made him more acutely aware of how bad he must reek.

He stood up and took several steps away from the computer. He couldn't believe she'd done all that in the what, four *hours*, since he'd last seen her?

He'd sound like a complete idiot if he told her he and Dr. Roberts had held off using the new system because they'd assumed all the patient records would have to be input individually—a task which would have taken *weeks*. But she apparently did it with the click of a few buttons?

She looked up at Hunter, eyes wide. Like she was waiting for him to say something. When he didn't, her eyes narrowed. "I think the words you're looking for are, *thank you, Isobel*."

Shit. Hunter lifted a hand to the back of his neck. This woman had him fucking tongue tied. Of course he was—she went to an Ivy League school. And yeah, he'd gone to Purdue, but he'd barely passed his classes because he was busy trying to work and pay the tuition not covered by scholarships at the same time.

But this woman—she was beautiful. Intelligent. Witty. So what the hell was she doing all the way out here?

"You know, what I don't get is why you lied." He stared at her.

She jerked back at his words. "What? I didn't lie."

"You said you grew up in a small town in New Hampshire."

"I did." She averted her eyes like she had something to hide. "Part of the time anyway."

He frowned. "Were your parents divorced?"

"No," she said quickly, then paused before adding with a slight cringe. "We had a summer house there."

Fuck. Him.

Beautiful, intelligent, *and wealthy*. This woman was probably more of a goddamned princess than even Janine.

Janine, the vibrant girl he'd met in college who was so determined to rebel from her rich East Coast roots by dating and then marrying a poor farm boy from the Middle of Nowhere, Wyoming.

Of course, the romance of a working man wore off real quick once she was living the reality of being married to a small town vet just establishing his practice. Almost from the moment they'd unloaded the moving truck, she hated it here.

She couldn't stand the people. The food. The lack of culture. How there was never anything exciting to do or places to go. Hunter had cut his hours as short as he could, he'd found special picnic spots, and he'd saved every penny so they could go spend weekends in the biggest nearby city, Cheyenne. He did everything possible to give her back something of the life she was accustomed to.

But even Cheyenne was horribly provincial to Janine's sophisticated palate. No matter how hard Hunter tried to make up for bringing her here and to please her, it was never enough. *He* was never enough.

"Look," Isobel said, "it doesn't matter where I came from. I'm not afraid of hard work." She jutted out her chin.

But all Hunter saw was another rich city girl, come to rough it for the summer on some lark. He wasn't going to be caught in the cross hairs again.

"I think you missed a spot back there." He gestured at the wall behind her.

Her eyes flashed and it wasn't hard to imagine that she felt like hurling the bucket full of dirty water at his head. Hunter had to turn away because Jesus Christ, she was even more appealing when she was pissed.

He should have just said no earlier when Mel proposed Isobel work for him. But how was he supposed to turn Mel down? Especially with her pregnant?

Plus, he and Dr. Roberts were actually desperate for the help. Dr. Roberts had just turned seventy and hadn't been doing farm calls for a couple years now. He only came in to the clinic three days a week and Hunter knew he wanted to retire. Ever since Janine... well, suffice to say Hunter had been happy to lose himself in his work for the past year. But even he had his limits. Still—why couldn't it have been *anyone* other than her?

"So we're really just not going to talk about last night?" she asked as he was almost to the hallway.

He paused and his eyes dropped closed. Why did she have to keep bringing that up? Images flashed of her underneath him. Her

83

responsive gasps as he licked deep into her cunt. The feel of her perfect breasts and hardened nipples pinched between his fingers and thumb. The way she clutched his shoulders when he finally thrust—

"Nope," he said without turning. Then he strode quickly down the hall before he did something really stupid like turn around, kiss the fucking daylights out of her, and beg her for a repeat of last night.

Chapter 8
ISOBEL

The *nerve* of that guy. Isobel threw the sponge in the bucket after emptying out the dirty, sudsy water in the clinic's bathroom.

She'd busted her ass all afternoon. First with figuring out how to make sense of their absolute *disaster* of a record keeping system— seriously, she could not believe that a modern day veterinary clinic could have such an archaic method of record keeping. Using a basic Excel spreadsheet instead of a database program was little more efficient than just using all paper records! Isobel had to research how to format the records to import them. It had taken her two hours and several botched attempts to figure it all out.

And then she'd taken on the herculean task of cleaning up that lobby that smelled like it hadn't had a deep scrub down in months.

But could Mr. High and Mighty acknowledge any of that?

I think you missed a spot.

She fumed about it the whole drive home.

The nice guy from last night was definitely all mirage.

Isobel mopped her sweaty forehead with her forearm and then wrinkled her nose when she caught sight of herself in the little mirror on the sun visor.

Or maybe he just got a good look at you in the light of day.

Because God, did she look like a wreck.

Mirror, mirror, on the wall, who's the ugliest of them all?

Her hair was coming out from her ponytail everywhere, except from the very front where sweat had slicked little wisps against her forehead.

She pulled in front of the ranch house and parked. She angled the mirror to take a better look at herself.

Oh God. No wonder Hunter was *so* eager to rehash last night. Ugh.

She slammed the visor back up and squeezed her eyes shut. She and mirrors had a bad track record and she knew better than to look.

"Enough." She gritted her teeth, then grabbed her purse and headed inside.

She was looking forward to a long bath and some time to decompress, but the first thing she heard after she walked in the door was her name being called out.

"Isobel!"

Startled, she looked over toward the open room and saw one of the twins jogging toward her. He was the one with the dreadlocks. What was his name again?

"You're just in time for dinner."

"Oh." She glanced around at the meatloaf and mashed potatoes heaped on everyone's plates. "That's okay, I'm not—"

"It's Reece," he said, pointing at himself. "I don't know about you, but I always mix up people's names when I first meet them." He smiled warmly. "Come on, you can meet everyone properly." He put his hand to her upper back and started herding her toward the table where they were all sitting.

He was being nice and she didn't want to come off as a bitch, just running away to her room the first night. She took a deep breath and pasted on a smile. Even though she felt like scuttling and hiding behind the curtains at the way all the eyes in the room were zeroed in on her.

Liam was seated beside Reece's twin Jeremiah. He gave her a blatant once over and then grinned unabashedly. She tried not to wince when she remembered that she looked like death warmed over. Mack just glanced over his shoulder at her then went back to his food while Nicholas gave her a welcoming head nod.

"Mel and Xavier have already gone up for the night," Reece explained. "I usually put the boys down before dinner. Bossman likes having the wife to himself in the evenings."

"To *think*, they actually need a break from our fabulous and magnanimous company," Liam shook his head.

"Hi again, everyone." Isobel gave a short, awkward wave.

Reece urged her toward the side table where the food sat steaming in heated chafing dishes. "What's your pleasure? We've got meatloaf tonight. Green beans, along with a vegetable medley over here to the right. Mashed potatoes and gravy. Biscuits. A little bit of everything?"

Isobel's eyes widened as she took it all in.

Calories.

Fat.

CARBS.

"Um," she swallowed, glancing from the food to everyone still staring at her. "No, thanks," she tried again. "That's okay. I'll just—"

"Don't be ridiculous," Reece laughed. "There's plenty." Then he started heaping food on her plate.

She made a strangled coughing noise but Reece just kept on shoveling food until Jeremiah jumped up from the end of the table.

"Enough already." He took the plate from his twin. "Sorry for my brother's enthusiasm," he apologized to Isobel, offering a warm smile with dimples identical to his Reece's. Apart from their hair and the way they dressed, they looked exactly alike. "He equates hospitality with feeding people. It's a Southern thing."

Isobel couldn't help but smile gratefully at Jeremiah as he scooped half of what Reece had put on her plate back into the trays.

Nicholas looked up from his food. "Texas barely counts as the South."

"Yeah, yeah," Reece said, waving a hand.

"I'll take more of the vegetables," she said as Jeremiah reached them.

"Are you vegetarian?" Reece winced. "Sorry, I should have asked."

"No, no. I just…" She scrambled. "You know. Being on the road. I've been eating a lot of junk food. Vegetables would be nice for a change."

God, that didn't come off too awkward, did it? Maybe it would have been easier to just say she was a vegetarian. But then she'd be locked into that and she *did* like meat. But rarely and usually only when it was boiled. She'd already cheated this week with the burger last night.

At least her neurotic thoughts weren't playing across her face, or if they were, the guys were too oblivious to notice. Jeremiah handed her plate back and then Reece tossed an arm around her shoulders, pulling her away from Jeremiah. He flashed a friendly grin down at her, dimples on display. "You're in for a treat. Nick cooked and the food's always the best on his nights."

"Because I grew up in the *actual* south and we do food the right way," Nicholas said.

"Stop hogging the beautiful woman all to yourself," Liam jumped up and pulled Reece's arm off Isobel's shoulders. He took Isobel's hand and dropped a kiss to her fingertips. "Will you please do me the honor of sitting beside me?"

"Oh, um," she looked around at all the guys. Then she shrugged. "Okay?"

"*Excellent.* Let me carry this for you." Liam took her plate with one hand and hooked his arm in hers. He led her over to the table and then waved at Jeremiah. "Move your books out of the way, ya gobshite." Liam shoved aside a couple of textbooks that were open beside Jeremiah's plate.

"Oh, I can just sit over—" Isobel started to gesture at the empty chair at the end of the table but Liam and Jeremiah were both shaking their heads.

"It's fine."

"Don't worry about it."

Jeremiah moved his plate along with his books and sat down. Isobel glanced at the books. One was Statistics and the other was Europe in the Twentieth Century.

"A little light reading?" Isobel lifted her eyebrows.

"My big brother's a college man," Reece said, taking a seat across the table from them, between Mack and Nicholas.

"Oh, is there a college around here?" Isobel asked, a little surprised. She hadn't seen anything except scrub brush and endless rolling hills the last hour of her drive yesterday. "Or do you commute?"

"I'm taking online classes from the U of W," Jeremiah said. Then he clarified. "The University of Wyoming."

"Oh, cool. I've taken a couple online classes before." She'd been so far into her advanced degree program at Cornell, she hadn't been able to take many—most of the upper level courses involved labs of one kind or another, but she'd taken a couple online biology classes during undergrad.

She was about to sit but then hesitated, thinking about her afternoon spent sweating while she scrubbed the reception area at the clinic. "I should really go grab a quick shower. It'll just take ten minutes and then—"

Everyone at the table laughed.

"Don't be ridiculous," Liam put a hand on Isobel's forearm to stop her. "If we all showered before dinner, we wouldn't eat until ten o'clock."

"Liam should be especially ripe since he was out raking the compost beds today." Mack smirked and crossed his arms behind his head, tattooed biceps flexing.

"Here we go," Jeremiah muttered under his breath, looking back down at his open Statistics textbook. He ran a finger down the page like he was looking for where he'd left off.

"And you're so much better coming in from an afternoon mucking out stalls?" Liam asked. "Where do you think the compost comes from, boy-o?"

"Man, we're trying to eat a meal here," Nicholas objected.

"That we are, that we are," Liam said. "Compliments to the chef, I meant no disrespect." Liam doffed an invisible hat at Nicholas, then angled his body toward Isobel.

"So how was your first day working for our illustrious veterinarian? And how do you come out of it smelling lemon fresh? I thought being a vet meant spending all day armpit deep up a cow's arse?"

Nicholas' silverware banged on the table as he slammed them down but Isobel just shook her head with a wry smile on her face. No one could accuse this group of not having personality.

She held up her hands. "No up close and personal encounters with bovines today. But there's always tomorrow to look forward to."

She shared a little about what she'd been up to instead, helping with the vaccines and updating the clinic computer records. Everyone seemed interested in what she was saying and as long as she was talking, she didn't have to worry about what was on her plate, so she told them a little about her road trip too when Reece asked about it. Honestly, she was surprised at how at ease she felt with all of them.

"Feck, you can't take a night off studying even when you have this vision of female perfection before you?" Liam suddenly asked, reaching across Isobel's plate to grab Jeremiah's textbook.

"Hey," Jeremiah said, reaching for the book. "I have a test next Monday. I need to study."

Liam rolled his eyes. "That's what Sunday night is for. It's Friday, for Jesus' sake. Take a load off."

Jeremiah got out of his seat and lurched for the textbook but Liam jerked it out of his grasp right before he could close his fingers around it.

"Christ, can you not take one day off from being an entitled son of a bitch?" Mack asked from across the table. "We don't all have a daddy who can bail us out if we bomb our classes."

Liam ignored Mack. He grinned magnanimously at Jeremiah. "But lucky you, you have me and I'm happy to throw away money on your education any time. Just say the word."

Jeremiah glared at Liam, his jaw locking. Yikes, Isobel could tell that was the wrong thing to say.

"We don't take charity." Jeremiah yanked his book back from Liam.

"Fucking rich people," Mack muttered under his breath, mopping up some gravy on his plate with his biscuit and shoving the rest of it in his mouth.

Liam narrowed his eyes at Mack. "You've got a little something." Liam motioned to his eyebrow. "Just there."

When Mack lifted his hand to his own eyebrow, Liam launched the rest of the biscuit he was eating straight at Mack's forehead, smacking him right between the eyes.

Mack shot to his feet, pushing his chair back. "You better watch it, pretty boy. I'd hate to have to rearrange your face."

"Whoa, whoa," Reece said, getting up and putting a hand on Mack's chest. "He was just joking around. He didn't mean anything by it."

Mack smacked Reece's hand away from his chest but Reece just lifted it back, though without touching Mack's chest this time.

Mack glared at Liam—who was smirking back like he couldn't be more amused by Mack's display.

"Hey guys, come on," Reece looked back and forth between Liam and Mack. "Is this any way to welcome a newcomer to the ranch? Poor Isobel is going to think we're a bunch of barbarians here. Look, you're putting her off her dinner." He pointed down at her plate, where she'd barely touched her food.

Damn it, why did he have to be so observant? She shoved a bite of squash and zucchini in her mouth. She even managed not to cringe when she realized the vegetables weren't steamed, but had been cooked in what tasted like *butter.*

Mack left his own mostly empty plate behind and stormed off in the direction of the stairs.

"What crawled up his arse?" Liam asked.

Jeremiah leaned behind Isobel to smack Liam on the back of the head.

Reece sat back down at the table, looking at Isobel apologetically. "I'm sorry about all that. I swear we're not all that bad. We usually get along great."

"Reece here is what we call an optimist," Liam said, shaking his head and stabbing his fork in the direction Mack went. "I'll get along with that arsehole the day hell freezes over."

"So, Isobel," Reece said brightly, obviously trying to cover the bad manners of the rest of his tablemates. "You said you drove here from New York?"

Isobel nodded, dabbing a big chunk of cauliflower against the side of her plate to try to drain off the butter that had collected on it.

"Which part?" Reece asked.

She put her fork down, giving up on the cauliflower. It was like a little sponge. There was probably a half a tablespoon of butter in that single bite. "I live in the city. But I go to college upstate in Ithica."

"So what brings you to our neck of the woods?" Jeremiah asked. He'd closed his books, apparently giving up on studying after all.

Crap. She should have anticipated this question. Why hadn't she thought up a good answer for it? She swallowed as she tried to think of something to say. God, her throat was dry. She smiled and held up a finger as she reached for the water pitcher in the center of the table and poured herself a glass. After taking a long sip, she still didn't have any better idea what to say.

"Um, I was just… in the mood for a change of pace."

"What about you two?" She gestured at Jeremiah and Reece. When in doubt, deflect. "Where are you from? You grew up in Texas, is that right? How'd you end up here?"

"Oh we were just in Texas for a year. We've been all over." Reece leaned back in his chair. "The question is—do you want the long story or the short?"

"Oh no, here we go," Liam muttered. "Don't get him going, love," Liam leaned in, bumping his shoulder against Isobel's. "Nobody loves telling yarns more than this one."

Isobel smiled. "Okay, how about something in between the long and short version?"

"Well, you'd have to start at the beginning, back when Jeremiah and I were just eight years old and our mother decided she wanted to join the circus."

Jeremiah shook his head but Reece ignored him. Isobel nibbled on a piece of celery while she listened.

"Mom decides she wants to join the circus. She was really good at gymnastics when she was younger, she says, and she's sure she'll be able to get a job. It's something she's always dreamed about doing and *carpe diem*! Seize the day!" Reece jabbed a fist in the air, his face enthusiastic and full of amusement.

"So she packs me and Jeremiah up in the car and we drive through the night and then all the next day. We get to this carnival right at dusk. I've never seen anything like it. There's a giant ferris wheel they set up, all covered in lights." Reece gestures with his hands, his face animated. "A man on stilts juggling. People selling candied apples and cotton candy and popcorn and hot dogs. I mean, to a little boy, this was heaven on earth."

"Mom gave us twenty bucks and Jeremiah and I spent the whole night riding every ride and getting so stuffed on funnel cake I threw up after riding the tilt-a-whirl." He grins nostalgically. "God, it was the best night of my life up to that point."

Reece's enthusiasm was infectious and Isobel couldn't help smiling along. "So what happened then? Did your mom get a job at the circus?"

"What? Oh, God no," Reece barked out a short laugh. "Mom was batshit. Totally nuts. She was lucky someone caught her before she took a flying leap from the trapeze. They called the cops. We didn't know until the carnival was being shut down for the night and went looking for her." He shook his head, still chuckling.

Isobel just stared at him, her mouth dropped open. "I'm so sorry," she finally managed to say. "That's horrible."

Reece waved a hand like it was nothing. "It was fine. We went to live with our Grandma Ruth then."

"So she raised you?"

"Oh, no," Reece laughed again, like the very idea was ludicrous. "Granny Ruth was a raging alcoholic. No, we only lived with her for about six months before we went into foster care."

"Oh." Isobel took another long sip of water.

"Now this is where the story really gets interesting. Jeremiah and I got to see all different ways of life over the next few years. I've never met anyone who had a more colorful childhood than we did."

Jeremiah let out a loud huff. "That's one word for it," he muttered.

Reece ignored him. "I mean, just the number of religions we got to personally witness was amazing. You can't really get to know a religion by just visiting a church or a temple on Sunday, you know. But to get to see a family living out their faith," he let out a low whistle, "You can really see where the rubber meets the road."

"Okaaaay," Isobel said, drawing out the word.

"Like, we lived with this really strict Baptist family first. Strict being the operative word." Reece shook his head with a little shudder. Considering how he described his crazy mom and alcoholic grandma with such fondness, Isobel hated to think what would actually make this guy shudder.

He brightened the next second. "But then came the Unitarians, and after them there was a family who wasn't very religious at all. But then we got to stay with the Hausers, who were Buddhists. They were these old hippies who showed us how to meditate and everything. They were very open souls."

"Too bad about the pot dealing that landed Mr. Hauser in jail our Junior year," Jeremiah cut in. He sounded less than amused but Reece just nodded sagely.

"It really was."

"So what'd you do then?" Isobel ate more of the vegetables and even a little bit of meatloaf, so interested in Reece's bizarre story that for once she'd stopped obsessing over the calories going in her mouth.

Reece shrugged. "Jeremiah and I figured we'd go it on our own at that point. We worked odd jobs. We were in San Francisco at that point and it's pretty chill there if you want to do the outdoor alternative living situation thing."

Alternative outdoor—? Did he mean... *homeless*?

He moved on before Isobel could ask, though. "That got old after a while so we headed east doing different jobs that included room and board. That was when we hit Texas. We worked a ranch there for about a year but then we," his eyes flicked toward his brother and for the first time in his disastrous tale the slightest shadow entered his eyes, "we wanted a new scene." It sounded like the vague non-answer Isobel had given about why she'd come here. Hmm.

But then Reece smiled again. "Jeremiah saw the notice online for this place and we hopped on the first bus headed north. And here we are." He held his arms out.

"And here we are," Isobel echoed. She looked down at her plate, startled to find she'd eaten almost half of her food. She was full but not stuffed and she didn't feel guilty or like she'd binged. She felt... well, *normal*.

She looked around the table. "I'm really happy to be here. It's great to meet you all." She hoped they could hear the sincerity in her voice.

She'd come here looking for an escape and if she read between the lines, it sounded like she might not be alone in doing so. She didn't know anyone else's story other than the twins, but Liam was obviously rich and not from around here, so what could have tempted him to come live out in the middle of nowhere, Wyoming? Then there was Mack, tattooed from head to toe. He didn't exactly look like a rural farm setting was his natural habitat. Even Nicholas—why had he abandoned his home down south that he seemed to have so much love for to come here?

Maybe she'd never know why they were all here. But in this one evening she'd felt more at home with them than she had in the last year living with supposed *family*. This place was supposed to just be a rescue for horses, but it seemed like they just might take in lost strays of the human variety too.

Chapter 9
HUNTER

Hunter scraped the mud off his feet on the side of the concrete step by the back door of the clinic.

Right as he was about to open the door, it was yanked open from the inside and he was face to face with an irate Isobel.

"Where have you been? People have been waiting since I opened the doors at 8:30!"

He paused, taken aback. The whole drive here he'd been trying to tell himself she couldn't possibly be as lovely or mesmerizing as his memory kept painting her. But here, standing in front of him looking pissed, with two spots of color high on her rosy cheeks, her black hair flying around her like a silky cloud that he just wanted to bury his hands in and—

He grimaced and pushed past her into the clinic's small break room.

"Clinic doesn't open 'til 9:00." He needed coffee. Now.

"And it's 9:03." She emphasized the *oh-three* like he'd committed an unforgiveable crime.

He was a grown man. He didn't have to explain himself to anyone. Still, he found himself growling, "Had a call out at the Johnson farm that took longer than expected. Had to extract a dead calf." Second one in two days. Happened like that sometimes. People didn't call for the vet when everything was going peachy.

"What?" she spat, then paused as if only just then processing what he'd said. "Oh." She blinked. "I'm sorry. That's horrible."

He shrugged as he reached for a mug from beside the sink. "Happens." He pressed the coffee dispenser pump but only a tiny amount of liquid came out before it sputtered. Damn it. It was office policy to run another pot whenever it ran out. He glared at Isobel as he jerked open the cabinet underneath the coffee maker to pull out a packet of grounds.

So he saw when Isobel's back went stiff. "If you had a case this morning, why didn't you call me? This is supposed to be an

96

internship. How am I supposed to learn how to do the job if you don't let me know about calls?"

He scoffed as he set the new pot of coffee brewing. "Because experience working on heifers at a quarter to six in the morning is going to be *so* helpful when you end up back in New York City."

If he thought she'd gone stiff before, it was nothing to how ramrod straight she went at that comment. She took a step forward and pointed a finger into his chest. "You don't know anything about me." Her voice was arctic.

He held up his hands. "Fine."

"Fine," she snapped back.

Then he realized just how close they were standing. Her face was about six inches away from his.

He had the absurd impulse to shove her back against the door and kiss the living daylights out of her.

Her eyes widened suddenly and she yanked back. "Your first client is waiting in exam room one." She picked up a file from the counter beside the sink and slapped it in his hand.

He glanced down at the folder. Mr. Buttersworth. He was Mrs. Jones' overweight, pampered cat. The cat bore a striking resemblance to his owner with his shock of orange hair and overlong whiskers. The woman had a mustache the bearded lady would be jealous of.

"Fine," he said.

"Fine." She glared at him for another second and then as if realizing she didn't have any other reason to still be standing there, she spun on her heel and stomped toward the exam room.

***

The morning passed with the regular bevy of cats and dogs cycling through. Hunter did his best to ignore Isobel and focus on his job. A bit difficult when he had her holding his four-legged patients down while he examined them.

Did she wear her hair down today on purpose? To distract him? He'd swear she kept flicking it over her shoulder just so that whatever fruity shampoo she used would waft his direction.

Mr. Buttersworth was only in for shots, a quick and simple enough procedure. Their second patient, a huge St. Bernard named Bernie, however, was a bit more challenging. It took both the dog's owner and

Isobel to hold the big dog down so Hunter could pry his mouth open to see what was causing him so much pain. And in spite of the giant, slobbering, whining dog who tried to yank back each time Hunter touched his mouth, half of Hunter's brain was distracted by the warmth of Isobel's thigh against his as they wrestled the dog on the floor together.

He finally got the dog to sit still long enough to see that it was an abscess tooth causing all the trouble. That meant surgery since he needed to get down to the root of the tooth. Hunter gave Bernie a shot of antibiotics and Isobel went out with Bernie's owner, promising her they'd find a way to fit the surgery in the schedule for the next afternoon.

It was just what Hunter would have done, but he was annoyed at her presumption. She should have at least asked him when was the best time to schedule the surgery.

A difficult to diagnose case with a molting parrot distracted him from thinking about her too much for the next hour.

They were down to their last appointment for the morning, a case of mange in an indoor/outdoor family cat when there was a knock on the exam room door.

Hunter set the cat back down in the box her owners had brought her in and called out, "Come in," but Isobel was already halfway to the door. She opened it to Sandra, his receptionist.

Sandra seemed taken aback to find Isobel on the other side of the door. Hunter almost smiled. She had to stop startling people like that.

"What is it, Sandra?" he asked.

Sandra looked past Isobel and smiled at him. He and Sandra had both grown up in Hawthorne, she was just a year behind him in school. She'd been working at the clinic for about six months after Dr. Roberts long-time receptionist had retired. "Doctor, there's a family out here with a dog they say has a hurt leg. They don't have an appointment."

"I'll put them in exam two," Isobel said, striding confidently past Sandra. Sandra's mouth dropped open and she swung her head back to Hunter.

Hunter nodded. "We'll see them. Give me five."

He turned back to Mrs. Voorhees, explained the treatment regimen, and gave her the medication she'd need.

He washed his hands and went into the next exam room. He was about to order Isobel out to go clean and sterilize exam one when he saw her crouched on the floor cuddling a young Labrador retriever to her chest, stroking his head one moment and gently rotating his back leg to check for injury the next.

The dog whimpered and burrowed into her stomach when she'd only barely moved the leg. Not a good sign. Isobel's eyes leapt to Hunter's as soon as he came in and he could tell she was thinking the same thing.

He glanced around and saw a short, compact woman with three little girls crowded around her. "Hi guys, I'm Dr. Hunter."

Their eyes were all fearful as he came in. The littlest girl was sniffling. Hunter wasn't great with kids' ages but he thought they were all between five and ten, maybe.

"Who do we have here?" Hunter leaned down on his haunches and looked at the dog.

"That's Jupiter," the middle tallest girl said. She had big plastic glasses and frizzy brown hair similar to her mother's. "My dad ran over him."

The mother looked mortified and hurriedly stepped forward. "Hi, I'm Pam. My husband wasn't looking where he was going this morning. He was in a hurry and he backed out of the garage without looking."

The youngest girl burst into tears and the mom stopped and turned to her daughter. "Oh honey, it's going to be okay. The doctor here is going to make Jupiter feel better."

"Let's see what's going on with him. How old is he?"

He reached for Jupiter, keeping his eyes on the dog and off Isobel as she transferred the dog into his arms.

"Just a little over ten months," Isobel answered.

Hunter shifted the dog in his arms and felt down along the problem leg. The dog whined the same way he had when Isobel touched him. Hunter suspected a break but there was only one way to be sure.

"Okay," Hunter stood up, holding the dog to his chest. "I'm gonna take this handsome guy to x-ray. We'll be right back with some more answers for you."

"Is Jupiter going to be okay?" the girl with glasses asked.

Hunter offered her a gentle smile of assurance. "We'll go get a picture of his bones and then we'll have a better idea of what we need to do to fix him up. Okay?"

She nodded reluctantly. Isobel hurried to open the door for Hunter.

The x-ray room was just a couple doors down and Isobel opened that door for him as well. He kept it clinical as he told her where the lead aprons were and put everything in place to get the images they needed.

He lifted Jupiter off the x-ray table when Isobel said softly, "You were good with the girls back there. It's got to be hard when you can't promise that their dog will be okay."

Hunter didn't say anything as the printer spit out the x-ray film. He silently handed Jupiter off to Isobel. She took the dog and scratched his head, being careful not to jostle his back leg.

"I mean, in college, they try to prepare you for that part of the job. I spent a semester volunteering at a clinic but I still never got used to it."

The room was dark apart from the light box on the wall that Hunter slapped the x-ray films against. The atmosphere was a little too intimate. He didn't want to bond with Isobel about the difficulties of being a vet. Because of course it was hard being part of the worst day in a child's life when they had to say goodbye to a beloved animal. But the truth was, he'd gotten so used to it, it bothered him less and less over the years. Which bothered him even more.

Hunter frowned when he saw the x-ray against the light. "I was afraid of that," he murmured.

Isobel came close. And flipped her hair behind her shoulder. Hunter gritted his teeth but pointed out the break even as she said, "Ouch. His femur. That won't be easy to brace."

She ducked her head down to nuzzle the dog.

"We can't just use a standard cast," he said. It was too high up on his back leg. "But we can try a Thomas brace to put the leg in traction. It'll at least give him a chance."

"Poor baby," she cooed into the dog's ear.

She was sensitive. Not always the best quality in a vet.

Which was a good thing, he tried to remind himself. He was supposed to be trying to get her to quit. Not be working with her like they made a good team.

Because they didn't. At all.

He turned and abruptly left the room without another word. Her footsteps followed behind him. He ignored her as he stepped back into the room with the family and explained the x-ray and the brace he'd be putting on. He also tried to set their expectations—only time would tell how the dog healed with the brace and lots of rest.

The girls nodded bravely and then they went to wait out in the hall while Hunter pulled out the coil of aluminum tubing he used for this sort of thing. With a small heating element, he started molding a cone-shaped frame.

"Oh." Isobel sounded startled. "You don't use a pre-made frame? You make it from scratch?"

"All different shapes of animals," was all he said. Plus, he saw no need for fancy equipment when he could make the same thing for ten bucks with materials from the hardware store. Folks around here could rarely afford the extra expense and sometimes any little cost saving measures he could find meant the difference between a client having to choose to put down a family pet or being able to treat them instead.

Hunter went over and gave the dog a sedative, then fit the round part of the cone he was shaping around Jupiter's hip joint to check the fit. The hoop needed to be a little narrower. He went back to his heating element and rod to shape the aluminum some more.

He ignored Isobel for the next thirty minutes as he set the dog's leg, then fit the Thomas brace into place and taped the leg down to keep it in traction. If Jupiter didn't overexert himself too much, the leg had a good chance of healing up just fine.

He finished the last bit of tape around the frame, then, on a whim, reached into his drawer and pulled out a glittery silver smiley face sticker and placed it on top of the tape right below the hip.

He picked up Jupiter and turned to go take him back to the little girls and their mom. Which was when he caught Isobel watching him. With this little smile and her eyes all soft. It made his neck feel hot.

He frowned and headed for the door. "Clean up in here. It's 12:45. We were due at the Anderson farm fifteen minutes ago."

Chapter 10
ISOBEL

Four farm calls and one hundred and thirty miles later, Isobel was ready to pummel Hunter Dawkins' handsome face in.

Had she actually thought he was sweet earlier today taking care of that family dog? Temporary insanity, that was her only defense. And she was definitely cured, that was for damn sure.

He hadn't let her touch another animal all day. She'd been relegated to watching him handle cases from the background. So far in the background, in fact, she'd barely been able to see what he was doing half the time.

I know you city folk think cows are cute and just part of the scenery, but they pack a nasty kick. It's best if you watch from behind the fence.

Hunter had said that right in front of the farmer who'd called them out. If Isobel's face had flamed any hotter she would have spontaneously combusted.

Then there were the endless hours on the road. Hunter was apparently the only large animal vet in two counties. And Wyoming? Yeah. It was a big damn state.

She'd thought he was joking when he told her how few veterinarians there were. Five and a half hours later, she believed it.

But she swore, if she had to spend *one* more minute locked in the cramped cab of Hunter's truck with him, she'd scream.

Did he have to take up so much *space*? He drove with his left hand on the steering wheel and his right arm draped lazily between them, taking up about three-fourths of the entire bench seat. She'd been crammed up against the passenger side door for several hours between all the farms because she didn't want to accidently touch him and have him thinking that she was trying to play handsy with him.

Not to mention, the *music*. God, if she heard another pop country singer twanging about how all they needed in life was beer, their truck, God, and the USA, she might just throw the door open and leap out of the moving vehicle.

A commercial for Chevy trucks ended and then the twanging steel guitar started up, followed by a man with a deep southern voice singing, "You can take a man's steer but don't you dare take his beer—"

Enough!

She reached over and pushed the off button on the console.

Ah. Blessed silence. Finally. She relaxed back in her seat with a relieved sigh.

Until Hunter flicked the radio back on the next second.

"—take your dreams but you'll never give up Jim Bean."

Isobel's mouth dropped open.

She punched the radio off again, then crossed her arms over her chest and glared at Hunter.

His hand shot out almost before she was even settled. He cranked the volume up and started singing along, picking up right in the middle of the line.

"—ever choke, you can rely on Jack and coke. Whoa-a, they're never gonna steal our pri-ide. We got the Lord on our si-ide."

"Fine," she said, having to all but yell to be heard over Hunter and the God-awful music. "Play your stupid music. Unlike some people, I'm not a *child.*" She huffed out so hard some of the shorter hair that framed her face flew up in a little cloud. Arms still crossed, she angled her body resolutely *away* from Hunter.

The music turned down and Hunter stopped singing.

"You sure throw a hissy fit like one."

It would be bad to punch the driver of a moving car, right? Instead she dug her nails into her arms and clenched her jaw, staring out at the passing countryside and not dignifying his comments with a response.

Thankfully, they arrived ten minutes later. She was out the door almost the instant the truck came to a stop.

It was a smaller farm unlike some of the bigger operations they'd been by today. They stopped in front of a ranch house with a large barn in the distance. The sun was low on the horizon and Isobel held her hand over her eyes to look out in the direction of the barn. It had a gated area off to the side where she saw several cows meandering.

104

She felt Hunter come up beside her but she didn't look at him. He passed by and went up to the door, knocking on it with several swift, decisive raps.

They stood waiting for several long moments before it opened, a baby's wailing greeting them. A harried man stood there with an angry, red faced baby in his arms. He bounced her up and down and tried to put a pacifier in her mouth, to no avail.

"Shh, shh," he said, looking over his shoulder. "Brenda, the vet's here."

Something was shouted back but Isobel couldn't make it out over more young children's voices screaming in the background.

The man hiked the baby up to his shoulder and rubbed her back, continuing to bounce, while he looked apologetically at Hunter and Isobel. "Sorry about all this. It's a bit hectic around here. The kids didn't get their naps today."

"Don't worry about it, Jonathan. You said you had a heifer that was giving you some trouble calving?"

Jonathan nodded. "She's out in the yard beside the barn. She's been in labor for a few hours and isn't moving along as quick as I'd like. Got two more that should be freshening any day now. I'd go down and show you but—" The baby on his shoulder let out a particularly ear-piercing wail and they all winced. "She's teething."

Aw, poor kiddo. And poor dad, if the bags underneath the man's eyes were any indication.

"We'll go take a look," Hunter said.

Jonathan nodded gratefully.

Hunter turned and headed back to the truck, where he hopped up and opened the big utility box he had installed at the back. Isobel took note of every instrument he grabbed—calf puller, chains, surgery toolbox, and the lariat.

"Are you going to actually let me within three feet of the animal this time?" she asked when he hopped back down from the truck bed.

"I've assisted with calvings before, you know. *Several* times." Okay, it had only been twice. And the first time she'd just watched from a distance. But the second time she'd been one of the people with her hands on the calf puller, yanking the baby calf into the world. As part of one of her labs at Cornell, she'd spent a week at a dairy farm in upstate New York.

Hunter didn't respond. He just kept walking out toward the gated off pen beside the barn. What, was he just going to give her the silent treatment now? And he'd called *her* childish!

"Melanie told me you were short-staffed," she had to all but jog to keep up with his long-legged stride, "and you yourself said I'd only be going on these calls with you until I was prepared enough to do them on my own. As a third-year veterinary student, I'm qualified to practice in a clinic part-time. But how will I be able to do any of that if you never let me touch any of the animals?"

He stopped walking, so suddenly it took several steps for Isobel to realize it and stop as well. She paused and looked back at him.

He had a patronizing smile on his face. "Fine. You want to be the veterinarian, working all on her own? Here's your chance. This is now your case." He dropped all the tools he was carrying at his feet and stepped back, his hands up.

She narrowed her eyes at him. What kind of trick was this?

But he just backed away and crossed his arms over his chest, watching her with that same stupid smirk on his stupid face.

She didn't try to hide her annoyance as she reached over and picked up the instruments he'd dropped. It was awkward to carry them all. She kept dropping one thing or other. She didn't dare look up at Hunter, knowing she'd just find him smirking at her.

She only managed to carry everything by tucking the calf puller and lariat underneath her arms, hanging the chains around her shoulders, and picking up the surgery kit. It was all heavier than she expected and the trek to the barn far longer than it initially looked.

But finally they got there. The heifer's plaintive mooing could be heard from the opposite end of the yard. She stood, pawing at the muddy ground, the whites of her eyes showing as she looked around wildly.

Shit. Isobel had forgotten how big cows were in person. She frantically tried to remember everything she'd learned on the couple occasions she'd seen this done.

First, get the cow in a stable position.

Both cows she'd seen give birth had been laid down on their side. But she knew that sometimes cows gave birth standing up.

She bit her lip, setting down her equipment beside the gate as they entered the yard. She felt Hunter's eyes on her as he hopped up to sit on the fence and watch the show. Judging her. But she refused to give him the satisfaction of looking his direction or showing him how much this whole thing unnerved her.

He was such a jerk. She'd just wanted to assist him, not have to do the whole thing by *herself.* Much less with him watching on.

You can't do this. All you'll ever be is a failure. Who are you kidding?

Isobel shut her eyes for a brief second and breathed in a deep breath to clear her stepmother's voice out of her head.

Turned out that wasn't the best move because the side yard didn't smell awesome. She'd forgotten that about her week at the dairy farm too. Animals stank. 'Shit happens' was more than just a saying on a farm.

Okay, time to stop overthinking this and just get it done.

She picked up the lariat and approached the laboring cow. Lassoing a cow couldn't be that big a deal. At least not for a cow about to give birth. Right?

Isobel walked toward the cow, her arms out to the side, the loop of the lariat ready.

"Hi there, Bessie. We're gonna take this nice and easy, okay?" That wasn't a tremble in her voice. Nope. Not at all. She cleared her throat. "I'm here to help." She smiled.

Apparently the cow didn't buy it because when Isobel took another step forward, the cow skittered sideways and then past her, dragging her water bag with her as she went. In humans, women's water just broke. In cows sometimes, like with this cow apparently, it slipped out intact like a giant water balloon hanging out her back end.

Oh the joys of veterinary medicine.

Isobel approached the cow again. She crouched lower and tried to make herself seem as non-threatening as possible. "Nice cow. We're all friends here."

The cow bolted again. When Isobel jolted to run after her, she slipped in the mud—at least she *hoped* it was mud—and fell on her ass.

The loud masculine laughter from behind her did nothing to lighten her mood. She set her jaw, ignored the squelching mud that splattered all over her eight-hundred-dollar riding boots, picked up the lariat, and approached the cow again.

She finally got the rope around the heifer's neck on the sixth try. Which was good because she didn't think it would be very compassionate of her to start screaming four letter words at a pregnant cow. Hunter on the other hand, now *him* she'd be happy to give an earful. If she was acknowledging his presence, that was.

Which she wasn't.

He did not exist.

It was just her and Bessie.

"Sorry," she said, yanking on the rope to urge the cow back toward the gate, "I'm stereotyping by calling you Bessie, aren't I? I'm sure you are a very unique cow with your own individual spirit. How about you work with me to get this baby born and we'll come up with a name that reflects your incredibly complex and personal style, what do you say?"

The cow let out a plaintive *mooooo*.

"I'll take that as a yes."

"All right. Over here. This way. Atta girl."

Finally, Isobel managed to get the cow to the fence near the eight-foot long swinging gate door. Before the cow could run away or move again, Isobel dropped the lariat and hurried to the gate to pull it toward them to enclose the heifer. Finally the heifer was secure, nose toward the apex of the V created by the side of the fence and the gate. Bessie wasn't going anywhere till her calf was born. The whole close-the-cow-in-with-the-paddock-door thing was another trick she'd learned from the dairy farm.

"Maybe Cassandra?" Isobel offered conversationally while she knelt down to open up the surgical box and grab out a long plastic sleeve. She fit the glove on over her left hand and then pulled the sleeve all the way up her arm to her shoulder. "Or something classic, like Helen?"

Here goes nothing. She squeezed some lubricant on her hand. With her right hand she held onto the gate and with her left, she reached right up into the cow's hoo-ha.

And reached.

And reached.

She was almost shoulder deep before she felt was she was looking for. A little hoof, and further in, a head. She felt around. Nose, jaw, and there it was—the mouth.

She stuck her finger inside and the little mouth started sucking on her finger. A grin cracked her face.

The baby was alive.

You never knew when labor had gone on for an abnormally long time. Another of the tools in Hunter's truck was a calf-cutter. In the case of dead calves, sometimes you had to cut the calf up in order to pull it out and save the mother's life.

She liked that Hunter had left the calf-cutter in the truck and hadn't just automatically brought it out. It indicated a sort of optimism. Or at least a commitment to trying every other option before going to that extreme.

But this baby was alive, and Isobel was going to keep it that way.

She felt around some more. Okay, there was one front hoof and… yep, there was the second one. The calf was in the right position. It must just be oversized. If she remembered her statistics right, oversized calves were the trouble in ninety percent of problematic calving cases.

Which meant she was going to have to put that calf puller and her own muscles to good use.

She withdrew her arm and breathed through her mouth, trying to ignore all the goo that came out with it.

A glamorous job this was not.

She reached down for another glove and then grabbed the chains of the calf puller. They had little cuffs on the end to attach around the baby calf's front hooves.

Here went nothing. She dove back in, this time with both arms, each hand holding a chain.

The cow bucked forward.

"Oof!" Isobel was knocked off balance, stumbling forward with the cow. There wasn't far for the cow to go—unless she nosed at the gate to push it open. Which she immediately did.

The gate started to swing back, widening the V and making space for the cow to get loose. Isobel yanked her right arm out of the cow and grabbed the gate to pull it back in position.

"Cassandra!" Isobel yelled. "Naughty cow!"

Once the heifer was still, Isobel tried again. But the second she took her hand off the gate to try to attach the first chain around the calf's hoof, Bessie/Cassandra was taking off again.

Isobel grabbed the gate at the last second to stop her, again.

Hair had escaped Isobel's ponytail but she couldn't push it out of her face because, yeah, cow goo all up and down her arms. She tried to blow it out of the way but it just settled right back in place.

She pursed her lips and huffed out a breath. She needed three hands—two to put the chains on the baby calves hooves and one to hold the gate shut—but obviously, she only had two. And Hunter was just sitting there behind her, probably gloating and laughing at her.

Ugh!

Okay, well maybe she could get the cow to lay down. If she would lay down, that would solve all of Isobel's problems.

"Why don't you take a load off, honey?" Isobel crooned, pushing down on the cow's rump. "Let's have a lie down."

The cow just started to the side again, knocking into the gate so that Isobel had to grab it before it opened again.

Fine. Isobel would just attach the chain one handed. How hard could it be?

Turned out it was hard. Very hard.

The latch for the little cuff was almost impossible to do one handed. Especially with the plastic glove on. With her hand all the way up inside the cow, she couldn't see what was going on either. She ended up shoving both hands inside the cow and quickly latching one of the chains around the first hoof, then stumbling along behind the cow before yanking out and grabbing the gate to push the cow back into position.

Then she repeated the process with the second cuff.

Finally, *finally*, she had both cuffs in place. She was soaked in sweat and cow muck. A cow's back end was not the most sanitary place, suffice to say. Not to mention, she couldn't tell how many times she'd been smacked in the face by the cow's swatting tail. A tail that was coated in manure.

But she had the chains on, goddammit, and this calf was coming out, come hell or high water. She attached the chains to the calf puller, a long flat metal shelf she braced behind the heifer's hips for traction. It worked similar to a car jack. She started cranking the lever that gave her torque to pull the calf out by the chains on the hooves.

Isobel only got a couple good pumps in before the cow started heading sideways, pushing against the gate again. But dammit, Isobel was done with it. So beyond done. She was getting the damn calf out.

So she didn't stop gripping the calf jack. She dug her feet in and pulled until she felt the veins in her neck straining.

And then was yanked off her feet by the cow starting forward again. She stumbled forward after the cow.

"Dammit, keep still," Isobel shouted, digging her feet again when the cow came to a standstill. She strained, leaning backward, and thought she felt some give as the calf shifted. She reached forward to massage around the cow's opening to help ease the calf's way. The hooves and front nose were peeking out now. Okay, now to just crank it a few more times and—

But before she could get in position, the damn cow darted forward again. Isobel wasn't about to let go of the calf puller. The heifer was booking it though and—

Shit!

Isobel was yanked off her feet. The heifer started dragging her along behind it. Ugh! Oh. Fuck. Gross. They were halfway across the paddock before Bessie stopped. Meanwhile Isobel had been on a chest-first slip and slide through the mud and shit filled barn yard. Isobel spit out a clod of what she could only pray was mud as she got to her feet and grabbed hold of the calf jack.

"Stop fucking with me, Bessie!" Isobel jammed her heels in the mud, solidified her grip on the handle and then started pulling the lever and maneuvering the jack and then pulling some more.

Out came the calf's head. The jack's lever was so taut she could barely get it to move. She managed one more crank and then she just pulled with everything she had. More than everything she had. She gave a primal scream as she yanked and pulled and strained, and then when she had no more to give, she yanked some more.

Oh God, oh God. She couldn't do it. She didn't have any more in her.

No, dammit. Just a little more. A *little* more!

She started sliding in the mud as the fucking cow started forward again. But Isobel kept her feet dug in and just kept pulling.

Then the chains she was holding suddenly gave all at once and before she knew what was happening, Isobel was on her ass in the mud and a baby calf was on the ground beside her, afterbirth landing all over both of them.

Isobel started laughing in euphoria. She wanted to hug the little calf. She'd done it. She'd actually done it!

The mother cow turned around and immediately started licking the little calf. It was lifting its little head and nosing back at its mom.

Isobel was still grinning as she shook her head and then undid the chains around the calf's front hoofs. She crawled and checked underneath. It was a girl. She laughed then sat back on her haunches. But only for a second before scrambling to her feet and reaching back inside the cow to make sure all the afterbirth was cleaned out. It was.

She stepped back, grinning at the mama and baby cow. She'd done it. Her first ever solo calving.

It was only then that she heard the laughing.

She swung around and saw Hunter doubled over, laughing so hard he was actually slapping his knee.

Her mouth dropped open. And then closed, her teeth clenching. She leaned over and grabbed the calving chains and puller, then stalked back toward the gate.

Hunter was still laughing, actually wheezing from laughing so hard as she opened the gate and slammed it behind her.

"I saw a spigot and hose on the back side of the barn," he managed to get out, wiping his eyes with amusement. "Better hose down along with the tools. You're a bit too ripe to get back in my truck like that."

She glared at him. In all likelihood, she had a warrant out on her for attempted murder in one state.

Why not make it two?

She yanked the long muck-covered gloves off her arms and threw them at his feet before grabbing the equipment she'd used and going in search of the spigot he'd mentioned.

She finally found it after walking around almost the whole barn. Because of course Hunter couldn't have been more specific, the bastard. She turned the spigot on and sprayed water at the chains before turning it toward her own boots.

She'd been so caught up in the moment with the calving, she hadn't really been paying attention to just how gross she'd been getting. But now that she had a chance to look down at herself, she almost gagged. She was covered in—

She jerked her head away. *Nope.* Better not to think about what she was covered in. She just turned the hose on herself.

"God!" she yipped, dancing away from the freezing spray for a second before closing her eyes, bracing, and aiming it back at her chest.

She didn't care if she had to ride home drenched, she didn't think she could stand herself smelling like the insides of a cow.

She dared a glance down at herself after spraying for several minutes. Ugh, the water was barely making a dent in all the shit covering her. Because she had no doubt there was plenty of actual manure mixed in there. The water was just turning it all into a brown slurry coating her previously light blue work shirt.

She gagged and threw the hose down, then ripped the shirt off over her head. Nope. Nope. Nope. She was not wearing the poop shirt for another second.

She stripped out of her boots and pants just as quickly. Her boots were dirty even on the inside. When she'd tripped and been dragged by the cow that one time, the mud and manure had caked up inside the top and run down her calves.

Ugh, *God*, could this *get* more disgusting? She put her thumb in the tip of the hose to make it spray high power at her disgusting clothes. Her poor boots. The supple leather would never be the same after this.

113

"Here, you can change into—"

She shrieked and covered her chest as Hunter came around the side of the barn. He paused, just staring at her while she stood there in nothing but her bra and panties, both of which were soaked through.

"It's not a wet T-shirt contest," she yelled at him. "Stop ogling me!"

His eyes jerked up to her, a lazy smile crossing his face. "If you say so, sweetheart." He tossed her a dark bundle of clothes. "You can change into this. But those boots go in the back of the truck." He hiked a thumb over his shoulder. "Now hurry it up, I wanna make it home before the first inning's over."

It would be justifiable homicide in this case. Surely any jury would agree.

"Get out of here," she cried when he continued just standing there looking at her.

He finally turned and moseyed back the way he came, moving so slowly she could have screamed. The instant he disappeared around the corner she unrolled the blue fabric and saw it was a pair of coveralls. She eagerly stepped into them. They were huge on her but still better than putting on the poop clothes. She pulled up the front zipper. The crotch sagged and she had to roll up the legs so they didn't drag on the ground, but that was fine. She grabbed all the equipment and her boots. Her boots were clean enough to hold underneath her arm, but she held her dirty, wet clothes between her thumb and forefinger as she headed back toward the truck.

She stepped carefully across the field back toward the driveway. It was muddy from recent rains and she had the disconcerting feeling that anything that looked like mud could just as well be more manure. A comforting thought, when she was walking barefoot.

That was it, tomorrow she'd ask Melanie if she'd mind using her Amazon account to order some work boots.

Isobel finally made it back to the truck and threw everything in the back. They'd disinfect the chains and cow puller when they got back to the clinic. In the meantime, she needed to dip her entire body in Purell.

When she rounded the truck, she heard voices.

"A live calf? That's great to hear."

114

"Yep. A little heifer. She was getting milk and feeding well when I left her."

"You always do a great job, Hunter."

"Not a problem. You have a good night now."

Isobel's hands clenched into fists. Did he actually just take credit when she'd—

Hunter was still smiling when he came around the truck and saw her standing there. If he noticed how furious she was, he didn't let it show.

He just looked down at her bare, dirty feet. "Clean those up before you get in the truck." He opened the driver's side door. Oh," he paused right before climbing up. "And next time," his smirk was fully back in place, "you might want to tie the cow to the gate with the harness so she stays in one place. Though I gotta say, I did enjoy the show."

Chapter 11

ISOBEL

Three weeks later, Isobel was still smarting about the mistake she'd made with that first calving. How *dumb* could she get? She couldn't believe she'd made the most basic of mistakes. Not tying up the freaking cow? Facepalm. And then she'd looked like a complete fucking idiot chasing that heifer all around.

She scrubbed shampoo into her hair as she thought about it.

Things hadn't gotten much better in the ensuing weeks. She'd backed off asking to help in cases and Hunter seemed just fine with that. Probably because he assumed she was an imbecile who couldn't even think to tie up a calving heifer.

During the daily in-clinic hours she felt a little more helpful. At least there she could direct the clients and their pets into the exam rooms. It had gotten so busy last Tuesday—one of Dr. Roberts' off days—that there wasn't any other choice except for her to help out. Several emergencies had come in on top of their regular appointments.

Isobel gave shots and dealt with minor complaints while Hunter took care of a collie with a major laceration and a choking llama that a man brought in with a trailer out back.

Then, without asking his permission—because screw him—she just started seeing and diagnosing clients on a regular basis. She was certified, damn it. So while he was dealing with patients in exam one, she took the next appointment in exam two. There'd only been one case so far that she'd wanted to check with Hunter on before giving treatment.

And he'd been civilized and professional about it. Maybe just because they were in front of the clients. She'd taken scrapings from a cat to check under the microscope, but wasn't positive about what kind of parasite the animal was carrying. Isobel had felt about ninety percent sure what she was dealing with, but she'd wanted to double check.

Hunter had coolly agreed with her assessment and then gone back to his own patient without another word. So he was *aware* she was seeing patients on her own and apparently didn't have anything to say about it. Yesterday, she'd seen him looking over the files of patients she'd seen that day. Since he hadn't said anything, did that mean she was doing a good job?

She closed her eyes and let the shower spray rinse the shampoo out of her hair. She'd been disgustingly filthy again when she'd gotten home today and the shower felt divine.

She sank back against the shower wall, shoulders slumping.

If it was just the clinic work, she'd be flying high. She'd get too busy and focused to obsess about food or anything else. Her ham sandwich was downed on the run between cases without any fanfare. Breakfast was much the same—she was always in a rush to get to the clinic. That in and of itself felt like a miracle.

But then, after the clinic closed each day around 1:00, the farm calls began. And as satisfying as diagnosing a case of worms was or stitching up a laceration after a cat fight, she couldn't help feeling the farm work was more important. Pets might be beloved members of a family household, but the farm animals were people's *livelihood.* Some of the farms they visited were small enough operations that every animal counted.

And she had no confidence in herself with the large animals after the calving fiasco. Hunter wasn't doing anything to help either. He seemed constantly annoyed by her presence. Which was a problem since, you know, they were spending a *lot* of time together.

Hours and hours in the car every afternoon. Sometimes the calls lasted into early evening. She knew Hunter went out in the morning before coming into the clinic. And he'd been called out for an emergency foaling in the middle of the night a couple days ago. But she didn't complain anymore about him not calling her in for these. The endless afternoon trips with him were bad enough.

Earlier today she'd finally grown the lady-balls to insist he let her help again. After all, the only way he even acknowledged her presence was when she forced him to.

She didn't even know *why* he was being such an ass. She'd thought maybe he had a God complex and he treated all his interns this way. At least until last Monday when one of his former interns dropped by the clinic. He and Hunter had laughed together and sounded like best friends. In fact, with the receptionist, with clients, with everybody else in the universe that Hunter interacted with, he was the friendly, nice guy she'd first met at the bar.

Until it came to her.

She didn't get it. Yeah, so she'd slept with him and okay, she hadn't been one hundred percent transparent about where she was from when she first met him. But so what? Get over it already. They had a professional relationship and it was time he started treating her with the respect she deserved as his assistant.

She wanted to say all that to his face.

She'd been about to.

She really had.

But then they'd arrived at the Newton's farm and she saw the gelding that was in pain from colic.

Colic was scary and life-threatening. It was a build up of gas in a horse's stomach that they had no natural way to get out on their own. Isobel hated seeing the horse suffering. But it was something she felt confident she knew how to treat.

"I'm going to help you with this case," she announced to Hunter as he grabbed the tubing and plunger from the equipment box at the back of his truck.

She was ready for an argument but all he did was toss her a big plastic bucket and say, "Okay."

Infuriating man.

He hadn't thrown her into the deep end on her own again. They'd actually worked together. He'd gloved up and then felt inside the back end of the horse, then gestured for her to do the same. She winced when she felt how much gas had built up inside the poor gelding. It felt like a bunch of balloons pressing against her arm.

Hunter let her feed the tubing up the horse's nose and down into its stomach. He filled the bucket up with water.

Then she started flushing a mixture of water and mineral oil into the horse's system. She had to hold the plunger and tubing over her head in order to get the leverage she needed since the horse was so tall. She worked until her arms were exhausted from holding them up. Then, without a word, Hunter took over.

They worked and worked while the owner held the horse's reins. The horse was sweaty and his eyes were wide with pain. He stomped where he stood, trying to get relief. No gas was passing, though. One time he looked like he was going to go down and Hunter took over the reins, pulling at the horse until he came back to his feet. They both knew that if a horse went down with colic, chances of recovery diminished dramatically.

After several hours, there was nothing more they could do. They had to leave the horses and farmer behind to wait it out. It was a horrible feeling, driving away, not knowing if the horse would live or die.

Hunter hadn't turned on the radio when they got back in the truck, so the ride had been silent for the hour-long drive home, both of them stinking of horse sweat and their clothes half-soaked with the water and mineral oil solution.

He'd pulled up in front of the clinic where her truck was parked.

She had opened her door and was about to step out when she paused. "Do you think he'll be okay?"

Hunter just kept staring ahead out the windshield. "The horse or his owner?"

"Either. Both."

Hunter shrugged briefly. "It'll be a long night. It's hard to say goodbye to the ones you love."

She frowned. He said that like he had some experience with it.

"You getting out?" He finally turned her way, looking annoyed. "I don't have all night."

Her eyes narrowed and she held up her hands. "I'm gone." She'd gotten out of the truck and slammed the door behind her.

She turned around so the shower spray blasted her face. God, she could use some ice cream. She'd grabbed a plate of steamed vegetables and some brown rice from the fare set up for dinner on her way upstairs and been proud of herself. *Look how good I'm being. These pounds are going to keep flying off.* Her fat pants were finally starting to fit more loosely with all the hard work and running around she was doing now.

But… ice cream.

She wondered if there was any left or if the boys had demolished it all already like last time. Mel shopped on Thursdays but that was no guarantee there'd be any ice cream left now that it was Friday.

She turned off the water and flipped her hair over to twist a towel around it. She dressed in record time, pulling on leggings and an oversized tee and socks. Then she jogged downstairs and toward the kitchen.

Maybe none would be left. Then there wouldn't be any temptation. She'd already had her allotted sweets for the day. Two sticks of gum earlier. She didn't need ice cream. That would blow all her extra 'cheat' calories for the week... and she'd sorta already spent them on Tuesday with the two Snickers bars she'd shoved in her face after an especially stressful afternoon of farm calls with Hunter.

It was fine, though. She'd just have one scoop of ice cream. *If* there was any. No big deal. Just a little something sweet to kill her craving.

She crept down the stairs, on the lookout for any of the guys. They'd all but tackled her when she'd come in earlier, trying to get her to sit and eat dinner with them.

They seemed especially thick about grasping the concept that she didn't want to sit down with a bunch of fit, attractive men when she smelled like the back end of whatever cow, horse, or pig she'd been spending the afternoon with. Even when she wasn't arm deep in the animal herself, she inevitably ended up walking away from the farms and ranches they visited reeking of animal, mud, and manure.

She got to the bottom of the stairs and heard the guys screaming at the flatscreen. It sounded like a game was on. She bit her lip and stepped even more lightly. The bottom of the staircase was visible from the big open den, but if she was really careful—

She darted from the staircase to the foyer, breathing hard once she got to the wall that hid her from the den. Oh thank God, they hadn't seen her.

She opened the front door, cringing at the small creaking noise it made. But she slipped out and shut it behind her. Whew, she made it. She ran around the house to get to the back door. It was unlocked and she stepped into the kitchen.

Ah, and there it was, the industrial size freezer in all its glory. She threw open the door and then felt a rush of exhilaration when she saw inside.

Ice cream, ice cream, and more ice cream. Mel had really outdone herself this week. There were all different flavors along with three large buckets of vanilla. She grabbed one of the buckets and then looked closer at the individual pints. There was coffee. Cookies and cream. Cookie dough—her favorite. Mint chocolate chip. Gross. She put that one back. Double dutch chocolate. Um, yes please.

Before she could think any better of it, she'd grabbed a spoon and had the tops off of all the containers. Then she was shoving large spoonfuls of ice cream into her mouth.

She would just taste a little bit of each one. She hadn't had ice cream in so long. And didn't she deserve a treat? After what she'd been putting up with from Hunter? But even thinking his name made her cringe and take another spoonful of ice cream.

Wow, the cookie dough was really to die for.

She was smart. You didn't get into Cornell without being smart. She bet Hunter's first few weeks on the job he'd made mistakes too.

Yeah, but he probably knew enough to tie up whatever animal he was treating.

She jammed her spoon into the ice cream. The chocolate mixed with the cookie dough tasted even better.

And why was he so determined to ignore her and treat her like crap, anyway? Was it just that he thought she'd make a bad veterinarian and he didn't see the point in even investing the energy to teach her anything? Or was it because she'd been so bad in bed that even the memory of their one night together was enough to put him off his lunch at the sight of her.

Not that *she* was ever put off her lunch. Just look at her. God, she'd eaten almost all of the cookie dough pint. All by herself.

There was no fucking point trying to fight it. She was useless. She couldn't do anything right.

That horse she'd tried to help tonight would die.

She reached over and shoved another spoonful of chocolate into her mouth. Useless. Ugly. Fat. An embarrassment.

Failure.

Failure.

FAILURE.

She dropped the ice cream and ran to the side of the sink that had a garbage disposal. She leaned over, finger ready to go down her throat.

"Shit!"

She jerked her hand back at the last second as big, fat tears burst out of her eyes.

No. She was better than this, goddammit. She was—

"Fine, I'll get it this time, you fuckers, but next time's on you."

Isobel stood up straight at the voice behind her and swiped at her eyes. Oh God, the last thing she needed right now was one of them to see her like this.

She stood up straight and was ready to make her excuses when a low voice said from behind her, "You doing all right, beautiful?"

She pasted a bright smile on her face and turned around, surprised when she saw it was Mack standing there. No wonder she hadn't recognized the voice right off. The big, tattooed man rarely had much to say. He seemed to prefer glaring as his main form of communication. She never took offense since he glared at everyone equally and seemed perpetually pissed off with the world.

"I'm fine. I'm just putting these away and then I'll—"

"You've been crying."

She froze. Didn't he know it was rude to blurt things like that out? But he just stood there, staring at her and frowning.

"Is there someone's face I need to go bash in?"

That made her crack a a real smile. She shook her head. She looked past him at the ice cream and felt her face heat with shame. They were all probably melting like crazy. She needed to get them back in the freezer but she didn't want to do it in front of Mack. Surely he had to wonder why she had so many containers open all at once. It was a freak thing to do. She was a freak.

But before she could decide what to do, he walked over to the containers. "You finished or do you want me to scoop you a bowl?"

Her cheeks were on fire. "I'm done," she managed to squeak. Then she ran over and tried to push him out of the way with her shoulder. "But I'll get these. You just go on with whatever it was you came in here for. I didn't mean to—"

122

"A couple of us were thinking of going out to Bubba's. You're gonna come out with us." He said it as a statement.

She looked up at him—he was over a foot taller than her. She paused where she was putting the lid on the cookies and cream.

"I am, am I?"

He nodded, his dark eyes alight. Wow, she didn't know he had an expression other than the glare, but there it was. He seemed amused by her. All he said was, "You are."

She felt like cocking a hand on her hip but instead she just went back to the ice cream. "And why would I do that?" She grabbed several containers and opened the freezer to put them back.

"Because you need to do something other than work. It's important. Socializing and shit."

She laughed again, closing the freezer door and looking at him. Did he realize the irony of him telling her *she* should be socializing? "Socializing and shit?"

He gave a decisive nod. "It'll be good for you." He took the last big bucket of ice cream and slid past her, his hand brushing hers as he opened the freezer.

She took a step back. "Is this— Are you trying to flirt with me?"

He laughed, a deep, glorious bass, and she didn't know whether to be insulted or not. When he closed the freezer, he leaned in, one hand on the cabinet over her head. "Oh honey, if I ever decide to flirt with you, you'll know it."

She sucked in a breath. Damn, the man was pure sin and sex when he wanted to be.

He pulled back and nodded. "Now go on upstairs and put on something tight and sexy. We're leaving in fifteen. You're gonna drink some tequila, let loose, and have some fuckin' fun tonight."

"Doctor's orders?" She arched an eyebrow.

He grinned that sexy grin of his again. "You bet your ass."

She just shook her head at him and left the kitchen. The other guys called out to her as she walked through the den and she smiled and waved back.

She considered just going upstairs and tucking herself in bed with her e-reader. But then she thought about how Mack had distracted her from how miserable she'd been feeling moments before he'd come in

123

the kitchen. If she stayed home tonight, she'd just retreat back in her head and get all stupid and self-involved again.

So, with that in mind, she walked to her closet and shoved aside all the practical, farm-worthy clothes and pulled one of the few dresses she'd brought off its hanger. She breathed out and bit her bottom lip as she undressed and then pulled the slinky black dress over her head.

When she'd ordered her work boots off Mel's Amazon account, she'd also used the opportunity to order all the basics she might need. On impulse, she'd used the last of her money to throw a cute little pair of strappy black pumps into her cart.

She slipped them on and they fit perfectly. She went to the bathroom and tried not to look at herself too closely. She leaned in just long enough to apply some mascara and lipstick. She hesitated only a second before choosing her siren red lipstick. Because why the hell not? She was going to go have fun, dammit.

She rubbed her lips together and then popped them. She stood up, allowing herself one look at the full effect. Her hair was mostly dry and not too much of a disaster. She pulled it up and looked at her face left and right, puckering her mouth.

And for once… the woman reflected back at her actually looked sort of… pretty.

She spun away from the mirror, shaking her head at the strange thought. Grabbing her purse, she opened her door.

Well, here went nothing.

Chapter 12
HUNTER

Hunter scrubbed a towel through his damp hair as the microwave beeped. He tossed his towel on one of the chairs at his dining room table as he went to retrieve his food. A real dinner of champions. Microwaved beef lo mein. Oh yeah, he was living the life.

"Ow, shit." He dropped the steaming hot tray to the counter, then shook out his stinging hand. He grabbed a kitchen towel and used that to hold it still while he peeled back the lid. More steam erupted and he grabbed a fork.

It was pretty tasteless shit but nobody bought Mr. Foo's Instant Beef Lo Mein if they were looking for an amazing culinary experience. He stood at the counter and wolfed down the food as fast as he could without burning his mouth.

He was done with it all too fast. He looked at the clock. 9:00. He ran a hand through his damp hair and looked around his empty cabin.

Late evening was always the worst time of day.

He tossed his empty food container in the trash, grabbed a cold beer, then headed for the living room. Flipping through the channels was less than inspiring. Red-faced people bitching about politics. Stupid reality TV shit. Who'd be next to be voted off the yacht? Here's an idea—anybody pretentious enough to be on a show called Hot for the Yacht.

Next. He finally came across a baseball game.

He settled in to watch. He'd already missed half of it and while usually a game was enough to distract him from shit well enough, today he couldn't seem to get his mind off of a certain dark-haired beauty.

Isobel had given it her all today with the colicky horse. He could see how upset she'd been when they'd left without being able to give a positive prognosis. She might be a city girl but she did have a way with animals. He'd peeked in on her at the clinic a few times—just to make sure she wasn't screwing up his practice. But she'd been doing great each time. Treating both the animals and their human owners with compassion, intelligence, and understanding.

He tipped his head back on the couch and took a long swallow of beer.

Truth was, what had seemed so simple—trying to alienate her so she'd leave quicker—was turning out to be much more difficult than he'd bargained for. Not to mention he hadn't counted on feeling like such an asshole about the whole thing.

Which was bullshit. He was the one in the right.

She'd lied to him and then foisted herself on him as his intern when he clearly hadn't wanted it.

But... he couldn't say she hadn't proven herself. Other than that hilarious misstep with not tying up the heifer while pulling the calf, her work had been impeccable. And it wasn't like other interns committed anything more to him than a single summer.

So why was he holding her to some higher standard?

Because you slept with her.

He winced, then stood up and started pacing behind the couch, his hand going to the back of his neck.

Shit. Was he really *that* asshole?

Goddammit, he wished he had someone he could talk to about all this. He'd always been a fuck-up when it came to women. His phone was sitting on the shelf beside the entryway and he stalked over to it. Then, before he could think better of it, he punched in the number he hadn't dialed in months.

It rang.

And rang.

And rang.

Then a long beep sounded.

Hunter sank against the bookshelf, his eyes closing and his head tilting back.

"This is Janine. I'm not around right now. Leave a message and I'll try to get back to you." Slight pause. "I'm shit at checking my messages though, so if you don't hear from me within a couple days, just call back again. Catch you on the flip side."

Hunter pulled the phone away from his ear and hit end call.

Then he looked around his empty house. Jesus, he couldn't stand another Friday night alone here, drinking beer and watching a fucking game. He turned and grabbed his keys and boots, stuffing his feet into them as he was already half out the door.

***

The parking lot at Bubba's was packed like always on Friday night. Bubba's was the only watering hole for twenty miles and Bubba was happy to make a buck off people's desperation for entertainment and alcohol, not always in that order.

Hunter pulled open the door and would swear the raucous noise that spilled out was a few decibels louder than normal.

The bar had a lot of floor space and people had pushed back tables to clear out an area for a dance floor. They only did that on Fridays and Saturdays. It was being put to good use and when Hunter looked closer, he saw why. Looked like the boys from Mel and Xavier's had come out for the night. A couple of those boys were genuine hell raisers and the town couldn't have loved them more for it.

Well, apart from the sheriff, Marie—but even she couldn't do much more than watch on since they'd never done anything *outright* illegal. Though the bar top striptease down to his boxers Liam had performed a couple months ago might have straddled the line of public indecency. It was certainly an image Hunter didn't think he'd scrape from his memory any time soon.

Tonight Hunter actually welcomed their shenanigans. Distraction was the name of the game, after all.

Until he saw the object he was trying to distract himself from right in the middle of the crowd, dancing with the manwhore in chief himself—Liam O'Neill. And not just dancing. For Christ's sake. Talk about public indecency.

Isobel's back was to Liam's front and one of his hands was tucked right below her breast. With the other, he lifted hers high overhead, then he skimmed down her body as they shimmied down, dropping low to the floor. Her black little nothing scrap of a dress rode even higher up her legs when she crouched down low like that. Liam grasped her waist in both hands and they shimmied back up to standing.

127

The song ended and Isobel jumped up and down, laughing and clapping. She threw her arms sloppily around Liam's neck and Hunter wanted to deck the bastard. Just how much had she had to drink?

None of your damn business. She's nothing more than an employee.

So why couldn't he look away from her? She never smiled like that around him. And he hadn't seen her with her hair down since the first night he'd met her, when she'd pulled it out of her ponytail for the shower. Her eyes were bright too, probably because of the alcohol.

That bastard Liam better not be trying to take advantage of her. They'd had a hard case with the colicky horse and maybe she was upset—

Nope. He turned away from the dance floor. None of his goddamned business. He pushed past people standing around the dance floor to get to the bar.

There was one open stool and he made a beeline for it.

He'd just grab a quick drink, then head back home. It was stupid to come out tonight anyway. What, was he some whiny little bitch who couldn't stand a little silence? So his house was quiet. Boo hoo. So he'd made his wife so miserable she'd left him in the middle of the night. It happened. Who didn't have problems?

Bubba came over to where Hunter was sitting. "What'll you have tonight?"

"Whiskey."

Bubba turned to get his drink.

In spite of himself, Hunter kept looking over to the dance floor. Now she was dancing with Mack. Christ, if there was anyone he'd trust a woman with less than Liam, it was Mack. "How long has that been going on?"

"About an hour." The answer wasn't from Bubba. Hunter swiveled on his stool and saw that Cal was sitting beside him. It would be easy to mistake Cal for a man—she always walked around in oversized men's overalls with big flannel shirts underneath. Her hair was cropped short too, or at least, it usually was. Hunter was startled to realize it was a little longer—there was a small ponytail peeking out the back of the baseball cap she always wore.

"Hey Cal," Hunter said. He'd known her ever since grade school. She was quiet, but a good sort.

Bubba set Hunter's drink and must have heard Hunter's initial question, because he looked out over the dance floor and smiled. "They've been livening up the joint for about an hour now."

"And how many drinks have they poured down her?" Hunter growled

"Hey there." Bubba braced his hands on the bar and narrowed his eyes at Hunter. "Don't be disrespecting me in my own bar. You know I don't put up with shit. That girl's only been drinking what she's ordered herself. And having a fine time of it." Bubba's eyes tracked back to the dance floor, his ruddy cheeks bright as he smiled. "Sure don't make 'em like that round here. 'Cept for my Dottie, of course, God rest her soul." Then his eyes flicked over to Cal. "No offense, Cal."

Cal just waved her beer. "None taken."

Hunter's mood soured as he watched Isobel. He swallowed a healthy swig of his whiskey. It was biting, but he got it down without coughing. Soon his throat and belly were warmed by the liquid. His muscles relaxed. He angled his back toward the dance floor.

Maybe coming here wasn't such a bad idea after all. He'd just ignore Isobel and have a nice little drink, shoot the shit with Bubba and—

Bubba's eyes were on the dance floor behind him and he let out a low whistle. "Damn that woman's a firecracker. If I was a young buck, you can bet I'd be—"

"For the love of God don't finish that sentence," Cal implored.

The temptation was too great and Hunter looked over his shoulder.

Now Isobel was sandwiched *between* Mack and Liam and their hands— Christ, they were all over her. Mack was chest to chest with her, his knees slung between hers and again, her back was to Liam. They were all dancing so close together, Hunter had no idea how they were managing to stay upright. She was staring into Mack's eyes, a wide smile on her face as she talked animatedly.

Mack was staring back like he wanted to devour her. Mack's eyes flicked behind her to Liam and it was as if they were having the same thought.

Hunter's hands clenched into fists and he was half off his barstool when someone came to stand in front of him. Hunter was about to order them out of the way when he realized it was Sandra, his receptionist.

"Well, it's just selfish of her to take two of them," Sandra said, looking toward the dance floor.

"It's obscene," Hunter shot back without really thinking it through.

Sandra's eyes brightened and Hunter immediately wished he could take it back. The gossip mill could be vicious in Hawthorne, like any small town. Another reason for Isobel not to be making such a spectacle of herself.

"So, I was thinking," Sandra leaned over Hunter to get her drink at the bar. Hunter frowned and tried to angle around her so he could keep an eye on Isobel. Who knew what those two bastards had up their sleeves. He did *not* like the way they were looking at her.

"We should go out sometime."

Isobel had flipped around so that now her chest was to Liam's. His hands were so low on Isobel's back he was practically grabbing her a—

"Hunter?"

"Huh?" he looked up at Sandra. "Sorry, did you say something?"

She giggled a little and pushed some of her frizzy, over-processed red hair behind her ear. "I said we should go out sometime. Remember how much fun we used to have in high school?"

"Oh." Shit. Hunter straightened on his barstool. He hated situations like this.

He and Sandra had dated briefly their junior year. Well, if you counted a drunken hook up after Matt Davies' field party the year they won Homecoming *dating*. He had taken her out to eat a few times afterwards because he'd felt like a major tool once he'd sobered up the next morning. Maybe there was more to her than the vapid cheerleader she portrayed on the surface? You couldn't judge a book by its cover, right? *He'd* certainly hoped to be more than just a dumb jock all his life.

Three dates and too many hours to count later with an earful of gossip about a ton of shit he didn't care about, he decided that in some cases, the cover was a perfectly accurate representation of what was inside.

And after ten years, other than a bad dye job and skin that advertised she was averse to sunscreen, Hunter didn't think much about Sandra had changed.

"Look, Sandra," Hunter began, backing away from her on his barstool, "I'm really not looking to date anyone right n—"

"Everything with Janine was over a year ago," Sandra said, leaning over so he could get a peek down her plunging neckline, no doubt. "You've got to get back up on the horse again." God, he could barely breathe with all that perfume she was wearing. "And cowboy, I'm happy to help break you back in."

Beside them, Cal choked on her beer as she audibly bit back a laugh. Sandra glared at her.

You're too late anyway, he wanted to tell Sandra. Another woman already had that privilege. His eyes skirted past Sandra's shoulder toward where he'd last seen Isobel dancing, sandwiched between Liam and Mack.

Only to find Isobel staring directly at him. The two guys were still on either side of her but she'd stopped dancing. The smile was totally gone from her face. She looked stricken, in fact. Her eyes went from Hunter, then to something right beside him.

Hunter turned his head to see what she was looking at.

And ran right smack into Sandra's lips. She'd stepped in between his legs and was right there, just fuckin' landing one on him. He got the brief ashy taste of cigarettes before he yanked back, launching backwards off the barstool.

"Christ, Sandra." He swiped at his mouth. His hand came away with a smear of her red-orange lipstick.

But she was still coming at him, her eyes lowered in what he assumed was her come-hither look. With all that black make-up around her eyes and her orange middriff baring halter top, she just looked like a dead-eyed hooker.

"Oh come on, Hunter. You don't have to do that coy cat and mouse bullshit with me." She put a lacquered orange-nailed finger on the center of his chest. She grinned at him. She had lipstick on her teeth. "Take me home and I'll make sure you get a very happy ending."

And a venereal disease, he thought.

Sandra tried to dip forward again but he held out a hand and gave a firm shake of his head. "I'm sorry, Sandra. This is never gonna happen between you and me."

Suddenly her bottom lip began to tremble. Aw, shit. Was she going to cry? He never knew what to do when women cried.

"But I thought…" she hiccupped. "When you hired me on at the clinic—"

Over her shoulder, Hunter saw Isobel fleeing down the back hallway in the direction of the restrooms. She didn't stop at the ladies, though. No, she blew past the restrooms and shoved open the back door, then pushed into the night.

Hawthorne was a pretty quiet town but they weren't that far off the interstate. What was she thinking, running out there all alone when she was drunk off her ass?

"—that we had a real connection. You gave me that *look* when we were scheduling the surgery for Mr. Bartlett's poodle. I knew you wanted m—"

"Sorry, if you'll excuse me," Hunter cut Sandra off midsentence and went to chase after Isobel. What the hell was wrong with her supposed escorts that they abandoned her right when she needed them most? He was going to have words with Xavier. If the man couldn't corral his men to act responsibly when they were out in town, something had to be done.

Hunter shoved people aside on the dance floor when they didn't get out of his way fast enough.

"Whoa, Hunter, why in such a hurry?" more than one person asked him. He ignored them all and just kept moving, finally jogging when he got to the hall corridor.

When he exploded out the back door, he looked left or right. Dammit, which way did she go?

But finally he heard the faint sounds of a woman crying.

Christ, that sound was enough to rip any man apart, but coming from her? What had happened? If one of those assholes had hurt her… His hands clenched into fists.

"Isobel?" he hurried toward the sound and found her crouched down against the wall behind the bar's dumpster, knees to her chest.

"Go away!" she turned her back to him when she saw him.

"What's wrong? Did one of those bastards touch you? I swear, if either of them laid a hand on you, I'll—"

"What?" She sounded both confused and incredulous. She stood up, using the wall for leverage. "God, no. Mack and Liam are great."

Hunter took a step back. "Then why…" his voice trailed off as she swiped at her cheeks.

"It was nothing. God, I'm just an idiot." She'd kept her face averted the whole time but suddenly her eyes flashed up to him. "What do you care anyway? Won't your date be mad you left her to chase after another woman? That's kind of an a-hole move."

"Date?" Hunter's mind was blank before it finally registered. "What, you mean Sandra?" He scoffed. "She's not my date. She just came up to me and—"

"Hey, no need to explain." Isobel held up her hands. "I'm not trying to get in the way of your next hookup. Your business is your business."

She took a few steps toward the club door like she was going to head back in.

"Wait," Hunter put out a hand. "Stop."

If she'd thought he was with Sandra and nothing had happened with Liam or Mack… was that why she'd been out here crying? He blinked. She'd been crying over *him*?

"It's not like that with Sandra and me." It sounded stupid, he knew as soon as he said it, but it seemed important for her to understand.

She shrugged. "Whatever. Like I said. None of my business."

"What if it was?" He took a step closer. Shit. What was he doing? He didn't know but his hand was drawn like a magnet to push a stray lock of hair behind her ear. Her breath hitched at the contact.

Her eyes searched his, back and forth. He could see confusion there. And something else. Longing?

Christ, she was beautiful. And more than that. She was kind. Patient. Compassionate. She was beautiful in all the ways that counted.

133

So it seemed like the most natural thing in the world when he cupped her jaw and drew her face down to his.

When his lips pressed against hers, his blood lit on fire.

She gasped and jerked away. "You've been nothing but an asshole to me ever since that first night." She glared at him.

Fuck. Why had he kissed her? Everything that made him pull away from her in the first place was still true. She was a rich, city girl. She'd be leaving at the end of the summer. She was far too much like Janine for comfort. Not to mention that she was right—he'd been treating her like a class A jerk for weeks now.

He was about to apologize and walk away when she suddenly reached up, dug her hands in his hair, and yanked him back down. Then she started kissing him like he was a feast and she'd been starving for months.

All other thoughts took a flying leap.

There was only Isobel.

Real and warm and alive in his arms. So alive. She tasted like strawberry and lime and tequila. And when she yanked his shirt out of his jeans and her hands caressed up his bare stomach underneath, he'd swear she was so hot she was searing his skin.

"Fuck, Isobel," he growled, spinning them and pinning her against the brick wall of the bar. All the blood in his body was quickly headed south at her touch and continued frantic kisses.

"Yes," she whispered.

Goddamn. He hadn't meant it as an invitation but she was sure taking it that way. Her hands scrambled at his waist, undoing his buckle. Aw, fuck. His cock strained against his jeans toward her seeking hands. But shit. She was drunk. She didn't—

He pulled back from her. It took all his willpower. "I can't."

He shook his head. Her eyes flashed hurt. Christ. He hurried to explain, cupping her face. Her skin was so soft and he couldn't help dipping back down to kiss her moist, berry pink lips. "You've been drinking. I'm not gonna be one of those guys who takes advantage of a woman."

He went in for another kiss when she laughed. He pulled back, startled.

"Hunter, I had one margarita. I'm not drunk."

He paused. "But you were so…" He gestured back at the bar. "Smiley."

Her gaze went in the direction he indicated, a wistful expression on her face. "I guess that's just me," she shrugged, "when I'm happy."

She looked back at Hunter and he felt kicked in the guts. He'd never gotten to see her happy. Because he only made her miserable. Fuck.

But he didn't want to think about any of that. He didn't want to think. Period. Full stop.

He pressed her back against the wall. Her legs spread, one thigh hitching up around his waist. It was indecent. If anyone came out here and saw them—

But all Hunter could think about was her hot, wet core, the tiny cotton fabric of her underwear and the denim of his jeans the only barrier to him being buried deep inside her again.

How many nights had he lay in bed tormented by the memory of that sweet little cunt of hers. And here she was, hot and wanting, wrapped around him.

Her hands were back at his buckle again and his cock surged in his pants. Fuck, he was so hard his cock could punch a hole through a brick wall.

The second her tiny hands touched his cock, he was almost done for. He reached down and palmed her juicy ass, giving it a rough squeeze, before jerking her panties down.

His middle finger dipped inside her. "Fuck," he hissed. Her sweet little pussy was fucking drenched. His thumb immediately sought out her clit. It was already swollen and he strummed his thumb back and forth before pressing hard on it.

Her hand gripping his cock squeezed and little high-pitched gasps escaped her throat.

"Is this for me?" he asked, his jaw going tight. "Or was it because of them?" He shoved another finger inside, not bothering to be gentle about it.

Her head had been bowed but she jerked her face up at his question, eyes flashing.

"Fuck you," she whispered. At the same time, her hand on his cock guided him toward the slick lips of her pussy.

Jesus Christ. With one thrust he could be inside her.

"Fuck *me* is what I think you meant to say." He lined his hips up and reached down, pulling his cock out of her hand and rubbing it up and down her vulva and her clit.

Her mouth dropped open and her head sank back against the brick wall. "Fine. You win. Fuck *me*. Just get the fuck inside me already."

With the hand not on his cock, he grabbed her chin and pulled her face down so that she was forced to look at him. Her eyes flashed fury and fire and crazy lust.

He dipped just the head of his cock inside her. "You want this? You want me to bury my giant cock deep inside you? You want me to fuck you so hard you come till you can't see straight?"

With every word, her chest pumped harder, her breaths growing more and more shallow. "Yes. Fuck. *Yes.*"

He was about to give her exactly what she was begging for before he remembered. *Shit.*

"What?" She'd obviously seen the change in his expression.

He met her gaze. "I don't have any condoms on me. I didn't plan on—" he broke off. "I'm clean, but I get it if you don't want to—"

"Damn it." She squeezed her eyes shut. When she opened them, her blue eyes were bright with want and her pelvis arched toward him like it was an involuntary movement. "I'm clean as far as I know. But my ex was screwing around so I can't be a hundred percent—"

Fuck it. "Good enough for me."

He jerked his hips forward, jamming his cock to the hilt inside her with one quick thrust.

Oh Jesus, *yes*. Fuck. So tight. Tighter than he remembered. And she was fucking clenching around him. So good. So fuckin' good.

Her arms wound around him and she clutched his shoulders, digging her fingernails in. Meanwhile she made these little high-pitched whimpers like his cock inside her was the best thing she'd ever felt in the whole damn world.

He grabbed her underneath her thighs, pulled his hips back and then thrust in again, driving her up and against the brick wall.

Her other leg came up and locked behind his back. She squeezed around his dick and he about passed out. He jerked his hips back and then he shoved back in.

Then she let out the hottest fucking moan, arching her breasts toward him. But apparently that wasn't enough because she pulled one arm from around his neck and started tugging at her own nipple.

Fucking hell. His cock lurched inside her. As if this weren't already the hottest fuck of his whole life. She twisted and teased her nipple until the outline was clear through the thin material of her dress. First one and then the other.

He wanted to bite them. Fuck that. He *needed* his goddamned mouth on them. He jerked the neckline down so he could get at her lace covered breast. Fuck. Did she wear that sexy as shit red lace bra just to torment him?

But no. She hadn't known she'd see him tonight. So who had she worn the goddamned bra for? One of those other dumb bastards inside? He'd kill them.

He jerked the lace down and bit the soft flesh of her large breast.

She yelped and yanked at his hair. But she wasn't pulling him away—the opposite in fact. No, she was pulling him harder in to her chest. Smothering him against her gorgeous tits. Fucking hell.

He sucked her nipple into his mouth at the same time he rocked his hips back and then shoved back in deep.

Her surprised gasp was fucking indecent. The parking lot was just around the corner of the building. If anyone heard her, they'd know exactly what was going on here.

The thought made Hunter even harder. Which surprised him. He didn't know he had any exhibitionist tendencies. Maybe he didn't. Maybe it was just Isobel. Hearing those sexy as fuck noises coming out of her throat and knowing he was eliciting them? Fucking hot as sin.

Still, it was a small town. Reputation was important here. He didn't want to be the bastard who ruined anyone, so he held one of his hands over her mouth.

Her eyes widened and she clenched around his cock. Shit. Was she not okay with that? He wasn't trying to—

He started to remove his hand but she shook her head, grabbing his wrist to keep it in place.

Did she find the idea of being gagged sexy? That was so fucking *hot*. His hand flexed on her mouth. His balls slapped loudly against her, he was fucking her so hard and fast. And then all thought flew out the window apart from the basics.

Jesus *fuck*.

Felt so good.

His cock so deep inside her.

Fucking her so deep.

So.

Fucking.

Deep.

No, not deep enough. He bottomed out, his balls against her ass but he just kept shoving further and further inside her. She rolled her hips all around restlessly, wiggling like she needed to feel every inch of his cock.

And the way she fucking clenched on him. Clenched. Released. Then clenched. Holy fucking—

Suddenly she pulled away from the hand he had over her mouth. He started to withdraw but she shook her head and sucked his forefinger into her mouth.

She sucked it so hard. She bobbed up and down on his finger just like she would his cock.

Fuck.

Just when he thought she couldn't get fucking hotter, she went and did something like that.

Turned out he didn't know the half of it.

Because a second later, she let go of his finger with a *pop* of her lips. Then she leaned over and whispered, a lusty desperation in her voice, "Stick your finger in my ass. Please Hunter. Stick it in my ass."

Fuuuuuuuuuuuuuuuuuuuuck.

Going to blow. Fuck. Her ass. His finger in her ass. His cock in her ass. He'd fuck her there next. Grab her ass cheeks and bend her over, then plow her like—

No. Christ. Hold it back. Hold it back.

There were an average of three hundred and nineteen bones in a dog's body. The epiphyseal plates were the soft areas of a puppy's bones that—

Fuck, it was no use.

His cock jerked and got harder than it ever had in his fucking life. Then he mashed Isobel against the wall and kissed her until she was gasping for breath. But all he could think about was her puckered, forbidden little asshole.

With one arm underneath her thigh, he supported her weight against the wall. And then with his other, he reached underneath. He teased along the bottom of her slit where his cock was buried.

She squeezed around him. Anticipating.

Fuck she wanted it bad.

"Tell me again," he growled. "Tell me what you want."

She made a restless whining noise. "Stick your finger in my ass. I want you everywhere."

He teased his forefinger around her back hole. His spine tingled and he had to stop fucking her so he didn't blow early. He wanted to fucking savor this.

She trembled as he teased the tip of his finger around her asshole.

"This?" he hissed in her ear. "This is what you want?"

"Yes." She shuddered and started wriggling on his cock again.

He continued teasing around the rim. Fuck. If he'd thought she was hot before... He leaned his chest back, his pelvis still pinning her to the wall. But he wanted to see her face while his finger teased her ass.

"Beg me."

Her eyes flashed with momentary rebellion. But then she bit her lip and looked skyward. She settled her gaze back on his. She didn't look away but kept her eyes leveled on him. She grabbed both of her breasts, plucking at her nipples. She arched and looked at him through a half-lidded gaze. "I want to come with your finger fucking my asshole and your cock in my cunt. I need it now. Give it to me, Hunter. Fucking please."

Well fuck. Again he was about to bust a nut. He gritted his teeth to hold it back as he slowly inched his forefinger up her ass. She squeezed around him like a fucking vise, both his finger and his cock. He should really have some lube for this but Isobel's little whimpering noises told him she was just fine with everything he was doing.

He dragged his finger back out and pushed it in, back and forth a few times. It was only when he pressed a second finger in with the first that Isobel's eyes popped open and he really started fucking her again.

"Look at me, Isobel," he demanded. "Your climax belongs to me."

She obeyed and he saw the myriad of emotions playing out across her face. Just like the first time they'd made lo—he shook his head, *had sex*—he felt like he was seeing straight into her, like in these moments she was incapable of hiding a single thing she was feeling from him.

He saw her discomfort when he added a third finger and he saw the moment she decided to accept and roll with it. He saw how she abandoned herself to pleasure and how her little gasps grew shorter and shorter as she approached climax.

And he was right there with her when her eyes widened in surprise as it hit. Her hands fisted in his shirt and she clenched everything. Her ass. Her cunt. Her fingers.

She was fucking milking him.

He reared back and then slammed inside her. Once. Twice. He bared his teeth. Every muscle tensed as his cum shot out of his cock, landing deep inside her.

Fucking marking her.

As his.

Fucking *his*.

His.

It was all he could think, over and over as they both gasped for breath in the aftermath.

"Izzy? You out here?"

Shit. *Now* one of those fuckers decided to check up on her? Isobel's eyes went wide and she started pushing at Hunter's shoulders. He still had her impaled against the wall.

He pulled out and set her as gently as he could back on her feet. When he tried to help smooth her dress down, she slapped his hands away.

He recoiled. What the hell?

"Izzy?" the male voice called again. "It's Reece."

"I'm fine, Reece." Isobel responded, kicking her underwear under the dumpster and running her fingers through her mussed hair. "Just give me a second."

Apparently Reece had no seconds to give because he rounded the dumpster right in time to see Hunter zipping up his fly and reaching for his buckle.

Reece's eyes went wide with surprise and he jerked his head toward Isobel. Her face went immediately red. "We've been looking for you everywhere. You had us worried."

She bit her lip. "I'm fine. I just needed some air."

"Did this asshole hurt you?" His eyes shot back to Hunter.

"Hey," Hunter took a step forward but Isobel cut him off.

"I said I'm fine." She strode toward Reece without a backward glance at Hunter. "Are you guys ready to go?"

What the actual fuck? Hunter's jaw tensed.

"Isobel." It was a command to stop as much as a demand for her attention. Her back stiffened but she didn't turn around.

"Let's go, Reece."

"Isobel." Hunter took another step toward her but Reece stepped in his way.

"You're gonna want to back up, pal."

Hunter clenched his jaw and he all but growled at the other man. He could do nothing but stand and watch as behind Reece, Isobel hurried to the back door of the bar, opened it, and disappeared inside.

"Fuck," Hunter shouted, turning and slamming an open palm on the brick wall.

"You better not have hurt her. If you hurt so much as a hair on her head, I swear we'll make you regret the day you were born."

Hunter swung back around toward the other man. He'd had dinner with Xavier's men a few times out at the ranch. All he remembered about Reece was that he'd seemed like a good-natured guy. He gave zero fucks about the fact now. He wasn't going to put up with anyone insinuating that he was the kind of guy to hurt women.

The fact that Isobel had left him just as coldly as Janine did after sex might have him feeling dangerous but it was nothing he'd ever take out on a woman.

Reece, however. He was fair fucking game.

"You're going to want to walk away now." Hunter's voice was low. "Without another word."

141

Reece kept glaring back. "Isobel's the sister Jeremiah and I never had. And nothing in the world's more important to us than family. You keep that in mind."

With that he turned and headed back inside the bar.

As soon as the door slammed behind him, Hunter yanked his phone out of his pocket. A few taps later, he had the phone against his ear.

He felt punched in the guts all over again when he heard her voice. "This is Janine. I'm not around right now..."

Chapter 13
ISOBEL

Isobel called in sick to work the next day.

Cowardly? Yes. But could she face Hunter after what happened last night? That would be a big fat *no*.

Besides, it was a Saturday and 'work' only meant being on call for emergencies so it wasn't like there were normal clinic hours she was shirking. She just couldn't handle being closed up in that truck cab with Hunter for hours on end today. Tomorrow was her day off and by Monday she'd have her shit together enough to deal with him again.

God, *why* had she given in to Hunter last night when he'd kissed her? She still didn't understand what the hell she'd been doing.

She hated him.

He was a jerk.

But the sex was *so* hot.

She'd heard about hate sex but had certainly never experienced it before. And there was no changing it now. So, yes, they'd had amazing, earth-shattering sex. The kind of sex that changed your entire view on life. Just like that first night.

But so what? And so what if she'd been completely shameless and slutty beyond all imagination while they were at it. Her face fired red when she thought about some of the things she'd asked him to do.

She'd never in her life asked a partner to do those things to her before. Sure, she'd fantasized about them plenty when she got herself off but actually voicing them out loud…

And yet somehow with Hunter, the last person on earth she *should* trust with her deepest, darkest desires, everything had just popped right out of her mouth.

She shoved her face in her pillow and squeezed her legs together.

She'd read that some people were genetically predisposed to addictive behaviors. Maybe she was just exchanging one obsession for another. Instead of a food addict, she'd become a nymphomaniac. Which meant Catrina was right and her DNA was predetermined to screw her over whether it came to food *or* sex…

God, she certainly wasn't thinking about food. No, ever since she'd gotten home last night all she could do was replay every moment of the sweaty, dirty fuck up against the back of the bar. She'd masturbated herself to sleep last night.

Then this morning, she woke up just as horny. Still, touching herself was nothing to the fullness of Hunter's thick cock filling her up. She squeezed her legs together.

She'd go nuts if she laid here in bed obsessing about this all day. She hauled herself to a sitting position and then swung her legs over the side of the bed.

She got dressed and combed her hair back into a ponytail. She'd showered when she got home to get rid of Hunter's scent last night.

Like always, she lingered in front of the mirror no longer than was absolutely necessary after brushing her teeth and making sure her ponytail was straight. She turned and went downstairs.

"Sleeping Beauty awakes," Reece said from the den when she made it to the bottom of the stairs.

"Wrong fairytale, dumbass," Liam said. "She's obviously Snow White. Look at her coloring. Pale, creamy skin. Rose-bud lips. Long black hair."

"Does that make us the seven dwarves?" Reece asked.

"So good to know they teach math skills to the kids these days," Mack said. "By my last count, there's only five of us."

Jeremiah gave him a sarcastic smile. "But you're such a clear ringer for Happy."

Mack flipped him off, then stuffed his scrambled eggs into his mouth. "Let's go, little girls. You can gossip and braid each other's hair another time. Those stalls aren't going to muck themselves."

The twins and Liam gave him the one-fingered salute in return. Nicholas just kept eating his breakfast, eyes quietly observing everything like always. Isobel gave him a pat on the back. "Morning Nick."

"Hey Iz. You off on calls with your Dr. Hunter this morning?"

She looked down at him sharply. "He's not *my* Dr. Hunter."

Nicholas didn't say anything. His eyebrows just went up slightly before he went back to eating.

144

Crap. She was being a freak. She tried to modulate her voice and sound normal when she said, "Nope, I'm hanging around here. Thought I might go spend some time with Bright Beauty and take one of the others out for a ride."

She and Beauty had gotten close over the past couple weeks. When Isobel wanted to get away from the noise of the house and the guys' boisterous heckling of each other, she'd steal away to the barn and spend an hour or two grooming and chatting with Beauty. She was a gentle-natured horse and the strict regimen of rest and massage seemed to be easing her pain as her ligaments healed. She'd never be able to compete again, but there was no reason she couldn't have a long, healthy life.

Spending time with the horses made her feel calm and collected, just like it always had. Animals were so much simpler than people. You looked in their eyes and you didn't have to wonder what they were thinking.

Look at me, Isobel. Your climax belongs to me.

She gulped as she put a bagel in the toaster and lifted the lid on the tray of scrambled eggs. She scooped a small spoonful onto her plate.

Yes, she far preferred animals to people.

"So, you and the redhead at the bar seemed to be hitting it off last night," Liam said. Isobel looked up just in time to see Jeremiah's face going red.

"I mentioned I was studying history and she said she really loved Game of Thrones. So we got to talking."

Liam burst out laughing. "She does realize that's not actual history, right?"

The back of Jeremiah's neck went a little pink as he picked up his toast. "George R. R. Martin said he based it on the War of the Roses. That's real history. We talked about that a little."

Liam winced. "Oh God, tell me you did not bore the hot chick with a history lesson. She was just trying to get in your pants, mate."

Jeremiah leveled him with a stare. "That's not all there is to a woman."

Liam waved his fork in a *maybe so, maybe not* gesture. "That woman, it's debatable. The shirt she was wearing barely deserves the title. It was more like an extravagant bikini. And she was all but

145

climbing your leg like a dog in heat while you were boring her with obscure English history."

Isobel's bagel popped. She took it and scraped a thin layer of cream cheese over it, then sat down at the table between Nicholas and Jeremiah. Reece and Liam were across the table from them.

Jeremiah was all out glaring now. "She gave me her number."

Liam laughed. "Of course she did." Liam leaned back in his chair, his hands behind his head. "The women in this town are all hard up and we're fresh dick." Then he winced and looked Isobel's way. "No offense."

She laughed and held her hands up. "None taken. Please, do continue with this fascinating argument. I feel it's my duty to all womankind to hear you out."

"Well, take a woman like your redhead. There are only so many options in a town this size. She starts out fucking high school boys. She's what, twenty-two? Twenty-three? If she went to college, she might have gotten a taste for some good sex. Still, for whatever reason, she ended up back here. Or maybe she never went to college and has been here the whole time. Either way, all that sad high school dick is starting to get mighty old by now."

He grinned wide and held his arms out. "Then we traipse in to town. A bunch of handsome bastards with our shiny new cocks. It's like when the carnival comes through town. They all want to take a ride."

"And yet you went home all alone." Jeremiah tapped his chin, pretending to be puzzled. "Shocking with such foolproof logic like that."

Liam waved his hand dismissively. "I wasn't putting any energy into it last night. I was just out to get ossified."

"Ossi-what?" Reece asked.

Liam looked around the table, and seeing everyone's bland expression, he clarified. "Ossified. Ya know—pissed. Smashed. Shit-faced. Twisted. Banjo'd."

"Banjo'd?" Isobel laughed. "Oh my God, that's my new favorite word for getting drunk."

Liam just grinned. "See, the accent gets 'em every time. If I'd wanted to get me hole last night, it wouldn't a been a problem."

146

"Get your *hole*?" Isobel choked, doubling over.

"Some of us are trying to eat a nice meal here," Nicholas said, glaring over at Liam.

"Hey, I'm just giving my public what they demand," Liam said.

Nicholas finished his toast and stood up. "Well what you ought to be doing is eating. The Dodgers Yankees game starts at 4:00."

Liam rolled his eyes. "Whatever will I do if I miss the first quarter of a bunch of fat-arsed men standing around waiting for a ball to be thrown at them."

Nicholas was not amused. "They're innings. And I'd like to see you say that to Clayton Kershaw's face while he pitches a ninety-five mile per hour fastball at you."

"Why would I do that," Liam pushed his chair back and stood, grinning a disingenuous smile, "when I could spend the day living the glamorous life style shoveling horse shit?"

"Oh right," Reece said after he finished chugging the rest of his orange juice. "It's compost day."

"One thing I never thought about when I dreamed of working a horse ranch," Liam shook his head, cringing, "was just how much actual *shite* was involved."

Isobel's nose scrunched too. She'd learned from the last 'compost day' that whoever was on compost duty ended smelling like, well, *shit*. How could they not, after hours spent in the compost shed raking the stuff that was in the early stages to aerate it? The second part was better—they got to use the four wheelers to take the finished compost and spread it over the fields as fertilizer.

"Just another reason I was so glad to get the manny job," Reece grinned. "Ya'll have fun with that today. I'm gonna have a quick drive down to Colorado to stock up on my... herbal remedies."

Isobel shook her head at him. Xavier and Mel apparently didn't mind him lighting up a blunt every now and then as long as he did it out of the house and after the kids were in bed.

"That's not legal here yet, is it?" she asked.

"No. It's not." Jeremiah's voice was flat as he stared at his brother. "You know if you get stopped with that shit on you, you could spend up to a year in jail."

"Relax, man. You're so freakin' stressed out all the time. When I get back, I can bake you some cookies that will totally chill you the fuck out," Reece's voice got all soft. The little shop I go to that's right over the border has the *best* hybrid called Blue Dream and it will change your *life* man, I'm telling you—"

"Yeah, it'll change your life," Jeremiah said, still glaring. "When you get picked up by a state trooper watching for dumbasses like you who are obviously crossing the border to stock up." Jeremiah reached out and tugged on a couple of Reece's bleach-blond dread locks. "Could you *say* I'm here to buy weed any louder? At least put a fucking cap on."

Reece jerked back from his brother and Isobel could see him losing his usually calm demeanor fast—something only his brother seemed to be able to provoke in him. "Why don't you butt out of what's none of your damn business? I'm sick of you always trying to run my life. You're only older than me by three minutes, jackass."

"Hey there. Okay." Isobel jumped in between them and turned to Reece. "Where are Dean and Brent anyway? Why don't you have them today?"

Reece's face immediately softened. "Mel and Mr. Kent took the kids to visit his folks back east. Another month and she won't be able to fly anymore."

"Oh, right," Isobel said. "She told me about it. Everything's just been so busy, I forgot it was this weekend."

"Well have fun with the compost." She raised her bagel like she was the other guys who were getting up from the table. "I'll be out to the stables in a little bit."

"I'd say see you out there," Jeremiah said, "but I'm pretty sure you won't want to come within ten feet of us without a hazmat suit."

***

Several hours later, Isobel was feeling great. She'd taken one of the sweetest horses on the ranch—appropriately named Sugar—for a long ride out into the countryside. Wyoming wasn't the kind of place she would have typically thought of as beautiful. It wasn't overly green or lush.

Instead, it had more of a stark beauty going for it. Wide open spaces. Scrub brush and hills that slanted into one another. Mountains in the far distance.

Being out there with just her horse for company made life feel bigger. She couldn't take in the scope of the big, wide world and not feel like all her problems were... well, *small*. God, why did she let herself get so neurotic about everything?

Food.

Sex.

Hunter.

Why? Why did she do that? Why did she obsess?

Then again, crazy might just be in your DNA.

She squeezed her eyes shut and breathed out. Breathe out all the toxic shit. Breathe in the beauty of the world around her.

She reached down and patted Sugar's neck, squeezing her thighs together to nudge the horse forward. It wasn't true. She wouldn't let it be true.

Perspective. That was what she needed. She needed to ride out here as often as she could so she could put her shit in perspective.

The world was big and beautiful.

She needed to stop taking all her own drama so seriously and step back and smell the wildflowers.

Maybe the way to change was to stop trying so damn hard. Just let change happen naturally without analyzing it all to death. Trust that everything would be okay.

Stop being so damn afraid all the time.

She laughed. "Easier said than done, huh, Sugar?" Still, she felt carefree as she patted Sugar's neck again, then she gently tugged on the left rein to turn Sugar back around to head back.

Rain clouds had started to gather across the big sky and she didn't want to get caught in the downpour.

The ride back was just as calming. When the Kent's ranch came back into view, she felt centered. Sure she could take whatever came her way in stride.

Even going back to work on Monday.

Okay, so she might need to take another long ride tomorrow to *really* make sure she was centered but she'd never felt more confident in her ability to take on the future.

A light rain started to fall right as she reached the stable.

She grabbed the shoehorn and swung her right leg off Sugar, dropping to the floor. "That's a good girl." She rubbed along Sugar's wither and gave her a pat. She was such a sweet horse. Which made her want to check in on her other favorite.

She needed to brush Sugar down and get her some water but as they passed by Bright Beauty's stall, Isobel went up on tiptoe. "Hello beautiful gir— Beauty!" she shouted in alarm.

Beauty was on the ground, rolling back and forth, a sheen of sweat covering her glossy coat and a pinkish foam at her nostrils.

Quick as she could, Isobel wrapped Sugar's lead around the stall peg and then opened the door.

"Beauty!" she went down on her knees.

Oh God. Beauty had seemed fine only hours before—though granted Isobel had barely peeked in to call out hi before her ride. Dammit. She'd been so involved in her own worries she hadn't been paying attention.

Beauty tried to roll but couldn't get very far in the confines of the stall. These were all the classic signs of colic. Which could kill a horse within hours if not treated correctly.

Isobel swiped at her eyes and tried to think. First, she needed to get Beauty back up on her feet. Then take her vitals. Okay. She could do this.

Isobel jumped up and grabbed Beauty's halter from a hook right outside the stall. She slipped it over Beauty's head, buckled it, then attached a lead to the halter.

"Come on, girl. Up." She tugged on the lead rope with all her might. "Up you go."

Beauty pulled against her. Isobel dug in and tugged hard. And finally, after a few more tense moments, Beauty climbed to her feet. She immediately yanked against Isobel's hold though, twisting her head toward her flank and dancing back and forth.

Then she reared back, kicking at her own stomach with her forelegs.

150

"Whoa, girl!" Isobel cried, letting out more slack on the lead and flattening her back against the stall door as Beauty came back down again.

Crap. Having a twelve-hundred-pound horse rear right in front of you was never a comfortable feeling but Isobel knew showing how freaked she was would only make Beauty more tense.

"Shhh, shhhh," Isobel tried to quiet the horse down. She drew the lead rope back in and stepped close to Beauty's nose. "Shhh, that's right, girl. I'm going to figure out what's wrong and make you feel better, okay sweetheart?"

Maybe it was just her imagination but she thought Beauty calmed a little at her voice.

"That's right, that's right," Isobel soothed.

She ran to grab some equipment and then hurried back so she could take the rest of Beauty's vitals. Her temperature was okay but her heart rate was almost double what was normal.

Not good. Not good at all.

Then Isobel did an internal examination. Was it just gas? That was the best-case scenario. Or was there a twisted intestine causing the blockage? That was the worst-case scenario because it required surgery.

What she discovered instead was the middle possibility. There was an impaction—a thick section of intestine that was hard with what was most likely undigested feed that had gotten all clumped up in a six-inch section.

"Okay," Isobel whispered. "Okay, okay, okay."

She withdrew her hand and peeled off the glove, taking both it and the thermometer out of the stall. She rushed back over to the sink, throwing out the plastic glove and scrubbing both the thermometer and her hands.

"Okay," she whispered to herself. "You can do this. This is going to be your job." But somehow it felt like there was less at stake with other people's animals. And Hunter was always there if she screwed up.

She paused mid-scrub. She could go call him. Get a second opinion.

But no. She'd felt the impaction. She *knew* what to do next. And she'd just helped him with that other colic case the other day.

Yes, that one had been a little different. They'd suspected it was a twisted intestine but the owner hadn't wanted to pay for surgery— understandable since it could cost more than the horse was worth.

When Hunter had called later to follow up on the case, the owner told him the horse hadn't lasted the night.

Isobel squeezed her eyes shut against the possibility. No. That wouldn't happen to Beauty. Beauty had already survived so much—a cruel owner who had held her to an impossible standard, pushing her past her limits even when she was injured.

Now Beauty was finally getting the life she deserved. She was getting her happily ever after here on this horse farm with owners who cared about her and were happy to just let her be herself.

Then to have that all threatened *now*, right when her legs were barely even healing up so she could actually enjoy her new home?

It was cruel. It was wrong.

Isobel wouldn't let it happen. She set her jaw before getting to work.

First she gave Beauty some oral pain reliever. Then she started trying to flush her system with the mineral oil.

"Come on, girl. You can do it."

An hour later, Isobel was still trying. She was damp with sweat and the mineral oil/water mix that had sloshed out all over her.

Beauty was slightly sluggish from the medication and not jerking around as violently. Isobel was glad Beauty wasn't in as much pain, but she also wasn't sure if that meant the mare's gut would keep working the way it needed to in order to pass the gummed up food.

"Okay," Isobel whispered to herself, looking around the stable. She wished one of the guys was around to ask them their opinion. She'd run out to check the compost shed, but all she saw were the missing four-wheelers.

She couldn't help feeling like she was doing this all wrong. Yeah, she was going by the book, but still? Why wasn't Beauty passing the food?

Isobel looked Beauty over. Maybe another walk?

After an hour and a half of trying to flush her system, Isobel had stopped and taken Beauty for a short walk up and down the barn. She'd hoped that might loosen things up. They couldn't go outside since the rain had started in earnest. Not that it mattered much because even in the limited confines of the stable, Beauty had been stiff and not keen to move far. They'd barely made two lengths of the stable before returning to her stall.

Then Isobel had reinserted the tubing and started again with the mineral oil.

And now another half an hour and still nothing. No stools. Not even any passed gas.

"How about another break, sweetheart? You've been doing so good." Isobel patted Beauty on the side of her neck, then withdrew the tubing from her nose. Beauty snorted and shook her head as it came free.

"I know," Isobel sympathized. "That can't be comfortable. You don't deserve any of this. We'll get you better. I promise."

But even as she said it, Isobel was terrified it was a lie.

You're such a failure at everything you try. Do you have any idea how disappointed your father is by you? Like mother, like daughter.

Isobel squeezed her eyes shut against the memories. Why was it always the horrible words that lodged in her head and never any of the nice ones? She was sure her dad had said nice things to her over the years.

Hadn't he? She didn't know. She was terrified that all he saw when he looked at her was her mother. History that was bound to repeat itself. He could barely even look her in the face.

"I'll be right back." Isobel's throat was thick as she mumbled the words before stumbling out of the stall.

She wouldn't do Beauty any good if she had a breakdown right in front of her.

Enough. She couldn't do this. Not alone.

She lit out for the house, her boots sticking in the now soggy mud with every step. Farm calls took Hunter all over this county and the two surrounding it. It might take him hours to get here depending on what emergencies he already had on his docket. And that was without the rain. *If* he was close enough to the highway to have cell service.

Meanwhile, colic could turn on a coin and become deadly.

Oh God, she should have called him as soon as she realized what was happening with Beauty. Would Beauty die because she'd been too proud to call for help?

She yanked open the back door and then sprinted to the phone, ignoring the mud she was tracking all over the floor. She pulled the wall phone off its cradle and had Hunter's number punched in seconds later. She bit her lip and paced back and forth in the kitchen as she waited for it to ring.

And ring.

And ring.

"Dammit." She raked a hand through her hair.

"Hullo." Hunter's easy greeting came over the line.

"Hunter! Is that you? Like really you and not just your voicemail?"

Silence for a second. Then, "Isobel?"

"Oh thank God, Hunter. Bright Beauty, one of the mares, is colicky. It's bad. There's an impaction in her small intestine. It's bad, Hunter. I've been trying to flush it with mineral oil for an hour and it hasn't moved an inch. I don't know what to do. I tried to walk her too, but nothing—"

"Whoa, whoa, whoa. Slow down there. When did she start presenting symptoms?"

"I don't know. I just found her down in her stall when I got back from a ride on another horse at, I don't know," she searched out the wall clock. It was 3:15 now. "Maybe 2:00? I glanced in on her a few hours early and didn't notice anything off. But I wasn't really looking. If I would have just—"

"You give her a painkiller?"

"Banamine. 10cc orally. Heart rate sixty-five. Hunter, I'm really worried." She took a quick breath. "Can you come out?"

There was no hesitation. "I'll be there in forty-five minutes."

Isobel sank against the wall as she fought off tears. "Thank you, Hunter." She swallowed hard, her fingers going white-knuckled around the phone.

"Yup."

She thought he'd hung up but then his voice came back over the line. "We'll take care of her. She'll be okay."

154

Isobel nodded fervently, then realized Hunter couldn't see her. "Okay." Her voice was little more than a whisper.

"Okay," he said.

Still she didn't hear the click that meant he'd hung up.

"You want me to stay on the line till I get there?"

Sometimes when he wasn't being a world class asshole, Isobel thought Hunter Dawkins was kinda perfect.

She swiped at a tear that crested before it could fall down her cheek. "I should go be with Beauty and I'm not sure the phone will go that far." It was a landline. They were so far out there was no cell service here. "Thank you, Hunter." She hoped he could hear how much she meant it.

"Not a problem." This time he did hang up.

For a long second, Isobel clutched the phone to her chest. Then she set it back down on its cradle and hurried back outside.

Chapter 14
HUNTER

Hunter had been having a shitty day.

Isobel had run out on him after sex. Again.

Just like Janine.

He'd been cursing his luck with women while he delivered the Juarez's foal and then spent the rest of the morning testing cattle for TB out at Ben Fenton's place. He'd just made it back on the highway heading north when his phone rang.

He had his phone on Bluetooth and answered without looking at the number.

And then came the last voice he expected to hear. When he heard how frantic and panicked Isobel was, his gut clenched.

It turned out she was only upset about a horse and wasn't in any trouble herself, but his immediate instinct to protect had already been activated. He was due out for pregnancy checks at the Pimentel farm but they could wait. It had started raining anyway and he might have postponed on that basis alone—or so he told himself

He pulled off the highway and turned around at the next overpass, pushing ten over the speed limit so he could get to her as soon as possible.

She'd sounded so upset. The horse was important to her, that was clear. To her, this wasn't just another case.

But then, even on their regular cases, he'd seen how she connected with the animals. She had that way about her. Only the really great vets had it. They loved the animals. It could be a liability as much as a positive trait.

In school they talked about developing a detachment from your patients, probably just like doctors with human patients were supposed to. It always rubbed Hunter the wrong way. Animals in pain just felt wrong on a basic level. People might lie to you and betray you but animals didn't cheat or steal or manipulate. They'd hurt you, sure as hell—you never took your eyes off a cow or you were liable to get

156

kicked for your trouble. But animals were rarely malicious—and if they were, it was only because humans had twisted them up that way. Like a couple of dogs from an illegal dog fighting ring he'd taken pro bono a few years ago.

He used to pride himself that he loved animals the way he saw in Isobel. But he'd lost it. It had all become routine the past year. Mechanical. He was a robot in a Hunter suit.

Until her. He used to say the way a person treated animals told you everything you needed to know about them. So what did Isobel's obvious empathy for all their patients tell him about her?

Rain had started pounding his window so hard his windshield wipers could barely keep up. He almost missed the turnoff for the Kent's farm.

The Florida Georgia Line song on the radio was cut off by three long beeps. "A severe thunderstorm warning is now in effect for Natrona and Carbon counties until nine pm."

"No shit, Sherlock." Hunter pulled the key out of the ignition and pulled on his rain slicker from the floor of the passenger side.

He was glad for the distraction from thinking about Isobel. Which lasted for… all of three point two seconds.

She'd left. No goodbye. No nothing.

What do you expect after you treated her like an ass for weeks?

His jaw clenched as he pulled in beside the few vehicles parked in front of the ranch house. He hopped up in the truck bed and grabbed his tools, then slammed the tool box closed.

He was just here to help a sick horse. That was all. He'd do the same for any horse owner who called so panicked. It didn't have to be anything more than that.

He jogged around the side of the house. He was familiar with the ranch. He'd come out here for years. The horses Xavier brought in were often in rough condition. He'd helped horses riddled with parasites to difficult foalings to lacerations and other injuries to cases of laminitis. And several cases of colic. Not all of which ended well.

When the stable came in sight, he saw one of the twins, he couldn't tell if it was Reece or the other one, standing just inside the stable doorway. He disappeared as soon as he saw Hunter. No doubt to announce his arrival.

157

Isobel came flying out seconds later, ignoring the pouring rain.

It was definitely inappropriate to be noticing how good she looked in a tight pair of Wranglers and a damp maroon tank top that hugged every one of her luscious curves.

Yep. Completely fucking inappropriate.

His eyes still lingered for too long.

He managed to jerk his attention to her face when she came right up to him. Especially when she threw her arms around his neck.

"Oh thank God you're here." The hug was over almost as quickly as it began. She let go of him and then jogged back toward the stables, waving at him to follow.

He was still processing the feel of all that warm female wrapped around him, but he did manage to find his legs to follow her.

Four men were standing around the stall of the horse in question.

"Thanks for staying with me, guys. I know your game is starting. I'm good now."

"We're happy to stay," said the biggest of the four. Nicholas, Hunter thought his name was. He'd never actually heard the guy speak before today even though he'd been out here every few months.

Isobel placed her hand on Nicholas' arm, her eyes softening. "It's okay. There isn't anything to do except stand around. But I really appreciate you helping calm me down until the vet got here."

"You're the vet," said the twin.

Isobel just shook her head. She waved Hunter toward the stall. "Don't be ridiculous, Jeremiah."

Aha, so it was wundertwin number two. He was glaring at Hunter as he pushed past him. Apparently Twin One had shared what he'd seen out back of the bar. Which made Hunter bristle because it was Isobel's business and he didn't like the idea of anyone talking about her like that.

Hunter glared right back, then opened the stall. Right now it was most important to check on his patient. He set his tools down and then entered the stall.

He could tell immediately by the look of the mare that it wasn't good. Isobel appeared right beside him.

"I just checked her pulse and it was seventy," she said in a small voice. "She's getting worse."

158

Hunter pulled out his stethoscope and then went to the horse's side, gently palpating the gut and listening for activity.

It was quiet inside. Too quiet. Not good. A healthy gut should be gurgling away. The blockage was stopping normal functions.

He pulled out a plastic sleeve and pulled it on, then did a rectal exam. He found exactly what Isobel had described over the phone.

"When was the last time you tried walking her?" He withdrew and pulled the sleeve off, balling it in itself to contain the muck.

"When I called you."

Hunter nodded. "Let's try taking her out again."

Isobel bit her bottom lip in worry.

"Come on, sweetheart, let's take another walk." Isobel tried to hand the reins over to Hunter but he just shook his head.

"She'll be more comfortable with you."

Isobel nodded while Hunter unlatched the stall door. All the other men had gone inside.

The mare took several stiff steps forward. Then her eyes went wild, the whites flashing.

"Let go!" Hunter grabbed Isobel and yanked her behind him right as the horse reared and then threw herself on the floor, rolling and writhing on the ground.

"We have to help her!" Isobel cried out but Hunter kept her firmly behind himself. The mare rolled back and forth, clearly in extreme pain.

But where Isobel only saw a beloved animal hurting, Hunter had enough experience to see a twelve hundred pound creature of instinct ready to lash out at anything and anyone.

"I've got some Xylazine in my tool kit. Go get it." He'd set it down behind them near the door of the stall door. Anything to get her further away from the volatile horse.

She was eager to help and he relaxed the second he felt her move away from his back. Only then did he venture toward the writhing horse.

He kept his breathing slow and easy. The only way to deal with a panicked or pained horse was to emit an aura of calm. And you couldn't bullshit them. Horses were the best lie detectors out there.

Though if a horse was in enough pain, it wouldn't matter if you were the Dalai Lama, they'd still lash out at you.

In all her rolling, the mare's lead had gotten twisted up underneath her. Hunter leaned down, making sure he was approaching slightly to the left so the horse could always keep him in her view. Sneaking up on a horse was a bad idea for all involved.

The mare stilled slightly on seeing him approach.

"That's right," he whispered. "Let's get you back on your feet. Then we can give you some more medicine and see if we can't get you feeling better."

He reached out to the harness around her nose. This would either work or he'd get bitten for his trouble. You didn't work with horses for as long as he did without enduring a few horse bites along the way.

He tried not to think about it. Instead he kept up a slow stream of conversation. "That's right, girl. Let's get you back up on your feet. Here we go. Let me just get to this lead that's underneath—" He traced down her harness to where it clipped to the lead line, then gently tugged. "Upsy daisy. Let's go, honey. Up you go." He added more command to his voice as he pulled on her lead line and she flipped back over to get her feet underneath her. Finally, she scrambled back to a standing position.

She let out a groan and then blew air sharply out her nostrils. Horses only groaned like that when they were in severe pain.

Dammit. He ran his hand up the lead so he had tight control of the mare and then led her back to the stall.

He breathed a little easier once he had her confined inside again. Only to find Isobel waiting anxiously, syringe in hand. "Is Beauty going to be okay?"

He could tell by the tightness in her throat that she was afraid of his answer. She was intelligent and she'd just witnessed what he had. None of those were good signs.

"Let's get her this shot and see how she responds." He reached out and she placed the syringe in his hand. He pulled off the cap and entered the stall again. Isobel followed. He tried not to think of her at his back. He knew she was hoping he'd pull off a miracle. He wished he could.

Why couldn't this just be a run-of-the-mill colic case?

160

He couldn't change things he had no control over. Hadn't he learned by now how immovable the universe was when it had decided on a course of action? Grant him the serenity to accept the things he could not change, yada fucking yada. Wasn't that what he'd spent the last year trying to convince himself of?

His jaw tensed and he forcibly relaxed it as he administered the shot.

"What now?" Isobel asked.

"We wait and see if she responds to the pain medication. It's only in severe cases that horses keep showing pain after giving them the Xylazine. In the meantime, let's check the color of her gums."

"Oh my God, I forgot about that." Isobel wrung her hands.

"It's fine. We're doing it now."

Hunter lifted the horse's lips to examine the gums and he breathed out heavily. Shit. They were supposed to be a salmon pink.

Beauty's were a dark red. Isobel's head swung toward Hunter, eyes wide with fear.

If a horse's gums turned all the way purple, it meant the impaction in the gut was cutting off so much blood flow to the intestines that they shut down. At that point, the horse's death was likely imminent within fifteen to thirty minutes.

"We have to get her to surgery." Isobel's face went white as she backed up quickly, banging into the stall door. She barely seemed to notice. Her hands went to her hair and she spun around. "Oh my God. The trailer. We've got to get the horse trailer. It's not hooked up to anything. But if I go get the guys, they can help and then we can—"

"Isobel." Hunter ushered her out the stall door and then he put a hand on her arm. She was so emotionally involved but they had to be realistic. And safe.

"I'm not sure that's the best idea. I don't have the set up for large animal surgery at my clinic. I contract out with the large animal hospital in Casper when I need to. But Casper's an hour and a half away on a good day." He gestured out the open stable door to where it was still coming down in buckets. "With the storm." He shook his head. "I don't like hauling a horse trailer in weather like this."

Isobel's features went livid and she threw his arms off her. "We have to try. She'll *die* if we don't do anything. I'll pay for everything, I don't care how much it costs."

"That's not what I—" He'd pay for it if it came down to that.

"You're wasting time Beauty doesn't have arguing about nothing." Isobel turned and stalked off into the rain.

Hunter threw up his hands. Goddamned infuriating woman.

He jogged through the rain to catch up to her, his boots squelching into deep mud with every step.

Chapter 15

ISOBEL

"Can't this thing go any faster?" Isobel leaned over to glare at the speedometer. "Forty-five miles an hour? Seriously?" She glanced out the narrow back window at the trailer they were pulling behind them.

Please let Beauty be okay.

Hunter didn't look her direction but she saw his jaw clench. "Don't push it."

He'd been grouchy ever since she refused to stay behind at the ranch while he rode off with Beauty in the trailer.

She shook her head. What the hell had he been thinking? He'd barely been willing to do the surgery in the first place. Like hell she was going to let him go off alone with her horse.

She bit her lip. Okay, that wasn't fair. She trusted Hunter's skills when it came to his veterinary practice. But still.

She'd had to threaten to drive behind him in her own car before he relented, his jaw tight. Between the boys bringing the trailer around, getting it hitched to Hunter's truck, and getting the distressed Beauty into the trailer, almost forty-five minutes had passed, just at the ranch alone.

If Isobel was honest with herself, though, she knew it wasn't him she was angry with. How had she not seen Beauty was sick *earlier*? And then she hadn't called him right when she finally realized there was a problem. And God, if she'd only checked Beauty's gums right away…

Her eyes pricked and she blinked rapidly. She would *not* cry. Beauty was going to be fine. She was going to have the life she deserved. A life full of long afternoons grazing in the fields under the wide, blue Wyoming sky.

Isobel glared out the windshield at the unrelenting downpour. The truck's windshield wipers were on their highest settings and rain still poured down the glass. There weren't many other cars out on the small rural highway—they'd even seen a couple pulled off the road, like they were waiting for the rain to slow down before continuing.

163

If only today was one of those ideal Wyoming days. For Christ's sake, almost every day she'd been there had been clear weather. Then the *one* day Beauty got sick and they needed to get somewhere fast—

Three low beeps sounded over the radio. Hunter rolled the dial up—he'd had it on his normal country station, but it had been so low she'd barely heard the music playing. The robotic announcer's voice came through loud and clear, though.

"The national weather service has issued a tornado warning for Natrona and Carbon counties from 7:00 pm until 8:15 pm. A severe thunderstorm capable of producing a tornado was located ten miles south of Bessemer Bend at 6:55, moving southeast at thirty-five mph. Radar indicated rotation."

"Shit," Hunter said, turning the knob so the radio was louder.

"Impact: Flying debris will be dangerous to those caught without shelter. Mobile homes will be damaged or destroyed. Damage to roofs, windows, and vehicles will occur. Tree damage—"

"Isn't that a little dramatic?" Isobel scoffed. "They just say this every time there's a bad storm."

"Quiet," Hunter hushed her sharply, turning the knob up even more.

"Take cover now. Move to a basement or interior room on the lowest floor of a sturdy building. Avoid windows. If you are outdoors, in a mobile home, or in a vehicle, move to the closest substantial shelter and protect yourself from flying debris.

"Repeating, a tornado warning has been issued until 8:15 pm for the following counties, Natron—"

Hunter turned the knob down and then hunched over to look out the front windshield, flicking on his flashers and slowing down.

"Hunter," Isobel rolled her eyes. "Don't make a big deal out of noth—"

"I don't like the look of that sky."

Hunter turned off the road and Isobel swung around to gape at him. "What are you doing? We have to get Beauty to the hospital. Every minute counts."

"Not at the expense of your safety," Hunter barked, his whole body tense as his eyes focused ahead. "Weren't you listening? That storm'll be on top of us any second. With tornado conditions."

Isobel's teeth clenched. "They have to say that to cover their asses." Was he really going to risk Beauty's life for some stupid, paranoid—

Hunter slowed the truck and put it in park. In the middle of nowhere. Just right there, in the road. Isobel looked around. They were beside a big lake. No, it was a dam.

Which she could see pretty easily because the rain had finally let up.

"Look, it's barely even raining anymore." She jerked a hand toward the windshield. "Now can we please get back on the road?"

She turned back to look at the trailer. She could just make out the tip of Beauty's head. She was still on her feet. Thank God. There was time to save her yet.

"Get out of the car." Hunter's voice was strained.

Isobel swung her head back around to look at him. "Wha—"

"Isobel, get out of the car. Now!"

He pushed open his door and sprinted around the front of the truck. What the hell was he—?

But then she saw it.

Holy—

Off to the right, opposite the dam, a funnel cloud was just touching down to earth.

The next second, Hunter was yanking at her passenger side door. But it was locked. Shit. Shit. She fumbled for the button to unlock it, her eyes never moving from the tornado. Hunter screamed at her and pounded on the door.

Finally she managed to get it unlocked and Hunter pulled her down from her seat. She barely landed on her feet but had no time to get oriented before Hunter was dragging her forward. She stumbled along behind him.

There was a tornado. An actual, real, bona fide tornado. Like in the movies. Holy shit. Fuck. Shit fuck.

Hunter dragged her toward a steep grassy embankment when she suddenly remembered. *Beauty*. She jerked her hand out of Hunter's.

"Beauty!" The wind had started whipping around them so loudly she had to shout to be heard above it. "We have to get Beauty."

165

"No time," he shouted back. "And if you stop again, I'll fucking carry you!"

Then he grabbed her wrist and yanked her so that she was forced to follow him. The rain had started up again and not just rain, but small pebbles of hail. She used the arm Hunter wasn't holding up to shield herself.

When she looked toward the tornado again, her heart stuttered. Oh God. It was headed right toward them. And it seemed bigger now. At its base was a dark brown cloud. It was ripping and twisting up debris as it went.

They were going to die.

"Careful now!" Hunter yelled as they reached the steep embankment.

Isobel tried to focus. No, they weren't going to die. She had Hunter. He grew up around here. She thought she could see where he was trying to take them. At the bottom of the embankment was the dam's base where there were several concrete culverts. The sturdiest place around to take cover, though still open on onc side to the storm.

Hunter took her waist as he stepped sideways down the steep grassy area. But they were rushing and the grass was slick from the rain. Her foot slipped once and he caught her, pulling her tighter against him.

They were almost halfway down when—

"Oh!" Isobel slipped again. Her feet went out from under her. Then, the world went topsy turvy— Ow! God. *Ow!* She rolled and slid and then rolled some more until she landed on the concrete at the bottom of the hill. All the air was knocked out of her lungs on impact.

She gasped for breath, feeling dazed and looking around. Where was Hunter? Was he okay? The tornado. Oh God, the tornado.

"Isobel!"

The next thing she knew, her body was being lifted. Cradled against a warm chest.

"Isobel, talk to me!"

She tried to say his name, but she still didn't have any breath. Hail pelted her legs in painful stings though Hunter shielded most of her upper body. She couldn't see the storm, couldn't see anything but his chest. Her body jolted with his every step and with how fast he was moving, she knew the danger was far from over.

A few moments later, Hunter set her down. Concrete, hard at her back and underneath her. They'd made it to the culvert.

She sucked in another breath and finally managed to take in air.

"Hunter," she gasped out. The wind was so loud, she doubted he could hear her.

He must have seen her lips move, though, because she saw the relief on his face right before he pulled her into his body. Even though he was as rain soaked as she was, he still radiated warmth. It made her feel safe. False comfort, she knew.

"Tornado?" she managed to ask, getting in more air with each breath now. She was less disoriented too and could make out the huge concrete box created by the structure of the dam. It would have been perfect—except for the fact that the tornado was heading toward them from the one exposed side.

Hunter pushed her into the corner and was trying to cover her body with his but she strained her neck to look over his shoulder. What little air she'd managed to gain whooshed out again.

"Oh my God," she whispered, shrinking into the corner. Not that she could hear her own voice over the storm. It roared like a locomotive racing past at top speed. It was almost on top of them, and it had gathered momentum so that instead of a spindly little funnel it was a wide cone, tearing up swaths of land as it went.

"Hunter!" She flung her arms around his waist and tried to pull him as tightly as she could into the corner with her.

The roar got even louder and debris was flung into the concrete wall of the dam. Isobel screamed as wood chunks and tree branches crashed all around them. Hunter hunched his body over her, both of them curled into the corner as tightly as possible.

They were going to die.

They were going to die.

And it was all her fault.

If she hadn't dragged Hunter out here. He knew it was a bad idea. She hadn't taken the storm seriously, but his instincts were spot on.

And now here they were.

For all the miserable times in her life when she'd thought it just wasn't worth continuing on—dammit, she just wanted to go back and smack herself now.

She wanted to live.

She wanted it so badly.

There was so much to live for.

Please God. Please. I want to live.

The wind howled. Debris continued to slam the walls. It piled up all around them. It felt like the world was coming to an end.

Chapter 16
HUNTER

Hunter curled his body as tight as he could around Isobel as the storm raged on. He had to keep her safe. Safe. *Safe.* It was all he could think.

Pain ripped at his back but he only noticed it peripherally.

She had to be kept safe.

If it had to take someone, let it be him, not her.

Christ, *not her.*

But then, all of the sudden, the screaming wind quieted. The junk and debris that had been continually flying at them stopped. The punishing rain became a light sprinkle.

Hunter's eyes were clenched shut and he held his body around Isobel's like an immovable cage. It was only when she stirred beneath him and asked, "Hunter? Hunter, is it over?" that he dared look over his shoulder.

And saw that the tornado had turned and was moving east. Not only that, but the funnel was narrow again. Losing momentum, it seemed.

Isobel tried to push out from under him but he wasn't about to let her up yet.

"Stay down."

She stopped struggling and settled for craning her neck to look at the retreating twister with him. As they watched silently over the next minute or two, it grew smaller and smaller and then dissipated entirely.

Isobel started laughing. It had a hysterical edge to it but he couldn't blame her. Jesus, how close had the goddamn thing come to them before it turned? He finally released Isobel and sat back on his haunches, looking around them.

Debris, mostly tree limbs and churned up earth, cluttered the ditch running up to the culvert. But there was also a ripped-up car tire and the twisted frame of what might have once been a bicycle just a little to their left. Shit. If either of those had hit him and Isobel…

He shuddered. Better not to think about the 'what ifs.'

169

Isobel was standing and she held down a hand to help him up. He took it and got to his feet, the whole while checking her up and down for any damage. But other than being covered in mud and a few scratches she probably gotten from her tumble down the hill earlier, she looked fine.

She was okay. She was safe.

She looked around them at all the damage, shaking her head in wonder when her eyes suddenly widened.

"Beauty." Then she took off like a shot, jogging through the twisted tree limbs and—damn, was that a tractor?—to scramble back up the embankment.

"Isobel," he called, but she didn't slow down. Damn fool woman. If she wasn't careful, she'd fall and break her neck on that damn hill. He hurried after her, wincing at the stiffness in his back. Looked like he'd have some cuts and bruises of his own.

She was already halfway up the hill by the time he made it to the bottom, scrambling up with her hands and feet like she was a monkey. He almost called out to her again but then stopped himself. He didn't want to break her concentration. And within another minute, she made it to the top.

He had a slower time of it, but when he finally got back to the road, it was to find a beaming Isobel. He immediately saw why. While there was some debris on the road, it wasn't nearly as much as there had been in the culvert below. And his truck and the trailer stood pretty much untouched.

"Beauty's still okay. Come on," Isobel waved him toward the truck. "If we get going we can still make it to Casper in time." She ran to the passenger side and hopped in.

Her and that damn horse.

Hunter let out a deep breath. He wasn't sure if it was relief or exasperation or what. All he knew was that this woman was going to be the death of him.

He walked toward the driver's side of the truck, grimacing as he hauled himself into the seat.

He turned the key and the truck fired to life, no problem. But before he pulled it into gear, Isobel suddenly launched herself over the bench seat and wrapped him in a fierce hug. His back was still

170

sensitive and he winced. The feel of warm, *alive* woman was enough to make him not care, though. He wrapped his arms around her and breathed her in.

He wanted to say a hundred things to her in that moment.

Like: Don't you ever scare me like that again.

And: I'm sorry for being an ass the last few weeks.

And: Let's both get out of these muddy clothes and celebrate being alive. While naked.

And: I'm terrified I'm falling in love with you.

But before any of those fool things could come out of his mouth, Isobel broke the hug and pulled back.

Then she screamed.

Because her arms were covered in blood.

His blood.

Oh.

Shit.

That was when he passed out.

Chapter 17
ISOBEL

Isobel paced up and down the hospital corridor, her nails chewed to nubs. It was an obsessive habit she hated, but compared to the alternatives, it was one she could live with.

What she couldn't live with, however, was Hunter not being okay.

The ER waiting room was loud and chaotic all around her. Babies crying. *People* crying. The news on the big screen in the corner of the room. The tornado warning was finally over but it had touched down near a mobile home park. The whole ER was buzzing about it and there had been a load of patients who'd come in with minor to severe injuries.

It was all just freaking insane. And the rush and chaos meant no one was telling her anything about Hunter.

But he'd be okay. He *had* to be okay.

God, when she'd hugged him and her arms had come back covered in blood… And then his eyes had rolled back in his head and he'd just sunk against her—

She leaned against the wall, feeling out of breath all over again just remembering it. She'd never felt more terrified in her life. Not even after she'd swallowed all the pills from every bottle in the house she could find that horrible night back when she was sixteen. It was only after she'd finished downing them that she'd realized she didn't want to die—but she'd been terrified she was too late and that she was just minutes away from death.

But no, not even that trauma compared to seeing all the blood and being positive that Hunter had just died in her arms. She'd been so busy worrying about the damn *horse* she hadn't checked to make sure that he was okay. What was *wrong* with her?

She pushed off the wall. It had been *hours*. She was just about to go to the nurses station and ask *again* if there was an update.

But then the double doors swung open.

And Hunter himself strolled out, wearing an oversized blue T-shirt with a giant yellow smiley face.

Isobel's mouth dropped open. Yes, he'd only passed out for a short time in the car, but he'd still been so woozy and out of it when she dropped him off. The nurse who did triage had taken one look at Hunter's back after Isobel had helped him stumble in and sent him straight into surgery. His shirt had been shredded and his back wasn't much better.

Therc'd been so much *blood.*

Isobel shook the images from her head and ran up to Hunter, automatically sliding her shoulder under his arm to prop him up like she had on their way into the hospital. "What are you doing up? You should be in a wheelchair." She looked up at him. "Actually, you should still be back there in a bed. What's going on?"

"Aw, I'm fine." Hunter swung his arm over her shoulder easily enough but didn't lean nearly as much weight on her as he had earlier. He headed toward the exit. He was a little stiff but walked with far more ease than Isobel would have expected.

She moved with him, completely confused. "But your back!"

"Just needed a little stitching up."

"A *little*—" She started, incredulously. His back had looked cut to pieces, especially that deep gash on his upper shoulders—just a few inches to the left and it would have hit his spinal cord. She shuddered and reached up to clasp the hand of the arm he had around her.

"What about the mare? Did you get her to the animal hospital?"

She turned her head to gape at him. Was he seriously asking about a *horse* right now? "You could have *died.*"

He looked down at her with a wide, dopey grin. "Aw, you worried about me, Isobel? Isobel? Ma belle?" Then he tipped his head back and started to sing a butchered version of that old Beatles song *Michelle, Ma Belle*, except inserting her name. "Isobel, *ma* belle—" then he'd sort of start humming along, obviously not knowing the French lyrics before busting out with *qui vont très bien ensemble* at the end of each line.

"Oh my God." Isobel shouldered more of his weight when he stumbled a little. "What the hell did they give you?"

Hunter immediately started shaking his head. "Oh not that much." They were nearing the hospital exit. "I told them to do a local where they were stitching and I think that's all they did. But they were really good. I didn't even feel it. I think I even fell asleep."

Riiiiiiight. Isobel was pretty sure from both what she'd seen of his back and the way he was acting now that he'd been knocked out from anesthesia.

She looked back over her shoulder. "Are you sure you're all right to leave the hospital? Aren't they supposed to wheel you to the exit or something?"

"Phsh." Hunter said sloppily, then waved a hand. "I'm walking just fine."

Right then he tripped over his own feet and almost took a header face-first into the glass exit door.

"Hunter!" Isobel managed to catch him right before he got a face full of glass.

"Whoa. Thanks." He started laughing high-pitched in a way she'd never heard before—like he'd gotten a case of the giggles.

Grouchy Hunter Dawkins. Was giggling.

Okay, the world had officially gone nuts.

But he'd pulled away from her and was walking out toward the darkened parking lot and he did seem a little steadier on his feet. Would wonders never cease.

It was eleven o'clock at night but the parking lot had enough street lamps lit so they could see where they were going.

She hurried to keep up with his long-legged stride when all the sudden he stopped. His momentum kept going forward and he stumbled a little bit, catching himself just in time before he toppled over.

"Whoa," he said again, then shook his head. He looked around. "Where's Rhonda?"

"Who?" God, what if he'd gotten hit on the head really hard and had a concussion or something in addition to his back and—

"My truck. Rhonda." He looked at her like, *duh?* and then kept searching the large hospital parking lot.

Now it was Isobel's turn to laugh. After the stress of the day, it was such a relief, she had to grab her stomach she started laughing so hard. "You— Named your truck—" she managed to get out through heaving gasps, "Rhonda?"

Hunter only looked mildly insulted. "Rhonda and me go way back. Certainly the best relationship with a female I ever had." All amusement fled his face with that last statement. He lifted a hand to the back of his neck but immediately winced at the movement and dropped his arm. It must have tugged at the wounds on his back.

Isobel sobered quickly. "Come on." She took his forearm and tugged him to the back of the parking lot where she'd parked his truck and trailer.

"I dropped Beauty off at the horse hospital after they took you in," Isobel said, finally answering his earlier question now that she had him steered the right direction. "They were ready for us since you called ahead and when you couldn't perform the surgery yourself, one of the vets there said she could step in." All the vets had been on call because of the storm and they were happy to get Beauty seen and fixed up so they could free up the operating bay for the flood of clients that would no doubt be coming in all afternoon and evening because of the storm.

"They called just a while ago to let me know that they removed the problematic portion of intestine and Beauty was doing great. They'll stable her for the night."

Hunter was nodding intently to everything she said. "You wanna stop by there and check on her before we head home?"

Again, Isobel stopped with her mouth dropped open. "No I do not want to— Are you *insane*?" Then she huffed out a breath and reminded herself that he was heavily medicated at the moment.

"You're in no shape for a two-hour long car ride." Isobel shook her head, looking out at the dark road. "Not to mention I wouldn't want to make that drive at night with a trailer hitched anyway." Then, more under her breath, "My luck, I'd hit a deer or hydroplane and manage to kill us both yet."

"Come on." She took his arm again. "We're going to go stay at a hotel."

He cracked a grin at this. "You tryin' to get me in bed, Ms… Ms…" His face screwed up like he was straining to think. "What's your last name again?"

Isobel rolled her eyes. "Such a charmer, you are."

They'd finally reached the truck and Hunter went to grab for the driver's side door.

"Oh no you don't, Mr. Dopey-pants."

He turned and gave her a spectacular grin that took her breath away for a second. It was annoying how handsome he was. "See, you can't remember my last name either."

Even heavier eye role. "Mr. Dawkins, would you please be so kind as to get your ass around to the passenger door because there is no way in hell I'm letting you drive in your condition."

He made a face at her like he was back in Kindergarten. "Who died and made you boss?"

The smile fell off her face. Because today, the answer had almost been: *him.*

"Get a move on." She pushed past him to unlock the truck and then climbed up inside. He just stared at her. Or more likely he'd been staring at her ass as she hauled herself into the cab. The fact that he was alive to ogle her made her slightly less snappish when she said, "*Now.*" Slightly anyway.

He finally got the hint and came around to the passenger side. He seemed to have some difficulty getting the door open, though. She saw him frowning in confusion at it through the window. Good lord, maybe she should have helped him up before getting in herself. She reached over and opened the door for him.

"Oh." He took a stumbling step back, reaching for the door to steady himself at the last second. Isobel about had a heart attack in the moment he faltered, though.

"Get in the *truck*," she all but yelled. For God's sake, if she survived today, it was gonna be a goddamned miracle. She just needed to get Hunter somewhere where there was a flat surface he could lay down on and not do any harm to himself. She'd swear she lost years off her life driving to the hospital with him half conscious and bleeding all over the passenger seat.

She grimaced looking down at the seats. They were a somewhat washable plastic-y material, and no doubt the truck had seen plenty in its tenure as Hunter's mobile veterinary office, but still. Seeing the brownish red stains along the seams leftover from her rush clean up job with the towels they kept in the back—

She jerked her eyes away from the upholstery and back to the man who was whole and healthy in front of her.

Hunter had his hand held in front of his face and he was staring at it like it held all the mysteries of the universe. "Have you ever realized your hand is as big as your face? Like, what does that *mean*?" He looked over at her, wonder filling his face.

Well, he was healthy enough.

"All right, space cowboy. Buckle up."

When he continued to stare at his hand, wide-eyed, she reached across him for his buckle. He nuzzled into her neck from behind. "You smell good. Did I ever tell you that?"

She jerked the belt sharply across his chest and pulled back, feeling her cheeks flush.

"I always thought so. Is it vanilla? No," his eyebrows hunched, considering, "it's got like a fruity thing. Vanilla fruit." He nodded, then looked at her like he was waiting for her to confirm his theory.

"Um." She was pretty sure she smelled disgusting at the moment. She'd only gotten a glimpse of herself when she'd run to the bathroom in the hospital earlier, enough to see that her clothes were muddy and her hair a disheveled mess. For once, she refused to allow her vanity to get the better of her, though, and she'd fled the mirror before any insecurities could take hold. Hunter's *life* was in danger and she'd refused to obsess over petty bullshit.

But Hunter was, for all intents and purposes, fine now. And he was staring at her far too intently for her liking.

So she put the truck in gear and pulled out of the hospital parking lot.

As soon as the truck lurched, Hunter grunted and jerked his torso forward.

Oh. *Ouch*. She hadn't realized it, but he'd been holding his body away from the back of the seat ever since he'd gotten in the truck. Until she'd started and the momentum pushed his sore back into the seat.

Her stomach knotted up when she thought of how much pain he must be in if it was still hurting through all the meds they'd doped him up with.

Speaking of…

"Hunter, did they give you a prescription you need to fill? To get more pain medication?"

Hunter made a dismissive noise. "I'll be fine. Dawkins men are tough as nails."

"Hunter," Isobel said with a warning voice.

"I'm fine."

Isobel gunned the engine so the truck jerked forward.

Hunter's pained grunt at his back hitting the seat again told her all she needed to know.

"Gimme." She held out her hand.

"Fine, fine." Hunter sounded like a chastened little boy as he pulled a piece of paper out of his pocket.

Isobel flipped it over. Vicoden. A month's worth. Damn, they weren't kidding around. She'd seen a Walgreens on the way back from the Animal Hospital.

She paused right before turning onto the road to flip on the GPS and click 'go' for the hotel she'd mapped earlier. Casper was a bigger metro area, if you could call a tiny city like this a 'metro.' But it had a Walmart and, more importantly, a hospital, so she was happy to count it as one.

Apparently this was the main hospital for all of east central Wyoming. Or so the nursing attendant had informed her over and over when she repeatedly asked for news about Hunter. As in, "we're the only hospital for *all* of east Wyoming. We deal with an *incredible* amount of traffic. Everyone wants to know about their loved one and I assure you, the doctors are moving as quickly as they can while also assuring each patient receives the best care possible. You'll be the first to know as soon as there's anything to know." The woman spoke like she was reading off a script. "Now, have you filled out your loved one's insurance information forms yet?"

Uh, Hunter wasn't her loved one and no she hadn't filled out the goddamned insurance information because she had no idea about any of that. She'd said she was his fiancé so they'd at least tell her about his condition. Except it turned out no one had ever come to tell her squat before Hunter himself came ambling out.

She stopped for the prescription and then they headed to the hotel.

Where there was only one room available—a single with one king size bed. They were lucky to even get that. The rest of the hotel was full of people displaced by the storm.

Isobel didn't care. She was just glad to get Hunter to their room. She helped him down from the truck and supported him under his arm.

Together, they made it toward their room at the end of the hotel strip. They were on the ground level, thank God. Isobel would have hated trying to get Hunter up the stairs.

Isobel fumbled in her purse for the key.

Meanwhile Hunter leaned in from behind her, all but sandwiching her against the door.

She felt a soft tug on her scalp and looked back to see Hunter rubbing the hair of her sloppy ponytail between his fingers, the corners of his mouth turned down.

"You never wear your hair down. My wife didn't either. She knew I liked it long. She said that was sexist." He huffed out a sad sigh. "Maybe so."

His eyes were apologetic as he looked up at her. "I still like your hair down."

His ex-wife. He never talked about her.

Isobel knew she shouldn't pry. If he didn't talk about his ex, he likely had his reasons. And he was probably only talking about her now because of the drugs.

But the little devil on Isobel's shoulder won out. "What was she like?" she asked as she finally got the door open.

Hunter let out another long sigh that expelled all the air from his chest. He winced at the movement and Isobel cringed with him. Was it too soon to take one of the Vicodin? What exactly had they given him at the hospital?

"Forget about it. Let's get you inside." She helped him in and over to the bed. She pulled back the comforter and then he flopped down on his stomach, boots still on.

Isobel started reaching for his boots when Hunter's sad laugh stopped her.

"Janie was beautiful. But hard. Like New York. Think that's why I liked her. She wasn't like any of the girls here." He closed his eyes. She wondered if he'd drift off to sleep.

179

It was ridiculous, she knew. But it still hurt in some stupid, unnamable way to hear him talking about another woman. Knowing he'd loved her enough to marry her. And what about now? Did he *still* love her?

"I visited there once, did you know that?" He flopped his head sideways, cheek landing on one of his hands. "New York."

Isobel shook her head but Hunter was already continuing. "And I thought, oh. I get it now. We never had a chance."

He looked so sad and he shook his head again, his eyes dropping closed. "New York women."

The next second, he shifted on the bed and let out a short grunt of pain.

"Don't fall asleep yet," Isobel said, her throat dry. "Let me give you some medicine."

Her hands shook as she got a glass of water from the sink and a pill from the bottle. "Here," she managed in a mostly steady voice. "Take this."

He lifted up and took the pill, lids half-mast. Once he finished gulping down all the water in the glass, he handed it back and then collapsed back to the bed, arms hugging the pillow.

New York women.

It was because she was from New York? He'd pulled the one-eighty after they slept together only after learning she was actually from New York and not New Hampshire.

He thought she was just like his wife. *New York women.*

"Come to sleep, baby," Hunter murmured, face half buried in his pillow.

Isobel jerked back from the bed.

Did he just…?

He'd just been talking about his wife. Was he so out of it he thought Isobel *was* this Janie woman? His wife?

Oh God. Isobel felt sick.

But so much made sense now. Why he'd been so instantly attracted to her. He just said his wife wasn't like any of the girls around here. So when a new woman showed up in town, with the sophistication of the city on her that reminded him of his wife even if he couldn't pinpoint exactly why…

Her stomach flipped. She shot to her feet and made a beeline for the front door.

But then she stopped as soon as her hand touched the doorknob. She looked back over her shoulder.

Dammit. She couldn't leave him alone right now. No matter how much she wanted to run away and try to clear her head.

Because running was always the answer, right?

She squeezed her eyes shut and leaned her forehead against the door. Shit. Was that really her go-to when things got hard?

After everything that went down that hellish year when she was sixteen, she'd run to Rick and Northingham stables.

Then she'd run away to college.

Then here.

But dammit, what had taking a stand and trying to get control of her future gotten her? Facing her problems hadn't exactly worked back in New York. And every time she tried to assert herself and take charge of her life *here*, she just caused more problems. God, she'd almost gotten Hunter killed because of her stupidity in insisting they go out despite the storm.

She was pretty sure that a tornado dropping down almost *literally* on top of her was karma's way of giving her the middle finger.

She banged her forehead once on the door before turning around and going to sit on the one chair in the room—the wooden one pushed in at a little desk top beside the TV. She pulled the chair out and stared down at it balefully.

She was exhausted. She needed rest if she was going to drive home tomorrow with the trailer. There was no way she'd even be able to catnap sitting on the uncomfortable chair. She looked over her shoulder.

Maybe she could sleep on the floor? But then her nose wrinkled. God, she was so tired. Her eyes lifted to the bed. Hunter was sprawled out, but mostly just on the left side. With the meds he was on, he'd be dead to the world all night.

She should take a shower. She'd done some spot-cleaning at the hospital but before she got in bed she should really—

Her shoulders slumped, the stress and weariness of the day finally hitting her full force. Oh fuck it. Housecleaning would clean the sheets whether she dirtied them or not.

She flipped off the lamp, then pulled off her jeans. After a second's hesitation, she pulled off her muddy shirt as well.

She'd wake up well before Hunter and slip out of bed without him ever knowing she was here. She got into bed, pulled the covers up over both her and Hunter, and was asleep within a few minutes.

***

Oh God, *yes*. Right there.

If he'd only—

But then Hunter's finger circled her clit.

Isobel moaned before remembering they had to be quiet. Hunter had pulled her into the women's restroom at Bubba's, then into the back stall, but it wasn't like there was a lock on the door.

Hunter's hand immediately slapped over her mouth, his hardness grinding into her ass from behind as he pressed her against the wall.

"Hush," his voice was a harsh whisper in her ear. "Those sexy noises you make are only for me. No one else gets to fucking hear them."

With his other hand he shoved her skirt up to her waist and her panties halfway down her legs.

And she was glad he had his hand over her mouth because she couldn't help crying out and pressing her ass back against him. She hadn't heard him undoing his buckle but his cock was already out. He rubbed it up and down between her ass cheeks while he sucked on the back of her neck.

Oh God, he was driving her so freaking insane. Every touch, the perfect pressure of his fingers at her clit, the feel of him hard at her ass—

But she needed more. More. "More," she groaned out. "Hunter. *More*."

She flipped so that she could face him and threw her arms around his neck.

"Ow." He flinched and pulled back from her.

Wait. What?

Oh God. His back. How had she forgotten? His back. The storm. The hospital.

This wasn't real. This was a—

Isobel startled awake.

Awake in a hotel bed.

With a very real Hunter.

Who very really had his hands down her pants.

"Hunter!"

"I'm gonna make you feel so good." Hunter was on his side, propped up on one elbow as he kissed down her jaw, his other hand at her core.

She should have pushed him away. No matter how good he was making her feel, he was on medication and might not be fully in the driver's seat at the moment. Plus, his back—

But in the hazy seconds between sleeping and waking, she wasn't processing information fast enough.

And that was when he dipped a finger inside her.

She almost came on the spot.

She'd been so primed by the dream. And it was Hunter. Who was alive. When he so easily could have died today.

That single thought had her grabbing his face and kissing him hard. His tongue was immediately tangling with hers. He kissed her so fiercely and with such urgency. Like he needed her for air. Like he couldn't live without this.

A second finger joined the first inside her and she bucked against him. Riding his fingers.

"Fuck, I'm so goddamned hard. Feel how hard I am." He grabbed her hand and put it on his cock. Which was indeed very, very hard.

"That's right," he hissed. "Fuck, baby. Grab me harder. Jerk it."

She did and he made a tortured noise of pleasure. Then his hands were back at her opening. "So fucking hot and wet. This cunt. Fuck." His fingers were less expert than last time he'd touched her there, but he never once stopped moving them. Exploring her outer lips, then thrusting inside and pressing against each wall like he was watching for her pleasure to find out which she liked best.

And oh God, she liked all of it. When her back arched in pleasure, he cursed. "I gotta eat this pussy. Move up the bed. You gotta give me that hot cunt."

"Hunter, your back," she tried to protest even as he kissed down her chest and latched on her nipple. I don't want to hurt y—"

He bit her nipple.

"Ouch!" She yanked back only to see him grinning up at her in the dim light provided by the bathroom.

"Then let me eat out the cunt that belongs to me."

He tried to bend to move his head down her stomach but his face went taut with pain.

The goddamned lunatic was going to hurt his back all because he was too horny to listen to good sense.

"Fine, fine," she said, pushing him back and scooting up the bed. She had to let go of his glorious cock, which was a shame. But as soon as her hips got near Hunter, he pushed her legs open and then settled between them, his face buried in her center.

He ate at her with abandon, all sorts of sucking and slurping noises as he'd suck her in and then let go with a loud *pop*. But it wasn't until he focused on her clit, his long, talented tongue repeatedly lapping forcefully at her small bud that the world split apart.

Oh God— It was— She couldn't—

"Hunter," she cried out, her thighs clenching around his head.

He continued suckling her all through the earth-shaking orgasm.

She collapsed back to the bed and for several seconds, Hunter continued suckling gently on her clit. Then he laid the softest kisses all over her pelvis. Up her stomach.

It was so good, so beautiful. He was so… She still didn't have words. All she knew was that she wanted to make him feel good in return. Better than good.

She scooted back down the bed with her legs open, ready to take him in her body. But as Hunter lifted to crawl on top of her, he grunted again in pain. His jaw flexed and he kept moving anyway

"Hunter, stop." She rolled off the bed and he immediately reached for her. But she shook her head. "I don't want to hurt you. Does it hurt when you stand up?"

"Oh." Hunter blinked, then frowned. "I don't know?"

"Try it." The dim lighting made Isobel feel brave. Or maybe it was Hunter that made her brave. He'd just been kissing her stomach and she hadn't stopped to freak out once about how he'd think it was too squishy or fat.

And all she could think about now was driving him absolutely crazy. It was always like that with him. She stood up straight as she reached behind her and unhooked her bra. Her breasts fell free and Hunter's nostrils flared.

He reached for the wall as he got to his feet.

"That's good. Hold the wall," she instructed, grabbing a pillow and then dropping to her knees in front of him.

His cock flexed toward her mouth. "Babe, you don't have to—"

She grabbed hold of the base and then sucked the head of his cock into her mouth. She hollowed out her cheeks as she applied suction and then pulled back with a loud *pop*.

"Jesus *Christ*." His legs wobbled and she pulled back.

"Is standing okay?"

"Yep. It's great. All good here. You can keep going," he spoke in a rush before pausing. "But you know. Only if you want. I'm not saying you have to—"

She shut him up by sucking his cock back in her mouth.

"*Fuuuuuuuuuck*," he hissed out, leaning against the wall and staring down at her. "Jesus, you're gorgeous. So fuckin' gorgeous. I love your body. You make me so hard."

He loved *her body*? He certainly wasn't lying about her getting him hard. He was like steel in her mouth. She hollowed her cheeks to get the best suction she could around his shaft each time his tip plunged past her lips. She was determined more than ever to drive him absolutely insane. She teased his slit with the very tip of her tongue as she slowly pulled back off again. A girlfriend had told her a trick once to try to spell out the alphabet with your tongue as a way to drive guys crazy.

She'd made it to Z twice before Hunter groaned and pulled out of her mouth. His features were twisted in strain as he looked down at her. He fisted his cock and jerked it up and down roughly. "Baby, I don't know if I can come. I'm so fuckin' hard. Christ I'm so hard."

His eyes briefly closed as he jerked his dick a little more roughly but then he opened them back up to look down at her. "But those pills or whatever at the hospital."

He kept jerking on his cock, twisting roughly when he got to the head.

Isobel had been getting a little fatigued. She didn't know how long she'd been at it but if she hadn't had the pillow, she knew her knees would be sore.

"But does it feel good?" she asked.

"Fuck yes," he said, squeezing his dick even harder. "I want to come so bad."

Which made Isobel's sex clench. God, he was sexy even when he wasn't trying to be. She bit her lip. Then took a deep breath. "I want to try something."

She reached up and batted away his hand, grabbing hold of his cock and gripping it as hard as she could before taking over and repeating the motions he'd just been doing.

He slumped against the wall, his eyebrows dropping and his mouth opening in pleasure as she jerked him off. "Anything." It was barely more than a whisper.

"You trust me?" She looked up at him, giving him the eye contact he was always so particular about.

"Anything," he repeated, his eyes burning into hers. "Always."

She smiled coyly up at him and then directed his cock back into her mouth. But then she started to finger herself. She moaned around his cock. God, she'd never before in her life found a blow job sexy but she was already on the brink again.

It was just Hunter's responsiveness. His thighs flexed each time she sucked him in. He was breathing so hard. One hand hovered near her head but it was like he was afraid if he touched her she'd disappear. It was sweet and fucking sexy all at the same time.

Which made her want to do bad, bad things to this man.

After getting her index finger lubricated with her juices, she sucked Hunter's cock in so deep the tip of him touched her throat. Then she teased the finger she'd just had inside herself at his asshole.

He jerked in her mouth like she'd electrocuted him. He pulled all the way out and she lifted her head to look at him. His gaze locked on hers. His chest moved erratically up and down.

186

"Do you trust me?" she repeated.

She could see the hesitation in his features but still his head bobbed up and down in a single nod. "Always."

"Then relax." She bobbed the head of his cock in and out of her mouth several times in quick succession until she had him groaning in pleasure again. Only then did her index finger go back to its explorations.

He went tense at first. But then, like he'd ordered himself to, his ass relaxed. When she pushed at his hole, her finger slipped inside.

She hummed around his cock in pleasure. She'd never done this before. Only read about it. The male G-spot. She'd read about it in a romance novel and then done a ton of research to find out just how to do it. Jason had never let her try it out on him. In his words: "all ass stuff is gay."

But Hunter was trusting her. And she intended to reward him. She pushed her finger several inches down his channel, feeling all along the wall toward the front of his body. And... *bingo*. There was a small walnut-sized bump. She began to gently rub and press it.

"Oh *fuck*." A shudder went down Hunter's legs and his hips thrust forward, sending his cock toward the back of her throat. And it was fucking exhilarating. She wanted him to lose control. She wanted him to go fucking crazy.

She continued her massage of the small gland while bobbing up and down on his cock.

He cried out an anguished, feral sound as he jerked his cock out and then thrust back in again. He grabbed the back of her head and roared as he came.

And came.

And came.

She tried her best to swallow his cum but she couldn't keep up and it spilled out her mouth and down the front of her chest.

No time to worry about it though because Hunter stumbled and almost fell to his knees.

"Oh! Hunter."

He grabbed for the wall, just managing to catch himself in time. His hand immediately went to his cock. "More," he growled through his teeth. With her finger still in his ass she kept massaging his prostate and he groaned as even more cum spilled out of his cock.

Isobel moved and extended her tongue, licking up the cum and watching Hunter through her lashes.

"Fuck. Gonna die. You're gonna kill me," he groaned, pushing his cock back between her lips already slick with his cum. He kept thrusting until long after he'd come all he was going to. She slipped her finger out of his back passage.

She got to her feet and started for the bathroom. He immediately pushed off from the wall and started following her. She turned back to look at him. "Lie down. I'll be right back."

But there was some look she couldn't read in his eyes. A wariness. Or… fear. "Don't leave."

She went up on tip toe and kissed him. "I just need to wash up. Get in bed."

She'd meant it to just be a quick peck, but he reached for her cheeks and he held her in place while he kissed her so deep she was gasping for breath by the time he let her go.

He closed his eyes and breathed out, his forehead to hers before finally letting go of her and stumbling toward the bed. He dropped onto his stomach before she could try to help him.

She ran to the bathroom and quickly washed up. Even so, she thought he might already be asleep by the time she got back. In her experience, guys usually went into an immediate coma about three seconds after coming.

But Hunter was awake, his intense blue eyes on her as she got into bed. He immediately pulled her to him, rolling slightly onto his side so he could wrap an arm around her from behind in a modified spooning position.

He must have just been fighting off the sex coma, though, because as soon as they were in place, she felt his entire body relax. And his voice was thick as he whispered the words that would have her awake the rest of the night:

"Love you, babe. Don't leave me again. Please." He snuggled into her neck, his arm cinching tighter around her waist. "I'll do anything. Just don't leave me again."

And Isobel went cold from her head all the way down to her toes.

She should have realized as soon as he called her 'gorgeous.' For God's sake, he'd said he *loved her body*. How had she not wised up, right then?

In his drugged head, the whole time he'd been having sex with her, he'd thought she was his ex-wife.

Chapter 18
HUNTER

Fuuuuuuck. Ow. Christ. Son of a mother—

Hunter's teeth gritted against the pain as his eyes blinked open.

"Goddamn it," he swore, stomach tensing as he tried to breathe through the pain. His back was on fire. Stabbing, painful fire.

He tried to sit up but even the tiniest movements pulled at his back and made it worse.

"Don't try to move." Isobel appeared in front of him like a dark-haired angel, her hair flying around her in a cloud.

For a second he could only stare. She must have taken a shower because she was cleaned up. She had on a pair of zip up coveralls they used in the field and always carried around in the truck—probably the only clean thing she had to put on. It was oversized on her but all he could think about was the fact that it would take one swipe of the zipper and she'd be naked.

Naked.

Suddenly the night before came back to him with the force of a hammer to the head. Her breathy groans. Her on her knees, mouth sucking his cock. Him pumping like a goddamned geyser down her throat after she—

"Hunter?" She held out a pill along with a cup of water. "Here, swallow this." She was looking toward him but wouldn't quite meet his eye. "It'll help with the pain. And this one's an antibiotic." She unscrewed another cap and handed him a second pill.

Was she really just going to pretend like last night hadn't happened?

"Don't give me any macho bullshit," Isobel said when he laid there unmoving. "Swallow."

Well, how was he supposed to refuse when she went all sexy nurse on him like that? He popped the first pill, then the second, cringing in pain when he lifted up on his elbows to drink the water.

Christ, he was thirsty. The water tasted great.

But it also made him aware of another pressing need. Looked like he'd be getting up from this bed after all.

He went to twist and sit up again. He gritted his teeth but couldn't keep the groan back as he pushed through the pain to pull his body up.

"Hunter!"

He hated hearing the alarm in Isobel's voice. Hated even more that he couldn't do anything about it other than mutter, "I'm fine, I'm fine."

He finally managed to get to a sitting position, his legs swung over the side of the bed.

"What are you doing? You need to lay back down!"

"Bathroom," was all he was able to get out.

She nodded and then sat down, sliding her slim body beside his and slipping underneath his arm.

Warm.

Soft.

Female.

And not just any female.

Isobel.

Again his short-circuiting brain was side-tracked from the pain. If he kissed her right now, would she kiss him back? Or keep pretending like last night had never happened?

It *had* happened… right?

He blinked a couple times. Could it have all been some Vicoden-induced dream? He watched Isobel even more closely.

She bit her plump bottom lip. How was that not a fucking invitation? Or rather, an invitation to fuck?

She was breathing hard and he felt the side of her breast brushing his chest every time she took in air. Was being near him affecting her the same way? Another flash of memory: her screaming his name, legs shaking with her orgasm while he ate her out.

Fuuuuuuuuuuck, he'd never forget the taste of that sweet cunt for as long as he lived.

But was his doped-up head just mixing up memories from the first time he'd had her? It was so vivid, though.

Then again, right before he woke up, he'd been reliving the storm. That had been vivid as hell too. The twister was coming toward them.

Only this time it didn't veer away. It kept coming and coming and he hadn't been able to save her—

At the thought, his chest squeezed until he couldn't breathe.

No. She was safe. Her body was warm. So, so warm. If he just turned into her, he could lean down and bury his face in her neck. Lick along the shell of her ear until her breath hitched in that way that drove him absolutely fucking insane.

"Okay," she said, her voice no nonsense. "Up in three. One, two—"

Well damn. Guess her thoughts weren't on the same page.

"*Three.*"

She stood up and he had to go with her or else he'd look like a damn fool. So as much as it fucking *hurt*, he lurched unsteadily forward. Again he couldn't help the groan of pain the movement caused.

Though it was actually more of a roar because Jesus *fuck*, that hurt. It hadn't been nearly this bad last night.

"Okay, I've got you, I've got you. You're doing great." Isobel's small hand went to his stomach to steady him. Low on his stomach. And that just made his brain a mess of cross-firing synapses.

A beautiful woman's hand close to his crotch made him want to grab her and grind his body against hers. Hellfire stabbing back pain made him want to collapse on the floor in a ball. Or pass out again. That would work for him too.

But goddamn it, he had to piss.

So he stumbled forward, Isobel struggling to help him toward the small bathroom.

Isobel shook her head. "They should have kept you another day at the hospital. What were they thinking?"

So this was probably not the best time to tell her he vaguely remembered the doctor saying something about strongly recommending that he stay another day for rest and observation. And Hunter being like, *screw that, I can walk, I'm just fine.*

Yeah. He was thinking Isobel didn't ever need to know that little detail.

He staggered the last few steps to the bathroom and then grabbed the doorframe to hold himself up.

When he stepped inside and flicked on the light, Isobel started to follow. "Whoa." He moved to block her path. "Where do you think you're going?"

She put a hand on her hip. "Don't be a baby. You need help."

She tried to slip past him but he held out his arm to bar her way. She must have seen the grimace on his face at the action—no matter what he did, it seemed to pull at his back. She immediately stilled.

"Are you okay?" Then her face fell. "Of course you're not okay."

Her lips pinched together and her eyes got watery. "I am so sorry, Hunter. I never even apologized last night. But I'm so, so sorry." She looked absolutely stricken. "You'll never know how sorry. I can't believe how *stupid* I was to risk your life when—"

"Hey." He ignored the pain it caused to lift his hand to cup her cheek. Her hand-wringing stopped and she went absolutely still, her large blue eyes coming up to meet his. "It's not your fault. These things just happen. We don't have any control over them."

That was one of the steps, after all. Acceptance. He couldn't go back and change anything that had happened with Janine—no matter how many times he called the number she never picked up to apologize to her.

What happened had *happened*. As sure as if it was set in cement. There was no time-travel to go back and undo it. No, 'if only I'd known then what I know now.' That was all bullshit fantasy.

Maybe everything had been fated before it even happened. Written down in some book in the sky, predetermined. So even if he *could* go back in time, nothing would have turned out any different.

Some days that thought comforted him.

Others it tortured him.

But Isobel was just shaking her head, eyes haunted. "If I hadn't been so stubborn, insisting we get Beauty to the hospital *right that second*—"

"Stop it." His voice was sharp. "There are no *what ifs*. There's just now. And we're both here now."

She stilled and he noticed her clenched fists loosen. She took a deep breath in. Was she letting go of her guilt? He hoped so. It was no way to live. He should know.

193

Her eyes dropped half-closed and she turned her head slightly, nuzzling her cheek into his hand as if without thinking about it.

This woman.

Fuck. Did she know what she did to him? And not just below the belt. Her sweetness. Her sassiness. Her intelligence. He'd never met anyone like her.

"I was so scared," she whispered. Her breath was hot on his palms. Her lips so close to his skin.

She was so beautiful. Delicate but strong. A winter rose, like his mom used to grow. His chest filled. He felt... She was just...

Her eyes widened suddenly and she jerked back from him. "Sorry. I'm supposed to be the one taking care of *you*." She dropped her eyes as she stepped out of the door. "I'll be right outside if you need me."

As soon as she closed the door, the pain that he'd been briefly distracted from made itself known again. He didn't bother hiding his grimace since Isobel couldn't see him now.

He turned his back toward the mirror and looked over his shoulder. He tried lifting up the back of his shirt to check out the damage, but twisting his arm like that hurt like hell so he quickly gave up. All he could see was the edge of a bandage anyway.

He went to the commode and quickly relieved his bladder. Then washed his hands and went back out to Isobel. She was making the bed. Unnecessary, since the maids would only strip it to wash everything once they left. Just habit or was she so uncomfortable around him she needed something to keep her hands busy?

"How long was I asleep?"

"You slept through the night." She punched a pillow to fluff it. "It's 7:30."

"Did you sleep?" Now that he was a little more awake, he noticed slight shadows under her eyes.

She waved a hand like it wasn't important. "Are you hungry?" She pulled the comforter over the bed and then smoothed out all the wrinkles.

He didn't miss how she immediately turned the questions back to him. But now that she mentioned it, he was starving. He hadn't eaten since before lunch yesterday.

"There's a Denny's next door," she continued. "I can go get you something and bring it back over—"

"How's the mare?" He felt bad for just now thinking of it, but he was a little slow on the pick up this morning.

Isobel's eyes opened wide at his question. Then she immediately jogged to her purse by the door. She quickly reached inside and rooted around for a moment before coming out with his phone. "They said they'd call this morning but I turned the ringer off so it wouldn't disturb you sleeping."

She walked back toward him, touching the screen. "Sorry, I had to use your phone. I didn't think to grab mine when we—"

She froze in her tracks. "Oh. Crap."

"What?" Hunter took a step toward her at the alarm on her face.

"Your mom has been calling. A lot." She looked up at him apologetically, then hurried over to hand him the phone. He hobbled toward her, meeting her halfway. He was getting better at this walking thing. It hurt, but not as much as it had when he got up. No doubt the Vicodin was starting to work.

Still, when he got the phone from Isobel, he leaned against the wall. He looked down at the screen. Shit. There were twenty-nine missed calls from Mom. A bunch of missed calls from other numbers too. He immediately dialed his mom back.

"Hunter?" Her frantic voice answered the line after the second ring.

"Mom, it's me."

"Oh thank God. *Tom,*" she yelled his dad's name, not bothering to pull the phone away from her mouth, "it's Hunter."

"Mom, I'm sorry I didn't—"

"Hunter Thomas Dawkins, are you trying to kill your father?" His mother's voice was irate. "You know he has a bad heart! We got a call last night from the hospital saying you were in surgery. Then nothing, for hours. We called and called, worried out of our *minds*. Then when they finally had something to tell us, it's only that you were out of surgery but that you'd disappeared! You didn't check yourself out. You were just gone!"

Hunter winced and held the phone away from his ear for a second as she continued her tirade. When he finally bit the bullet and put it back to his ear, she was midsentence.

"—to mention everyone's been calling the house all night long looking for you. I couldn't even take the phone off the hook because we were hoping you'd finally remember your poor mother and father. If you weren't dead in a ditch, that was. Do you have any idea—"

"Why were people calling the house?" Did the whole town know about his little hospital disappearing act? Jesus, that meant the town gossip train would be talking about it for—

"Well what did you think people were going to do when they weren't getting a response from the emergency clinic line? Mollie Sanders wouldn't stop moaning about her precious corgi who had mala-something-hooey stress because of the storm."

"Maladaptive stress response," Hunter corrected automatically. A fancy term that meant the dog was afraid of storms. Mrs. Sanders was sure it was a life-threatening condition that would shorten her beloved corgi's life. She called Hunter without fail every time there was so much as a distant rumble of thunder.

"Then Bill Sawyers kept going on and on about his prize heifer having trouble calving. I'm trying to tell them I don't even know if my *son* is safe, don't come crying to me about an *animal*!"

"Why didn't they just call Dr. Roberts?" Hunter asked.

His mom let out a huff. "I guess he reinjured his hip when he tried to help Bill with that damn heifer."

Wow. His mom must be really worked up if she was swearing.

He softened his voice. "I'm fine, Mom. Really." He ignored the biting pain in his back as he shifted his weight to his other foot. "I'm sorry I scared you guys. It wasn't surgery, just some stitches. I didn't realize the hospital had called you."

"Well they still had us as your emergency contact number on file from when you had your appendectomy there when you were seventeen."

Hunter smiled, shaking his head. And of course his parents still had the same number a decade and a half later.

"I'm sorry, Mama. I hate that I worried you." He was, too. After Dad's heart attack seven years ago and then everything with Janine…

196

well, Mom had had too much to worry about for too long. He hated adding to her burdens.

A heavy sigh came across the line. He heard tears in her voice when she next spoke and it about killed him. "We can't lose you. I feel like we've just got you back after…"

Hunter swallowed. "Don't cry, Mama. You know I can't handle that."

She sniffed loudly. "Who's crying? I'm not crying."

There was a brief pause and Hunter imagined her wiping her eyes with one of the kitchen towels. Her voice was strong and no nonsense when she continued. "Now tell me about this new woman of yours. Everyone's been seeing you around town together but you don't bring her to meet your own mother? What kind of son did I raise?"

"*Mom.*" He felt the back of his neck heating up. "It's just a work thing." His gaze flipped over to Isobel, who wasn't bothering to hide the fact that she was following his half of the conversation with rapt attention. He was not about to discuss his complicated relationship to his summer intern with her in earshot.

"I gotta go, Mama. But I'm fine and I'll call you back later today when I get home. It might be late since I'll be out taking care of all these calls."

He was already looking Isobel's direction and he saw her eyebrows pop up in surprise at his words.

"You do what you gotta do. Just be safe, baby. And if I call you again, you better answer! Or call back within an hour if you're somewhere without any reception. You promise me." Her voice was hard but he heard the thread of fear and desperation underneath. He felt horrible thinking about the sleepless night she'd just spent because of him.

"Promise."

"All right. Love you."

"Love you too, Mama."

She hung up without lingering. That was his mom. She was a marshmallow underneath, but you'd never know it for her mama bear fierceness. All she'd ever wanted in life was a big family she could love on. Instead she got his quiet, taciturn father for a husband and, after several miscarriages, him. Just one son to lavish all the love she had to give.

And life as an isolated rancher's wife wasn't an easy one—not that he'd ever thought about it growing up. He'd taken her for granted. Taken all of it for granted. It was only when his dad had the heart attack that he'd realized how much his mom needed him around.

How could he, her only son, desert her by moving away to the big city like Janine kept pressuring him to do when his Mom had given up everything for him?

Suffice to say, she and Janine had never gotten along.

"What did you mean by 'take care of these calls'?" Isobel asked as soon as he got off the phone.

"Just what it sounded like." Hunter tapped the phone to access his voicemails and put them on speaker phone while he walked over to the nightstand.

A robotic voice read out the time the voicemail was left: *8:19 pm.*

Hey Hunter, this is Ken Peterson. I'm having some trouble with one of my mares. She got riled up by the storm and smashed herself real good on the fencing—

Isobel had brought in his spare change of clothes from the truck. They were folded on the bedside table. He picked up the button up denim work shirt and shook it open.

Grimacing, he tried to shrug into it. The pain was a lot less sharp than it had been twenty minutes ago but *damn*, that still smarted.

"What do you think you're doing?" Isobel asked over Ken's voice talking about the cut on his horse's flank. "You need to lay back down. Right now." She stalked over toward him and grabbed his arm, trying to pull him toward the bed.

So anyway, if you could call me back and come on over. It's a nasty gash, bleeding all over the place and I don't want it to get infected. I'm hoping to get her bred in a few— The recording cut off, running out of time on Ken.

There was a *beep* and then the next message started.

8:33 pm. Bill Sawyers here. Need help with Blue's calving. She's one of my best Angus. Expect your call back within the hour.

Beep.

198

Hunter grimaced and this time, it wasn't from the pain in his back. Whatever had happened with Blue was over and done with now, more than twelve hours later.

He sighed and sat down on the bed.

"Good," Isobel said, relief clear in her voice. "Now lay down and I'll go get you some food."

Hunter reached for his work boots that Isobel had set beside the bed.

"Hunter!"

Isobel started to snatch the boots away from him but he jerked them back, grunting at the pain the move caused.

Isobel's hands immediately flew up and she stepped back. "I'm sorry."

Hunter gritted his teeth as he leaned over and slid his foot into the boot. Aw fuck, aw fuck, *aw fuuuuuuuck*, bending over like this was hell on his back wounds. He reached for the laces to tie them even though his breaths started coming short as he fought to breathe through the pain.

"Stop it! You're hurting yourself."

She dropped to the floor and knocked his hands away. She didn't pull the boot off, though. She just took over tying them. He breathed out in relief and sat up straight. So much better when he wasn't bent over.

She reached for his other foot and helped him slide it into the other boot. Then her fingers were tightening and pulling the laces. She yanked them extra tight. When he glanced down at her, her mouth was in a taut line.

Clearly, she wasn't happy. But goddamn she was beautiful. And her crouched down in front of him, just like last night, Christ, it was making his dick hard. The memory was fuzzy around the edges, but he'd swear the hardest orgasm of his entire goddamned life was no dream. But how could she act so nonchalant like nothing had happened.

"The animals don't take a day off," he said. "Ever. This is the job."

She jerked her head to look up at him, the sharp movement displacing some hair that had fallen over her neck. And revealing the

199

hickie beneath. Right at the base of her neck where it met her shoulder.

His nostrils flared. He *knew* it wasn't a dream.

"You think you can pull a calf in your condition?" she asked, eyes flashing. "Hunter, you can't even tie your own shoes. You're not going to be any help to anybody until you get the rest you need so you can heal."

It was on the tip of his tongue to bite back that she was singing a different tune last night when she was roughly shoving his face into her pussy.

But dammit, she was right. This morning he could barely walk. The magic combo of whatever they'd given him at the hospital plus Vicodin that had let him enjoy last night's activities without too much pain was long gone. The Vicodin alone was enough to curb the sharpest edge of it, but the truth was, he was gritting his teeth against the pain this very second.

And the thought of farm calls sounded like torture. That didn't mean there was any getting out of them. Isobel would have to drive, of course. And it was true, most of the practical realities of being a large animal vet were physical. It was why Dr. Roberts didn't usually do farm calls at his age.

But Hunter had something Dr. Roberts didn't. He had Isobel.

Isobel got back to her feet after finishing with his laces and she looked at him in alarm. "Why are you smiling at me like that."

"Do you trust me?"

Her whole body jolted at the words and her eyes cut to him, slightly widening.

It was the same thing she'd asked him last night.

Would she say something now? Acknowledge what was between them?

But she only nodded, eyes fastened on him.

Fine. She still wanted to keep running?

He supposed the real question was whether or not he was up for the chase. Was he willing to risk it all again for love?

He managed to keep his voice even as he said, "Well today's the day you get to jump in feet first, Dr. Isobel. You'll be the primary vet and I'll just be backup."

Her posture relaxed. She smiled but then quickly looked away like she was still gun-shy after the question about trust.

Should he risk his heart on such a skittish woman?

His knee-jerk reaction was *no*. Never again. But he had a feeling that where Isobel Snow was concerned, he might already be a goner.

Chapter 19
ISOBEL

A week and a half later, Isobel was still doing most of the heavy lifting on the farm calls, though Hunter came out with her for most of them in case there were any dicey situations. That first day had been the worst—mostly because Hunter insisted on coming even though she could see the strain on his face with every step he took.

He looked so pale he might pass out by the fifth farm they'd stopped at. She'd taken him home right after, then gone by herself to handle the last couple more routine calls.

And she had. Incredibly. It turned out there might be one thing in life she wasn't useless at after all. Suck on that, Catrina.

If only she knew what to do about Hunter.

That night between them at the hotel had been... well, she'd say *unforgettable*, but apparently Hunter had completely forgotten it.

That wasn't fair. He'd been doped up all to hell. But that wasn't the worst part.

While it had been happening, had it been *her* he was having sex with, or his ex? That was the question that plagued her. She'd been so certain that night he'd been thinking of his ex. But on the endless replay of the night, remembering how he'd looked her in the eyes and how *present* he'd seemed...

Then again, he couldn't recall a goddamned moment of it, so how present could he have really been?

Ugh, she was going to drive herself crazy. She'd been snippy all week because of it. She'd overheard Liam whispering that she must be on the rag. It was a testament to her newfound self-control that she hadn't crossed the room and smacked him upside the head.

If anyone was getting the brunt of her bad mood, though, it was Hunter. But how could she look at him and not hear his words in the back of her head? *Love you, babe.* Which may or may not have been directed at her.

She shook her head as she approached the next cow in the field. She had some truly thrilling work today. TB testing cattle. Woo hoo. There hadn't been a case of TB in Wyoming for over twenty years.

Isobel was just flipping up the second cow's skirt—i.e., their tail—to make the injection when she heard shouting from over at the fence line.

Hunter was waving his arms at her and yelling something. She couldn't make out what. The fastest way into the field had just been to climb through the wooden fence so Hunter had stayed on the sidelines since he was still pretty stiff.

"What?" she shouted back at him, moving a few steps away from the cow. "I can't hear you!"

He used his hands to make a little speaker around his mouth and yelled again, over and over. B something?

"Ball?" she yelled back.

A movement from the left caught her attention and her heart dropped to her feet as she finally understood exactly what Hunter was screaming about.

Bull.

Heading straight toward her. It was huge. It had giant shoulders and a giant hump on its back. Holy *shit.*

"Run!" Hunter shouted.

Isobel didn't need to be told twice. She started sprinting toward the fence.

The bull was already halfway across the field, though, and her second of hesitation had cost her. He seemed to be gaining on her and she pushed harder. The ground was uneven though. If she tripped or fell, she'd be trampled.

She watched the ground trying to avoid any divots or dips in the field. She looked over her shoulder. The bull was far too close. Shit. He couldn't be gaining on her.

People ran with bulls all the time in Spain. So a human could outrun one. Right?

Right?

She looked forward. The fence was close now. Maybe twenty feet.

The bull bellowed behind her.

Ten feet.

Hunter had jumped up on the fence and reached out his arms. "Run," he kept shouting, features screwed up in terror. "*Run.*"

The roaring bull noises got closer than ever behind her but she didn't dare risk losing momentum by looking back. When she got close to the fence she jumped, reaching for Hunter's arms even as he stretched over the fence toward her.

He caught her and dragged her over the top of the fence. Their momentum kept carrying them and the next thing she knew, she was flying toward the ground. She landed on her back and Hunter collapsed over her, his chest to hers. He barely stopped himself from smashing into her by catching himself with his hand on the grass beside her.

Isobel blinked hard and gasped, her breath having been knocked out of her.

"Are you okay?" Hunter asked, his eyes frantically searching her face. Then he pulled back and grabbed her cheeks. "Isobel, focus on my finger."

He lifted his index finger and waved it back and forth in front of her face. She followed his finger with her eyes, feeling ridiculous. She would have told him how ridiculous he was if she had the breath to speak with.

Instead she just flopped her head back against the grass as Hunter demanded, "Tell me if it hurts," while he felt down one arm and then the other, then ran his hands up and down her legs.

When he started up the thigh of the second leg she sat up and knocked his hand away. She took a deep breath and finally got enough air to say, "Normal to have," she gasped in more air, "two near-death experiences in two weeks," another gulp of air, "on this job?"

She closed her eyes and focused on getting several deep breaths. "Should have read the fine print."

She smiled and reached a hand out for Hunter to help her to her feet but he wasn't laughing at her joke. No, he was glaring.

"What the hell were you *thinking*?"

"Excuse me?" Isobel asked, affronted.

"I was waving my arms and yelling at you for a full thirty seconds before you started running. What the hell else do you think this—" he waved his arms in an overexaggerated motion that had to be tugging on his back stitches— "means?"

Was he seriously saying it was her fault that she almost got trampled by a bull?

"Are you blaming me for that?"

"You never enter a situation where you don't know the variables. The first thing you ask when you're dealing with cows is if there are any uncastrated males around."

"Well I didn't see you asking!" Isobel yelled back at him, finally getting to her feet on her own.

Hunter took a step forward like he was going to yell something else but he couldn't think of anything to say.

Instead, he turned on his heel and stomped back toward the four-wheeler they'd used to get out to the field.

Well, he wasn't the only one who got to be pissed and act like a preschooler. She stalked over to the four-wheeler and got on the seat ahead of Hunter. She felt more than a little smug satisfaction when his arms had to snake around her waist so he wouldn't fall off.

While she'd been overly cautious on the way out to the pasture to be careful not to go too fast because of Hunter's back, now she had no such qualms. She gunned it along the uneven dirt path all the way back to the farm house.

Hunter's arms tightened around her reflexively and for some stupid reason, it made her smile. It was nice to be in the driver's seat for *once* where Hunter was concerned. He always made her emotions fly all over the map.

As soon as they got back to the house, however, Hunter was vaulting off the four-wheeler and stomping up to the door. He about banged the thing off its hinges before the owner came out.

Hunter immediately lit into him for not warning them about the bull.

The owner hemmed and hawed about how the bull had never hurt anyone and was docile.

Isobel couldn't help arching her eyebrow at that and Hunter went through the roof. "Well you and your docile bull can find another veterinarian because I refuse to work for someone who endangers the life of my staff."

205

Hunter pulled out the check the man had written him earlier and ripped it in half before flinging it in the air. It fluttered to the ground as he turned and stalked away from the farm house.

Isobel just lifted her eyebrows again at the farmer because, well, what was there to say after that? She hurried to follow Hunter back to the truck.

His mood had not mellowed any, if the way he slammed his door and yanked his seatbelt on were any indication.

He was riding as a passenger since his back still wasn't healed up enough to lean back against the seat and Isobel tried to get him to rest in between stops. Not that she thought he'd be doing much resting at the moment. She pulled her seatbelt on and put the truck into reverse, executing a three-point turn in the wide gravel driveway and then heading back out onto the road home.

She'd heard that saying before—the tension was so thick you could cut it with a knife. Well, she thought she might need a hacksaw for how tense things were in the cab of the truck. Hunter looked strung so tight that he'd snap with the slightest provocation.

So she really should have known better before asking, "Was it really necessary to ream that guy out so bad? It was probably just an honest mistake, him forgetting to tell us about the bull."

Maybe it was the devil in her, wanting to poke the bull beside her, because he immediately erupted.

"Mistake? You call that a mistake? That asshole almost got you killed and you think it's just a fucking mistake?"

"Whoa, chill out." She waved one hand at him.

"Both hands on the wheel," he snapped.

Oh he did *not* just—

"I know how to drive, thank you very much." Picking. He was always picking at something. Yes, he might be further along the path in life than her but that didn't mean she was stupid. "And I know how to take care of myself. I saw the bull without any of your help. You yelling and calling all that attention probably just made him start running faster."

"Me. Yelling?" He enunciated each word and then angled his whole body toward her. "If I hadn't been yelling, you would have kept your nose up that cow's ass until the bull was trampling you. If I hadn't been there you'd be a goddamned—"

He took a deep breath but Isobel was already incensed.

"What?" She looked over at him furiously. "I'd be a what?"

"Pull over," Hunter snapped.

"What?" Isobel looked back at the road, then checked her mirrors. It was empty blacktop on all sides.

"I said pull over."

"Why?"

"Goddammit for once can you just do what I ask?"

"Fine!" Isobel yelled, slowly applying the break and bringing the truck to a stop on the side of the road. She jammed it into park and then glared at Hunter while crossing her arms over her chest. "Why are we stopped?" she demanded.

"Because it's not safe to argue while you're driving."

"Ok," she threw up her hands. "Now I'm so incompetent I can't even drive your precious truck right?"

"Stop putting words in my mouth. That's not what I—"

"You know what?" She swiveled back around to face front. "You don't want me distracted while I drive? Then how about we just don't talk at all?"

She reached for the gear shift to put the car back into first but Hunter grabbed her hand.

"Goddammit, woman."

She swung her head toward him, glaring daggers. So help her God, if he said one more thing about her driving or—

And then Hunter was kissing her.

He yanked her roughly into his arms and his mouth demanded response.

And oh God, she couldn't help but give it to him.

"You don't know how fucking terrified I was," he whispered frantically before kissing her again. Then he pushed her back against the car door, his elbow honking the truck's horn, but he apparently didn't care because he didn't stop.

He was wrong. She thought of the blood that had covered her arms when he'd collapsed in front of her. She *did* have some idea just how scared he'd been.

Thinking of that moment and then having him, hot and alive and demanding in her arms— Suddenly her need to have him was all consuming. Her core throbbed with needing it. Needing him. Needing to be filled.

Her hands scrabbled down to his belt. A second later, she was pulling his cock out. He was hot and hard in her hand. She squeezed him and he jerked in her fingers.

Oh God, that giant cock of his. She wanted to lick it and nip it and tease it, but even more, she wanted it inside her.

"Christ," he swore, his hands just as frantic to pull down her jeans and underwear. She lifted her butt so he could yank them down her thighs and off her feet.

As soon as she was free, Hunter pushed her legs open wide and positioned his cock at her pussy. He didn't even hesitate a second before shoving in. There were no sweet words. No preparation. He just speared her against the car seat.

Isobel moaned and threw a hand up against the back window. If anyone was driving by, if anybody saw them— But the next moment she couldn't care because oh *God*, he felt so good inside her.

"Harder," she commanded, shoving her pelvis up toward him as soon as he pulled back.

"Baby," was all he said before thrusting into her so hard his balls slapped her pussy.

"Yes," she cried out. "More. Fuck me harder. Hunter, I need it. I need you so bad. You don't know. You don't know."

She kept saying it over and over because he didn't know—couldn't know. How bad she needed this from him. After such a run of shit luck in her life and then to have almost lost him, too? She needed him to make love to her so hard that he fucking marked her. So that it felt *real*. With him fully aware of who was underneath him.

Maybe he felt a little of what she was feeling. Because the next thing she knew, he pulled out and then lifted her by her waist so that she was spread out beneath him on the long bench seat.

His eyes were dark and almost feral as he looked down from above her. Mr. Nice Guy Veterinarian that everyone else thought they knew had left the building. Or the truck, as it were. Instead here was a man who excited Isobel more than any other ever had before.

"I'm going to take every one of your holes until you know who you belong to. You're fucking *mine*."

Her nostrils flared at that. Okay, she couldn't decide if that was the hottest thing she'd ever heard or the most chauvinistic, but him dropping to an awkward perch on the floorboard and starting to eat her out was definitely winning him brownie points toward the hottest lover of the year award. Or you know, the century.

"Oh shit," she couldn't help cursing, dropping her hand and winding it in one of the seatbelts. Hunter had latched on her clit and that plus the sight of his dark head buried in her pussy—

Oh God, oh God, *yes*. Don't stop. Never stop. Never, ever, *ever*—

The hand not twisted in the seatbelts dropped to his head and she shamelessly thrust her pelvis into his face as her climax hit. One pulse of heat, then two. And she held it, that fucking perfect explosion of everything, the center of light and heat and—

When she finally sagged back against the seat, Hunter was moving, scrambling in the cramped space.

"God*damn*, I love it when you fuck my face like that. Do you know how crazy you make me? My dick is hard as fucking iron. I'm always having to hide stiffies around you. Not anymore."

He slid her even further down the seat and shoved her shirt up. Then he yanked down her bra to expose her breasts. "That's right," he hissed out. "Love those beautiful titties of yours."

He leaned forward and rubbed his cock in the valley between her breasts. Then he massaged and pressed her breasts together until her cleavage made a tight channel around his cock.

He thrust back and forth several times. Seeing his cock jump toward her face from between her breasts—God, why was that so freaking hot? Even though she'd just come, the sight of him using her body for his pleasure like that, holy shit.

She stuck out her tongue to lick the slit of his cock the next time he thrust forward through her breasts and his whole body jolted.

"Christ, I need your mouth, Bel. I need every inch of you." He shifted so that his cock was right at her mouth. He grabbed it and rubbed it back and forth over her lips, teasing her.

"Tell me you want it." His voice was so low and gruff and full of lust that Isobel would swear she almost spontaneously orgasmed on the spot.

In answer, she dropped her mouth open wide and sucked him inside.

"Shiiiit," he swore as his hips jackhammered forward, almost like he couldn't stop himself. Isobel didn't mind. She loved him like this. Unrestrained. Free in a way he could only be with her. Completely real.

She swallowed around him and he swore. He grabbed her head, but instead of using it to shove deeper down her throat, he stroked her hair. "Fuck baby, that's so good. Do you know how good that is? Christ your throat's like a vise. I just want to fuck you and fuck you and *fuck you.*"

He emphasized each *fuck you* with a thrust of his hips. The juxtaposition of his gentle hand at her head and his fat cock forcing its way in and out of her mouth, making her drool all down his shaft and over his balls—Isobel couldn't help groaning little needy moans around his cock. And when she did that it seemed to make him even crazier.

"Fuck, that's right baby. Let me know how much you love my fat cock. That's right. Christ, this is the best hummer— Isobel, shit, I'm gonna— Not yet— I—"

With a growl, Hunter pulled himself away from Isobel's mouth, using her shoulders to hold her still because she kept chasing after him with her tongue. He'd been about to blow and she wanted to taste him and suck him dry and make him beg at her mercy and—

He glared down at her like he knew what she'd meant to do. But the next second he was leaned down and kissing her so deep, she could taste herself on his lips.

"Fucking vixen," he whispered, and then thrust his tongue in and out of her mouth in an imitation of fucking.

Her legs squeezed together but then she realized—wait, that's stupid. She had the hottest fucking man in the universe above her. She reached for his cock and tried to guide him back inside her but was only met with his dark chuckle.

"Oh no you don't." He pulled his hips back from her grasping touch. Her eyes flashed up to his in confusion.

"I told you I was taking all of you. Right now."

His meaning barely had time to register before he was grabbing her and flipping her over on the car seat. "Hands and knees," he bit out.

Holy shit, he wasn't really going to— His hands were immediately on her ass, massaging the fleshy globes in his hands.

She squeezed her eyes shut in horror. Her giant ass was in his face. He must be disgusted. She should just turn back around—

But when she made a move, his hand came down in a *thwack* across her left butt cheek. She yelped and jumped on the seat.

"Goddamn but I love this ass. Do you know how many nights I've spent dreaming and jerking off over thoughts of this ass?" She felt his warm breath against her flesh and then his teeth nipped and bit at her, up and down all over her ass. She yelped but he just gripped two handfuls again and growled low.

"After the hotel and knowing what your sweet mouth and pussy felt like, it's all I've been able to think about. Maybe if I'd claimed you completely you'd stop playing these fucking games with me." He gave her ass another sharp smack.

"The hotel?" Her voice barely came out above a whisper as she looked over her shoulder at him. Did that mean he— "You remember that night?"

His mouth dropped open and his eyes narrowed. "You thought I forgot it?" The question was a mixture of disbelief and anger.

"You didn't say anything!"

"Neither did you."

She just stared at him. So he remembered. And he— He—

"You drove me so fuckin' insane that night." He kept her gaze as he dipped a finger in her pussy and dragged it along to press at her back entrance. "Now it's my turn."

He remembered that night. And he'd known it was *her*.

Her.

He'd called *her* gorgeous. He loved *her* body.

It seemed so obvious now with his body so hot on hers. They were a match. This was right. It always was between them. So why had it been so hard for her to believe it? Why was it always so hard to believe the good stuff?

He sank one knuckle, then two inside her. She clenched around him and moaned, her sex clenching too. Oh God, oh fuck, it was so hot. Was he really going to take her there? Would he fit? Would it hurt?

She was so caught up in him, in the craziness of everything they were doing, she didn't care. She wanted it to hurt if it meant what he said was true. If it meant it would mark her as his. She'd never belonged anywhere. And he wanted her to belong with him. God, that night in the hotel, he'd said he *loved*—

Nope. Couldn't think about that right now. Every nerve was on sensation overload. So instead she tried to shut her brain down and rely instead on her body and what it wanted.

And what it wanted was: "*More*," she groaned, twisting restlessly on the finger he had up her ass. "More, Hunter. You said you'd take me. Stop fucking around and do it."

He thrust his cock inside her pussy again. She cried out because *yes*, oh God yes. Not exactly what she meant but she'd take him wherever she could get him.

But then the next second he'd pulled out again. Slick with her wetness, the head of his cock pressed at her anus.

Her eyes popped open wide and her stomach swooped, both in anxiety and excitement as she wriggled her ass at him. An invitation.

His cock pressed in. He didn't shove. More like he kept up a constant pressure until her muscles gave way and let him in.

She grunted at the feel of him. His hands caressed her hips. "You're so beautiful. Christ, Bel, you're so fucking beautiful."

He leaned over and kissed along her spine even as he continued pushing in. Oh, *oh*, wow. It was— She felt—

"Bel, you giving me this, *Christ*." He groaned low once he was fully seated in her ass, squeezing her hip with the hand not bracing on the back window. "There's no going back."

He reached over her shoulder to tilt her head back so she was looking at him. And what she saw in his eyes was enough to have her catching her breath.

"No more running. No more games." He pulled out slowly and then pushed in again. Slowly, so achingly slowly. "You're mine now."

She was glad that he kissed her then because she didn't know what to— How could she— She kissed him fervently, hoping a kiss could communicate what she couldn't yet formulate in words.

"Touch yourself," he whispered. "I don't have a good angle and I want to feel you come around me while I'm in your ass."

Her whole body shivered in delight at his words. He stroked in and out again. She reached and started rubbing her clit just like she did when she was alone. But she wasn't alone now. And that made it so much hotter. God. Oh *God*—

"Fuck that's so hot," Hunter whispered, his breath hot on her neck. "Stick two fingers in your cunt. Fuck yourself with your fingers, baby."

She let out a tortured moan as she obeyed. She was drenched and her fingers slipped right inside.

Hunter's cock jerked in her ass. "Now three. Three fingers." His voice was hoarse. Isobel's breathing went shallow. He was close to losing control. God, she could hear it. And it made her own need spark like nothing ever had before.

"I'm fucking myself," she said, her voice high-pitched and strained. "What now?"

"Aw hell, baby. Tell me what it feels like."

"I'm tight," she gasped. "My little cunt is a tight fit. I bet my ass is even tighter, though." When he next thrust in, she clenched around him with all her might.

"Bel. Oh Jesus. *Bel*. I can't— It's so fucking good. I'm gonna—"

His movements got frantic. He yanked out and then jammed back in her ass. Over and over, just *reaming* her out and God, oh *God*, it was so dirty and so goddamned hot. She fucked herself with her fingers and rubbed her clit with her thumb.

"Fuck! Isobel!" He grabbed both her hips and shoved himself so far inside her, her eyes popped open wide. And she shoved her fingers in and out and ground at her clit until— until—

"*Ohhhhhhhhhh*—" She screamed, fingers digging into the seat as Hunter's cum pumped into her ass and she rode out her own orgasm.

213

He slumped over her, breathing so hard it was like he'd just run a marathon. They were both sweaty and she was being mashed into the seat, but she barely cared.

"Shit, sorry Bel. Am I crushing you?" Hunter withdrew. He rustled behind her but she barely had the energy to look over her shoulder.

She felt limp and sated and for once, like everything was *right* in the world. It was such an unfamiliar, wonderful feeling, and she didn't want it to end.

But a few seconds later, Hunter was helping her tug her pants back up her legs. It was awkward and she had to twist and stretch her legs at odd angles before she finally managed to get herself back in order. She avoided Hunter's eyes. Because what now? After that insanely intense sex? Were they supposed to just—

"Hey." Hunter's voice was confident as he pulled her over to the passenger side and up onto his lap. He put his hand underneath her chin. "I meant it. No more games or misunderstandings or whatever the fuck's been keeping us apart. You're mine now."

Isobel gripped his hand so tight she hoped it left a bruise. He wasn't the only one who could leave marks. "And you're mine."

She didn't know what all that meant. What kind of commitment he was claiming, if any at all. Maybe he just meant she was his in this moment. Right here, right now, they owned each other completely. That was true enough. As for the future…

But thinking of the future only brought up the past. Would Hunter be holding her so snugly if he knew what kind of person she really was?

Fear lodged in her throat. How long before she failed him just like she did everybody? No more running, he'd said. But it was what she did best.

Not this time, she whispered internally. Not this time.

But as Hunter kissed her shoulder blades reverently as he slipped out of her ass, she wondered if she'd ever be capable of staying and being the woman he thought she was. She knew better. She'd fall apart again and he'd see her for the weakling she really was. She could hardly bear the thought of it.

"We should get going," she said, slipping off his lap.

Hunter grumbled something that sounded like assent but the next second he was pulling her back and kissing her breathless. He kissed all other thoughts out of her head.

When he kissed her like that, for just a moment, he made her believe that anything was possible.

Chapter 20
ISOBEL

"Well look who actually came home for once," Mel teased Isobel over breakfast several weeks later. Isobel's cheeks went pink.

It was true, she had been spending more nights at Hunter's cabin than at home lately. But ever since they'd reconnected—as in really *reconnected*—in the truck that afternoon, well, they couldn't get enough of each other.

It was work all morning in the clinic, then out to farm calls in the afternoon. Hunter was finally taking a hands-on role in her internship and she was learning more than she would have ever thought possible back in her stuffy Cornell classes. There was nothing like up close and personal experience with the animals.

Hunter was patient as he helped her learn the difference between how a heifer's ovaries felt when she was ovulating and ready to breed and when she wasn't at peak cycle. They'd been called out for more calvings than she could count since it was the season for it—they didn't always end happily, but she learned more and grew more confident with each one. While there was nothing to be done about stillborn calves sometimes, they hadn't lost a mother cow yet.

Isobel had always known that working with horses made her feel good, but she hadn't expected the bone-deep satisfaction of saving an animal's life that people depended on for their livelihood. They were both saving an animal *and* helping people. It brought an insane rush of adrenaline each time. If she were doomed to be an addict, she might as well channel her impulses toward healthy obsessions.

"You just let us know if that boy isn't treating you right," Mel's husband Xavier said gruffly. Several of the other guys at the table chimed in, agreeing with him.

Isobel smiled at Xavier. "Hunter's great."

Xavier just grunted. "He better be."

It had taken Isobel a little while to get used to Xavier's scarred face. He was such a big man, and then with his face—it was hard not to be intimidated. But then she saw how clearly his wife and sons

216

adored him and after a few weeks she barely noticed the scarring anymore. His older son especially seemed to idolize him. Even though Reece was officially manny to both boys, Dean spent half his day out shadowing Xavier, imitating whatever his father was doing.

Currently, Dean was sitting across the table from Isobel, crammed in between his brother and his father. "Daddy, Daddy." He grabbed at his father's giant forearm while Xavier lifted a biscuit to his mouth. "Can we go now? Look, I finished my spinach." He held up his empty plate for his father's inspection. "You said I could ride with you if I ate it. Can we go?"

"Me come too!" said Brent, turning and standing up on his chair, holding the back of it for balance.

"Whoa, buddy," Reece said, snatching Brent up and setting him back on his bottom. The little boy jumped right back up again like a jack in the box. "I wanna go with Daddy and Dean!"

Dean rolled his eyes.

It was such an exasperated expression to see on a six-year-old that Isobel had to choke back a laugh.

"Tell you what, bud," Xavier stood up, wiping his mouth with his napkin as he went, "later today when I finish up my work, you and me will go around and pet the horses together. Just you and me. Deal?"

"I wanna go now!" the little boy shrieked.

"Whoa, Brent," Reece said, "that's not how we talk to—"

But Xavier already had Brent up in his arms, his face only inches away from the little boy. "Do you want to have special time with Daddy later or not?"

The little boy's lip trembled, his face uncertain. "I wanna go now."

Xavier arched a warning eyebrow. "Do I need to count?"

The little boy's eyes widened and he shook his head. "No, daddy. I be good."

Xavier smiled and his whole face warmed. "You're always my good boy. Daddy loves you." He rubbed noses with his son, then tossed him up in the air and caught him again. Brent shrieked and giggled.

"Xav, don't," Mel said when he went to toss him again. "All his breakfast will come back up."

217

"One more time?" Both father and son looked pleadingly at Mel. She waved a hand and rolled her eyes. "Don't come crying to me if you end up with pancake all over you."

Up Brent went into the air again. Then Xavier kissed him on the top of his head and patted his behind before sitting him back down in his chair.

Isobel took a last bite of her eggs and bagel before moving her chair back when Liam came and grabbed the seat beside her that Jeremiah had just vacated.

"So, birthday girl, what kind of cake do you want Nicholas to bake for dinner tonight?"

"Oh that's right," Mel said, raising a hand to her head, "I almost forgot. Happy birthday, Isobel."

Isobel waved a hand. "Oh. It's nothing."

"It's not nothing," Reece said, wiping Brent's face with a napkin. "Your birthday should be the most special day of the year."

"Which is why you've gotta tell us your favorite cake and liquor so we can have both on hand for dinner."

"That's so sweet, guys." Isobel put a hand on Liam's arm. "But Hunter's actually taking me out on a date tonight."

"Well of course he is. He'd be a brute not to wine and dine his girlfriend on her big day."

Liam's words made her freeze. Girlfriend? Yeah, she guessed she sort of was. Not that she and Hunter had sat down and made it official or anything.

Everything was just so wonderful... which was terrifying. It was like she was floating in some dream bubble and any second it would pop. Then she'd come crashing back down to reality. And it would be ten times more crushing to bear because she'd glimpsed what crazy happy could feel like.

"So we celebrate tomorrow," Liam continued. "Still need to know what kind of cake. Your American desserts are disgustingly sweet, but when in Rome," he shrugged and grinned. "I'm trying to develop my sweet tooth. So what'll it be?"

Isobel shook her head at everyone around the table staring at her expectantly. "Well, I actually don't like cake either. When I was little, my mom used to always bake me an apple pie on my birthday. It sort of became tradition."

"That's sweet," Reece said, hiking the little boy onto his hip. Only Reece could pull off such a maternal move and not seem a bit effeminate.

"Apple pie it is," Nicholas said. "Do you like crumble or pastry topping?"

"Crumble, if you know how. But really, you don't have to go through the trouble if you—"

"Consider it done."

Isobel couldn't help smiling as she walked out the door. The longer she stayed here, the longer everyone started to feel like the family she'd never had.

A thought which had the smile falling from her face. Because again, when was the other shoe going to drop?

God, did she have to be such a fatalist all the time? Maybe some people actually got to have a happily ever after?

Chapter 21
HUNTER

Hunter finished his pork chops and then just sat watching Isobel as she took dainty bites of her burger. He kept waiting for it to get old—watching her, finding out new little quirks of hers, waiting to find some habit that annoyed the hell out of him. Hunter hadn't done a ton of dating before Janine because well, he just hadn't found that many women that he wanted to spend time with.

Either they were interested in things he found mind-numbingly boring or they wanted more of his attention than he had to give. Or they wanted to change him. Or their voices were too shrill. Or they wanted to call him daddy in bed—

Yeah. He hadn't been big on the whole dating thing. But Isobel was just— Jesus, even when they were fighting he was still enthralled by her. And lately since they hadn't been fighting, he'd been able to find out even more about the way her intelligent mind worked. They talked for hours in the car between farm calls, and—

"What?" Isobel's eyes widened. "Do I have something on my face?" She immediately brought her napkin up and swiped around her mouth.

"No," Hunter laughed. "You're gorgeous as ever. The most beautiful woman I've ever seen in my life, actually."

She frowned and looked down at the tablecloth. She hadn't talked much throughout dinner. Actually she'd gone quiet about halfway through doing the rounds of farm calls this afternoon. Hunter hadn't pressed it because he knew there were days he didn't feel like talking much and he hated it when people constantly pestered him to know what he was thinking. Sometimes he just wanted to drive and let his mind wander.

But now he wondered if there wasn't more to it. Isobel looked upset.

"I wish you wouldn't say things like that." She set her burger down on her plate and pushed it away from her. Was she not hungry? He knew firsthand the burger tasted amazing. She'd offered him a bite earlier.

"Say things like what?"

She glanced up at him and then back down at her plate. "Never mind." She waved a hand but he could tell by the way her brow was furrowed that she was upset about something.

"Bel, talk to me. What's going on?"

Her jaw flexed and she grabbed her napkin, scrunching it into a ball between her fingers. He thought he was going to have to spend the next ten minutes pulling it out of her but she finally started talking. "Guys usually have a type when it comes to women, right?"

Um. What? Where was she going with this? Hunter slowly shrugged. "I don't know. I guess?"

Apparently that was the wrong answer. She nodded, looking like she was about to start crying even as she stood up and yanked her purse over her shoulder. "I'm tired. I'm gonna turn in early and—"

Hunter jumped to his feet and moved to stop her. "Bel. It's your birthday. We haven't even—"

But she was already hurrying to the door. And goddammit, all eyes in the diner were on them. Jesus. The diner was Gossip Central. Not the place to be having this conversation. Or argument. Or whatever the hell was going on.

Then again, Isobel was almost out the door. Swearing, Hunter fumbled for his wallet and threw a few twenties on the table, then rushed after her.

Outside on the sidewalk in front of the diner, he finally grasped her arm and spun her so she was forced to look at him. Only to find tears running down her cheeks. "Bel—"

She jerked out of his grasp. "I saw the framed wedding picture you keep in your glove compartment earlier when I was looking for hand sanitizer." Her eyes were both devastated and accusing as they flashed up at him. "You keep a picture of her in your *truck*? I guess you're not as over her as you pretend to be."

Hunter felt like she'd punched him in the chest. He couldn't help taking a step back from her.

She just started nodding rapidly. "That's what I thought. And I'm not exactly your type, am I? I'm not skinny or blonde or—" She broke off and shook her head. "Just forget it."

Hunter heaved out a deep breath and ran a hand into his hair. Christ. How did he even begin to untangle all this?

"Jesus, Bel, it's not about being blonde or— I mean, if I think about it I guess you and Janine do have some things in common." Speaking Janine's name hadn't hurt as much as he expected it to.

And suddenly he wanted to tell Isobel about her. As much for Isobel's sake as his own. He took a step closer to her, speaking quietly as he reached for her hand. She let him take it. "Janine was strong. And stubborn." He felt the familiar twinge in his chest every time he thought about her. "She was a good woman. Passionate. Rebellious." He smiled sadly.

"Do you still love her?"

Hunter let his eyes drift, thinking about the small blonde firecracker he had married. They'd made so many mistakes, but he liked to think the love had been genuine. He nodded. "I hope some part of me will always love her."

Isobel yanked her hand out of his and she backed up several steps. More tears shone in her eyes. Seeing her like that made Hunter's chest ache.

"Isobel, wait." Hunter started to follow her but she held up a hand.

"If you love your ex so much, maybe you should go find her and be having dinner with her."

Then, before he could grab her hand again, she turned and hurried down the sidewalk.

"Isobel. Isobel!" he called as she strode down the sidewalk, not looking back.

He jogged and caught up with her just as she reached her car that was parked on the street in front of the diner. "Isobel, stop. Shit. I didn't realize you thought—" He grabbed her shoulders and forced her to turn around when she didn't move.

Her mouth was pinched and she refused to look up at him.

Fuck. There was nothing to do but come out with it. "Janine died a little over a year ago."

If he thought saying her name was hard it was nothing to uttering that sentence. He felt like he'd been punched in the stomach as soon as he got it out. He dropped Isobel's shoulders and put a hand against her car to steady himself.

"What? Oh my God, Hunter. The night we met, you just said she left, so I assumed…" she trailed off and Hunter ran a hand through his hair.

"Yeah. I haven't been so great at being able to talk about it. Or deal with it. At all. I even kept on paying her cell phone bill so I could call and hear her voice. It's only just recently that I've been able to…" Hunter paused as a middle-aged woman walked past with a big dog on a leash. The sun had just set and while there weren't a lot of people around, there were still some.

"Want to take a walk?" He held out his hand to her.

She nodded and took it. As soon as he felt her small hand in his, he felt calmer. Like maybe he could tell the story after all. For the first time since giving his statement to the police that night.

"She hated living in a small town. Almost from the first day we moved in." He explained a little about how things had gotten worse and worse toward the end.

"It was one of those nights after we'd, well," he looked away, "been intimate. But then right afterwards, she left to go sleep on the couch. I got pissed. I followed her and we started fighting."

Hunter remembered every detail of that night. Janine had been wearing his ratty old Purdue shirt to sleep in. She was beautiful but he hadn't been able to see it. He was so *tired* of the rut they'd fallen into.

"What do you want from me?" he'd demanded.

She accused him of not loving her.

"Not love you?" he scoffed. "You think I'd put up with all this bullshit if I didn't love you?"

Her eyes flashed with fury and she got right up in his face. "You don't even know me! If you knew me at all, you'd know I could never be happy out here in the bu-fuck middle of nowhere, living with all these uncultured *hicks*. I want to talk to someone who's read this week's New Yorker. I want to go to the theater. I want to go to poetry readings and wine tastings and then I want to put on a skimpy sequin dress and go clubbing and then in the morning I want to go eat a bagel and lox at Benny's on the corner of Broadway and Bleecker."

"So, what?" Hunter threw up his hands. "You want to just up and move back to Soho?"

It was a rhetorical question but Janine shoved her hands on the table and shouted, "Yes! That's exactly what I want."

And then she'd gone to the bedroom and started packing.

"What?" Hunter had scoffed. "You're just leaving? Right now?"

"Right now."

"But it's the middle of the night."

"Well I can't stand spending another minute in this house."

Hunter took several steps back from the bedroom at her words. That was when he'd gotten it. She meant it. She was actually leaving him. It had come to this. How had it come to this?

His wife. His beautiful, neurotic, infuriating wife, was about to walk out the front door and out of his life.

And that was when he knew none of the rest of it mattered. Not the mortgage on the house. Not the veterinary practice he was in the process of taking over from Dr. Roberts. Not even his parents.

Janine was his *wife*. She was his first priority. And he'd failed her. He could deny it all he wanted her, but he'd known she was unhappy.

Hunter looked over at Isobel. They'd stopped walking right by the little city park along main street. Her eyebrows were drawn in compassion as she listened to him talk.

"Just a little more time, I kept telling myself." He shook his head at how stupid he'd been. "Just a little more time and she'll adjust."

"But if you realized that… Before she left, I mean," Isobel said, confused.

Hunter shook his head again. "It was too late. I tried to talk to her. I said that okay, we'd move to Manhattan. That I wanted to go with her. That I was sorry. That she was the most important thing to me."

But Janine had pulled away from him and grabbed her suitcase. She said she needed some time by herself. She said she had to think.

"And then she got into her car and drove off." Hunter's voice was bleak and Isobel reached out and took both of his hands.

"What happened?"

"Car accident," Hunter whispered. "It was winter. The roads were icy. Her car slid on a curve and she ran into a tree. Died on impact."

Hunter had to strain to get the next words out. It was the worst bit of all—the part that kept him up at night torturing himself. "But from the time of night and the angle of her car—" His voice broke but he shook himself, determined to tell Isobel everything.

"She wasn't leaving town. It was right before dawn. She'd driven about two hours away and had turned around. She was coming back. For me. She left because of me and came back because of me. She died because of me."

Isobel's hands went to his face. "No, Hunter, no, that's not true—"

"I know," he nodded, swallowing hard. "I know."

"Do you?" Her eyes searched his.

He huffed out a short, slightly bitter laugh. "Knowing in here," he tapped his head, "and believing in here," he put a hand to his chest, "are two different things."

He breathed out, feeling like a weight had lifted off his shoulders. "But I'm glad you know now. After Janine…" He shook his head. "I didn't think I could ever feel that way again. That I'd ever want to."

He reached up and covered one of her hands on his cheek. "But then you came to town. Even after that first night, I was already feeling so much for you. I'd been a dead man walking for a year and then—" He looked her in the eye. "It scared the shit out of me. *You* scared the shit out of me."

Isobel smiled, her eyes full. She flipped his hand so she could kiss his palm.

"But I'm not scared anymore." He moved back but still held her hands tight. "Bel, I love you. I can't lose you. It'll be August in a couple more weeks. I told myself not to think about the future, to just take this one day at a time. But dammit, Bel, I can't do that anymore."

"Because I want a future with you. I want it all. I want to wake up with you every morning and have babies with you and grow old together. I won't make the same mistake twice. We can live wherever you want to. Whatever will make you happy. As long as it's together."

And then he dropped to one knee. "Isobel Bianca Snow, will you marry me?"

Chapter 22

ISOBEL

"No!" Isobel jerked her hand away from his. She didn't mean to. It was just automatic.

But God, everything he'd just said, God. Growing *old* with her? *Babies*?

He had no idea. This man who'd already been so broken by the last woman he'd loved. He had no idea about her.

She saw the devastation hit his face at her rejection.

"Hunter, you don't—" She scrambled for words to make him understand. The last month had been the happiest of her life. Of course she wanted a future with him.

But that didn't mean it was something she had to give. God, look how obsessive she'd gotten after seeing the picture of his wife. All the old thoughts and insecurities had come roaring back in spite of the progress she thought she'd made since coming here.

She hadn't even meant to snoop. She'd just opened up the glove compartment and found the picture frame, face down.

As soon as Isobel flipped it over, all the air had swooped out of her chest.

In the picture, Hunter stood side by side with a gorgeous, petite blonde. Isobel's eyes had immediately zeroed in on the woman. She had such a tiny waist. Like impossibly tiny. Barbie tiny. And her clavicles. They were sharp, jutting out just like the models in magazines did. In fact, the woman might have well been a model.

The Hunter in the picture looked at the woman like she was his sun and moon and stars.

Like she was his life.

And Isobel's head had immediately jumped to the worst possible conclusions. Which was why she had to refuse his ridiculous proposal.

Didn't he see how screwed up she was? How *crazy*?

The furrow in Hunter's brow moved from pained to confused. But God, how did she even begin to explain? Apparently he was running out of patience, though.

"Talk," Hunter demanded. "Tell me why we can't have a future together. Do you not feel the same way about me? I know this is fast." He ran his hands through his hair. "I can slow down. Shit. I'm sorry. We can—"

"Hunter," she cut him off, pained. "Stop. There are things you don't know about me. About my past." She looked down at the sidewalk. "And my family."

"Then tell me." Hunter put a finger underneath her chin to lift her face. "I want to know everything about you."

Isobel pulled away from his grasp and walked to the center of the park where there was a white gazebo. A couple street lamps lit the path. "You say that now. But you don't know." She shook her head, tears pricking at her eyes.

"Don't tell me what I want." His voice was dark as he moved to keep stride beside her.

God, he wasn't going to let it drop, was he? She took a deep breath. He'd revealed things about himself tonight and now it was her turn to be brave.

"My mother committed suicide when I was eight years old. She hung herself from the ceiling fan in her bedroom while my dad was at work. I was the one who found her."

"Jesus Christ," Hunter hissed out and then the next thing she knew, his strong arms were around her, pulling her to his chest. "When you were just eight?"

Isobel nodded into his chest. For a moment, just a moment, she let herself absorb his warmth and comfort, but then she pulled away from him. She needed to get the rest of this out. She needed him to understand.

"That's not all." Her voice was little above a whisper. "My whole life everyone told me how much like my mom I was. I looked like her. I was quiet and bookish like her. But only my dad knew that I was emotional and had black moods like she did. Still, everyone talked. After she…" Isobel's voice trailed off. "Well, after that, it was like everyone was just waiting for me to turn out the same. To turn out crazy like her."

Hunter's nostril's flared. Isobel cringed, waiting for him to pull away from her. "People said that to you?"

Isobel shrugged. "It was just the way the grown-ups would look at me. But they must have talked about it behind closed doors because the kids would say it to my face." *Insane Isobel, gonna crack like crackers. Just like her mom.*

"I started seeing a therapist right after Mom died. Apparently I was very *at risk*. That was the term they used. At risk."

"Motherfuckers," Hunter spat. "Your dad was okay with that?"

Isobel shrugged. She didn't really remember a lot about Dad from that period. He worked a lot and she spent most of her time with the nanny and her therapist.

Isobel walked up the gazebo steps. Hunter hurried behind her and swiped a little dirt off the bench seat so they could sit down. It was easier, telling him all this in the dark where she didn't have to look at his face.

"Anyway, a couple years later, he got remarried. A woman named Catrina. I didn't get along with her very well. There were a few rough years." She didn't want to go into all that. It was hard enough to get this out as it was. She finally turned toward Hunter. "What I'm trying to get at with all this is that they were right. I did turn out just like my mom."

"What are you saying?"

Isobel's hands fidgeted in her lap. Then she took a deep breath. Now or never. "I tried to commit suicide when I was sixteen." Isobel squeezed her eyes shut. She couldn't bear to see if he cringed or pulled away from her. "It was right after I'd gotten out of a clinic for an eating disorder. I didn't feel like being there had fixed anything and when I got home, things with my stepmom were harder than ever. So I swallowed some pills. A lot of p—"

She couldn't even finish her sentence before one of Hunter's arms went around her waist and the other pressed her head to his chest.

"Christ, Bel, I'm so sorry you had to go through all that." He laid his cheek on her head.

The tears she'd been keeping back finally spilled over. She tried to pull away from Hunter but he just kept her pressed fast to his chest. Goddamn him. Didn't he realize every second he held her meant it would hurt that much worse when he didn't want her anymore?

"You're not listening," she said, pounding at him. "I'm trying to tell you how fucked up I am. My eating disorder relapsed just this summer after my dad died and—"

"Your dad just died?" Hunter finally pulled her back, only far enough so that he could look at her face.

She wiped furiously at her tears, hating that he was seeing her like this. "At the beginning of April. But Hunter, you're missing the point. I'm—"

"You were grieving," he said firmly. "Who wouldn't be screwed up by that." Then he cupped her cheeks, holding her face in a firm grip. "Do you still think about hurting yourself?"

"No." The response was automatic. And true. "Even when it's bad, I've never gone there again."

Hunter nodded, then pulled her tight to him again. "Because you know, deep down, you deserve everything. A good, full life. You're worthy, Isobel Bianca Snow. You're beautiful and you deserve every good thing life has for you."

How could he— Hadn't he just heard what she'd—

She jerked violently away from him, shoving him back and stumbling to her feet. "I'm broken. I'm no good for someone like you. No matter how hard I try, it won't make a difference. I'll always end up back there." She threw a hand behind her. "Don't you get it? I'm terrified all the time. Why do you think I run so much?"

Isobel put her hands to her head and looked upwards at the dark gazebo ceiling. "Every day I see her there, hanging. God, it was so horrible. How could she *do* that?" Her voice was getting hysterical but she didn't care. "How could she just leave me? Why didn't she love me enough?"

"No, Isobel, don't say that." Hunter got to his feet and approached her but she held her hand out to stop him.

"It's true. I wasn't good enough for my own *mother*."

"Christ, Bel. She was just sick, she didn't—"

"Exactly." She was crying so hard her tears nearly blinded her. "And I'm sick the same way. What if I did that to you? Or God forbid I ever…" Her hands went to her stomach. Oh God, she and Hunter hadn't always been safe when they'd had sex… Wait no, she'd just

229

had her period a couple weeks ago and they'd been using condoms since then. She dropped her hands and breathed out in relief.

But a man like Hunter deserved children. And she'd never trust herself around them. She sobbed so hard her chest hurt.

"Please let me hold you." Hunter's voice was ragged. "It's killing me seeing you like this and not holding you."

Isobel didn't have anything left so she just shrugged. Hunter must have taken that as a yes because he dragged her against him. Then he sat down on the bench and pulled her into his lap, cradling her to his chest.

He rubbed her back and whispered soothing sounds in her ear. "Shhh, you're going to be all right. It's all going to be okay. I promise. Do you hear me, Bel? I swear we're going to make it all turn out okay."

Isobel just buried her face in his chest. She hadn't even told him about Catrina or the real reason she'd come to Wyoming yet. She didn't have the strength for it right now. His arms around her felt so good, so safe. When he said everything would be all right, stupidly, impossibly, she wanted to believe him.

She knew better. Lord above, she knew better. Good things didn't last. She couldn't shed her DNA like last winter's coat. She couldn't outit at all aprun it, no matter how hard she kept trying.

Her hands fisted in Hunter's shirt as she tried to gather the strength to do the right thing—to push him away for his own good once and for all.

But before she could muster it, his phone started ringing in his jeans pocket.

"Shit," he swore. "I'm on call. I have to get that."

She nodded and climbed off his lap. To be honest, she was glad for the interruption. She was so confused. Being in Hunter's arms felt amazing. Like always, it felt *right*.

It was selfish to want him, though, when she was a ticking time bomb. She crossed her arms over her chest while Hunter stood up and answered the phone.

He nodded several times. "How long has the cow been down?" More nodding. Hunter sighed and pinched the bridge of his nose. "Okay Alex, I'll be out there in thirty minutes."

He hung up the phone and looked over at Isobel. She tried for a wan smile. "So we're off to look at a sick cow?"

Hunter breathed out. He clicked his phone back on and checked the time. "About that. I'm supposed to be getting you down to Bubba's for a nightcap."

"What?" Isobel asked in confusion.

"God, Mel's gonna kill me." He ran a hand through his hair. "But it'd be shitty to just send you in there like this. It's a surprise party."

Isobel's face must have shown just how horrified she felt by the idea because Hunter crossed the short space between them and took her hands.

"Look, it's shit timing. I'm sorry. I'm sorry about all of this. I was supposed to make you feel special on your birthday and instead I brought up all this heavy shit. And now I've got to leave and take care of this call." He winced. "Why don't I just call Mel and tell her you're tired and not up for it tonight?"

Isobel thought about Mel and all the guys waiting for her in the bar. They'd be disappointed if she didn't show. And they'd have questions.

She couldn't remember the last time she'd had that—people who wanted to celebrate the good times with her and noticed and cared about her enough to press when things were bad. If she'd ever had it at all, apart from the summer with Rick's family at the stables. In the short months they'd all had together, the people at the ranch had started to feel like family.

"No, it's all right," Isobel finally said. She could grin and bear it for a few hours. Who knew, maybe being around everyone would help her forget her troubles for a while? Or at least help her put off making a decision. She was, after all, the queen of running away from things she didn't want to face.

Her shoulders slumped at the thought but she stood and walked down the stairs and headed toward the sidewalk. Bubba's was at the end of the block on the other side of the road. There weren't any more cars parked out front than normal. They must have all either parked in the back or on side streets to keep up the illusion that it was just a regular night.

Hunter was quickly by her side, his hand sliding into hers. It was such a simple gesture, childish almost—holding hands. But Hunter's grip was so firm and solid that again, she was tempted to believe that anything was possible. That what if maybe, just *maybe*, her future didn't have to be as bleak as she always assumed?

How could a simple touch do that? But no, it wasn't just any touch. It was Hunter.

Ugh, she was tired of her rollercoaster thoughts and emotions. Didn't that just prove she wasn't stable enough to trust herself?

Before she could think on that too long, though, they were in front of Bubba's.

"Do you want me to come in with you?" Hunter asked, eyebrows furrowed in concern as he looked between her and the door.

"No." She shook her head and then went up on her tiptoes to kiss him. "Go see to the cow and then hurry back." She looked up at him through her lashes, trying to end the evening on a lighter note. "After all, I still need my birthday spankings tonight."

His eyes flared. "I'll hold you to that."

"You better." When he pulled her into him to kiss her, she couldn't help nipping at his lips. Lust flared through her body. At least this part was easy. There was zero confusion when it came to her body's response to Hunter.

Was it cowardly to ignore everything else and just revel in their connection for a little longer? She winced.

Gorging now and ignoring future consequences was an addict's logic.

Hunter's arms were around her again—how did she keep letting herself get caught in this position?

"I don't know what's going on in that head of yours," Hunter said, dropping his forehead to hers, "but I want you to think about one thing."

"What?"

"Look at me."

She'd had her eyes cast down but she leaned back just far enough so she could meet his gaze. He didn't say anything. She started to ask him what he was thinking but he just covered her lips with a finger. And stared into her eyes.

Like the first night they'd met.

They were fully clothed, standing on a public sidewalk in the center of town. But somehow it felt more intimate than the first time when he'd been naked and buried inside her. And far more terrifying.

She knew him now. She knew that when he slept he preferred the left side of the bed. But his favorite way to fall asleep was with his arm slung around her waist, right beneath her breasts, tugging her ass up against his groin. If they hadn't already made love that night then the position usually led to it.

She knew that while he could wake up as early as any of the farmers around, he was a bit of a bear before he'd had his first cup of coffee. She knew he loved animals but didn't have any pets because he didn't feel like he'd have enough time or attention to give them. She knew how he loved it when she teased him by ever so lightly scraping her teeth along the ridge of his cock right when he was on the edge of coming.

She knew all of that and a hundred other things. She'd found all that out in just two months. How much more was there to discover? She could spend a lifetime and not know him completely. Because he'd be constantly changing and evolving and oh *God*, how she wanted to be there to see it. To be part of it.

And in his eyes, she saw the offer—the offer of *everything*. No holds barred. No restricted access. She could have all of him if she'd just reach out and take it.

When she blinked, a tear streamed down her cheek.

Hunter finally spoke. "You keep talking about how you run away all the time. But what if you've been looking at it all wrong? What if it's not running *away* from the bad stuff? What if it's more about running *towards* something good?"

She could only blink at him. Everything she was feeling, and then his words… Could she really—

"I gotta go." He held her face and kissed her hard before pulling back again. He kept cupping her cheeks as he looked her in the eye. "I'll see you later tonight."

She nodded. She felt a bit speechless at the moment.

"Remember to act surprised."

She nodded again and he pressed another kiss to her lips before turning to walk toward his truck.

Isobel took a deep breath and then let it out through her teeth. After the emotional night of revelations and the freaking rejected *proposal*, all she really wanted to do was go climb in bed with a pint of Ben and Jerry's.

Hunter wanted to marry her. Could she even wrap her head around that?

Nope, she decided. Not at all. And there was still a surprise party to get through. So she tried to bottle up all her emotions as best she could, and then she turned toward the door.

"Surprised, act surprised," she whispered to herself.

Then she pushed open the door and put on her best surprised face.

Chapter 23

ISOBEL

The bar erupted as soon as she opened the door.

"Surprise!" was yelled from everywhere at once and a confetti cannon erupted right in her face. And into her open mouth.

Isobel coughed and waved confetti out of her face

"Jesus, Reece," Jeremiah said, smacking his twin on the back of the head. "Give the girl a second to catch her breath, will ya?"

"Oh no!" Mel laughed, coming forward and helping Isobel get confetti off her shirt and out of her hair.

As soon as she'd gotten most of the confetti out of her mouth, one server with a tray of champagne glasses handed one to her, and another approached with a big slice of apple pie. With a crumble topping.

Isobel took the pie and champagne, immediately looking around for Nicholas. He was always easy to spot in a crowd since he was a head taller than everyone else. He was standing toward the end of the bar near Liam, who was bent over his phone. She lifted the plate of pie toward Nicholas and mouthed *thank you.*

He nodded, then looked away, seeming embarrassed at the acknowledgement. That man. Mel was right. Whoever caught him would be lucky indeed. She handed off the champagne and took a bite of the pie—the waiter had brought a fork with it. It melted in her mouth it was so delicious.

People crowded all around to wish her happy birthday. Not just the guys from the ranch but everybody and anybody from the town who she'd even remotely had contact with through the veterinary practice. She was glad that Mel stayed by her side and helped her field all the well-wishers. She was glad too for the pie. Whenever she couldn't remember someone's name, she'd just take a bite. Except soon the pie was gone.

But then it was Liam to the rescue. He came and grabbed her arm right as one of the elderly farmers was starting in on how he was worried that switching to a cheaper feed might make his cows bloat.

"Sorry, I gotta steal the birthday girl away," Liam said, then snatched her and pulled her behind him.

Isobel waved at the disgruntled farmer. Then, after they were out of earshot, she whispered to Liam. "Thanks for the save."

"What?" Liam pulled her to the back corner of the bar where Mack was already waiting.

"Did you show her?" Mack asked.

"Show me what?" Isobel looked back and forth from Mack's grim expression to Liam's wary one. "What's going on?"

Liam tapped something on his phone before holding it out to her. "Do you know you're a missing person's case?"

Isobel grabbed the phone which had a video from one of the network morning shows keyed up to play. And there was Catrina sitting on the couch across from the famous host. Isobel's eyes widened and her heart sank through the floor.

"They're calling you The Missing Heiress," Mack said, reaching over and pushing play.

The camera focused on the hostess. "The public is fascinated by this case. Is it true your husband left your stepdaughter half a *billion* dollars in his will?"

The shot switched to Catrina. She'd had professional hair and make-up done but there seemed to be a few more lines on her forehead than Isobel remembered. What, had she been neglecting her botox injections?

"Yes, Isobel's father loved her so much. We both do. It's her birthday today." Catrina dabbed at her eye with a handkerchief. Isobel felt like hitting something. Catrina, crying over her? Yeah, when hell froze over. "I just want to know that she's all right. That she's safe and getting the help she needs so she can receive her inheritance and live the life her father and I always wanted for her."

Isobel's hands clenched around the phone so hard she was afraid she'd crack it.

"When you say 'the help she needs,' what exactly do you mean by that?" The hostess tilted her head and looked at Catrina with a compassionate expression.

Catrina swallowed and sniffled dramatically. Isobel scoffed. "Overplaying it a bit, aren't we, mommy dearest?"

In her periphery, Isobel saw Mack and Liam look at each other but she ignored them as Catrina began to answer.

"Isobel is a… a passionate girl. At times, troubled." Catrina's eyebrows came together. "But I'm afraid, sometimes she just…" Tears leaked out of her eyes. "Well sometimes she can become unstable. Violent even. Towards herself and others."

Catrina stopped and broke down in sobs.

The hostess reached across and put a hand on Catrina's arm. "I'm a mother too. And so are many of our viewers out there watching."

The screen went back to a shot of just the hostess, staring straight into the camera. "Again, Isobel Snow has been missing since April 22nd, last seen driving a silver Toyota Carolla heading west on I-80."

A picture of Isobel appeared on the screen.

Isobel winced. Oh God. It wasn't a bad picture. They must have gotten it from her phone, but it was one Veronica had snapped of her smiling at Jason back when they'd all been at Cornell. Had they been sleeping together even back then or had it only started after she left?

They'd cropped Jason out of the picture but Isobel couldn't help wondering if Catrina chose it because she was hoping to get a reaction out of Isobel.

"Do you have any last words in case Isobel or anyone who might know her whereabouts is watching this?" the hostess asked Catrina, who seemed to have barely recovered from her most recent sobbing fit.

The camera focused back on her. "Just please, please, Izzy bear. It's time to come home. Everything will be forgiven. Just come home and get what you're due." Then a number flashed across the bottom of the screen.

Isobel slammed the phone back into Liam's hand and turned away, barely managing to stop her scream of fury. *Izzy bear* was the nickname her mom—her real mom—had given her. It always set her off when she'd heard it after her mom died. And Catrina knew it. The bitch knew it and she was trying to goad her.

Plus, what was all that bullshit about Dad leaving her the money?

"Iz?" Liam asked cautiously.

"It's bullshit." She swung back around to him. "My dad didn't leave me squat." He couldn't even look at her in the end. "Catrina had

237

him so wrapped around her little finger." Isobel was shaking, she was so mad. "The first thing she would have done was made sure his will was changed so she'd be the sole beneficiary."

"I don't know what that shit was about." Isobel waved her hand toward the phone that was still in his hand. "Maybe some sort of trick to get me to turn myself in. Like I'd be stupid enough to go back just for the money."

"Turn yourself in?" Mack asked at the same time Liam said, "Whatever's going on, just tell us. We can help you. We can—"

"When did that air?" Isobel interrupted both of them.

"This morning," Liam answered.

She turned away from them, shoving a hand out behind her. "Just give me a second," she said, knowing they were following her. "I just need a second to think."

Her first impulse was to run.

Go get in her car and start driving. They knew she'd been on I-80. That interstate led in almost a straight shot across the country to Wyoming. She could go south. Bleach her hair blonde. Cut it short. Head to Mexico.

What if you're not running away *from the bad but are actually running* towards *something good?*

If she ran now, she wouldn't be running toward anything good. All the good was here. The good was Hunter. And Mel. And Liam and Mack and Nicholas and the twins and Xavier and the boys. It was the animals she got to work with every day. It was this tiny nowhere spot on the map that had embraced her.

She stopped pacing.

No more running.

All along she'd been looking for what she'd found here. A place to belong. Family who loved her unconditionally. People who built her up instead of tearing her down.

When Hunter got back tonight, she'd tell him everything. Whatever repercussions she had to face from her past mistakes, they'd face them together.

And if it was too much for him? Her heart hurt at the thought. But it was better to know that he couldn't handle all her baggage before she got even more of her heart invested in him. She was stronger now.

Every day built her confidence. She'd do her damnedest to handle whatever life threw at her.

And in the meantime?

She took a deep, cleansing breath in. In the meantime, she was going to enjoy the hell out of her party.

She turned back to Mack and Liam with a bright smile. "How about this? I promise I'll tell you *all* about it—tomorrow. Tonight, can we just kick back and have a great time? Can you guys do that for me?"

Mack and Liam exchanged a glance. Mack was the first one to speak up, stepping forward and offering her a quick embrace. "Whatever you need, beautiful. You just let us know."

She pulled back, laughing as she looked at the two of them. "Wow." She glanced over their shoulder. "Did I miss the flying pigs?"

"What?" Liam frowned like he was questioning her mental stability.

"The two of you." She gestured between them, laughing. "I thought the two of you would only get along when pigs flew."

"Ha. Ha," Mack said, completely straight faced, muscled arms crossed over his chest.

Liam laughed and pointed at Mack. "What, me get on with this tatted up bastard? You off your nut?"

"What are you guys doing over here in the corner hogging the birthday girl?" Reece came up and took Isobel's hand, then bowed over it and brought it to his lips. "May I have this dance, oh ye fair maiden?"

Isobel put a hand to her chest. "Why I would be honored, sir."

"I call dibs next," Liam said as Reece pulled her toward the area in the middle of the bar where people had gathered and started dancing to the music—country, naturally. But like Liam had said earlier today, *when in Rome.*

She spent the next half hour laughing, dancing, and mingling. She could really get used to this taking-life-as-it-came thing. Why did she spend so much of her life so damn worried all the time?

She took a break from dancing as the twanging notes of steel guitar faded. Her, actual enjoying country music. It was definitely a night of firsts.

She fanned herself as she headed toward the bar where Jeremiah and Nicholas were sitting together. She dropped to an empty barstool beside them.

"It's hot in here. Do you guys feel hot? God, I'm so hot."

"Well I could have told you that, love," Liam said, coming over and handing Isobel a tall mug of beer. She took it gratefully and pressed it against her heated cheek. Then she took a deep swallow. But she only felt more thirsty and hot afterward. She set the mug down on the table, sloshing beer over the sides. She barely noticed though, she was so busy fanning herself again.

She looked around the busy bar. "Where's Hunter? He said he'd hurry back."

"He's not coming back."

"What?" Isobel swung around. The voice had come from behind her, she was sure, but when she looked, no one was there.

"Isobel?" Nicholas asked. "You okay?"

"Huh?" Isobel turned around and looked at Nicholas and the others who were watching her. She swiped at the sweat on her brow but then blinked. Her hand felt weird. Swollen. Too large for her arm, like she had a giant lobster claw for a hand. What the—

She jerked her hand in front of her face and shook her head.

Okay. It was normal. Not swollen.

"Aw, is poor little Isobel finally going crazy? Cracking like crackers?"

"Who said that?" Isobel turned so fast her head felt like it moved more quickly than the rest of her body.

"Whoa," Nicholas said, reaching out and steadying her. "Honey, who are you talking to?"

"Hearing voices is how it starts, you know."

Isobel jerked away from Nicholas, looking all around her, trying to figure out who was talking. "Do you hear that?" she asked the guys who were all staring at her like… like she was crazy.

"Crazy. Just like me, baby girl."

Isobel spun around and then she screamed.

Because there, dangling from the neck by a rope, was her mother, her toes barely scraping the bar top.

Chapter 24
ISOBEL

Isobel tried to run forward to help her mom down, but her legs wouldn't work. They were distorted like in one of those carnival mirrors.

"Mom!" she cried out, reaching out. If she could just get to her in time, if she could cut her down before—

"Why didn't you save me?" her mom gasped, her hands going to the rope around her neck as her legs started to twitch horribly.

"Mom!" Isobel screamed, again and again, but it was like a faraway sound—a tinny recording on one of those old tape players her dad used to keep around.

Why couldn't she get back in her body? If she was human, she could cut her mom down.

She blinked and Mom was gone. But so was Isobel. Her body was gone. She was outside it. Separate from it. Separate from everything. Even time.

That meant she could go back and undo it all. She wouldn't let Mom leave them. She'd wrap Mom in her Supergirl cape to keep the bad thoughts away. And she'd always be a good girl so Mom would love her enough to stay.

Noises buzzed like insects all around.

Pulling her back.

No. *Mom.*

"Iz!"

"Isobel. Can you hear me?"

"Izzy, talk to us."

Hands.

Shaking her body.

"Isobel, talk to me. What's wrong?" Mack. Mack's voice. Mack's hands.

She looked down and it was like watching puppets. She watched the Mack puppet grab the Isobel puppet by the shoulders. But the

Isobel doll just stood frozen, looking over Mack's shoulder like a frightened rabbit.

She was dying.

No.

She was dead.

All of this—the little town of Hawthorne. Liam, Mack, the twins, Mel.

Hunter.

None of it had ever happened.

She was still sixteen years old, wasn't she? She'd just swallowed a bottle of pills. Her dad *hadn't* come home and found her in time.

People said your life flashed before your eyes when you died, but they never told you it was the future you got to see and not just the past—the future life you *could* have had.

But Isobel wouldn't get to live any of it.

There would never be a summer at the stable with Rick's family. There wouldn't be any of the years at Cornell or dating Jason or Dad dying of cancer. She wouldn't mind missing out on some of that.

But it also meant there would be no Wyoming. No Mel's Horse rescue.

No falling in love with the love of her life.

She'd miss it all.

And why?

Because she thought things were so miserable that she couldn't stand another day of it? Of living in that house with that woman talking down to her and making her feel two inches small?

God, there was so much more to life! It wasn't fair! She'd been just a kid. She hadn't known what choice she was making.

And now she never would.

So why? Why show her what she would never have? Why be so fucking cruel?

"Isobel! Thank God! I finally found you!"

Isobel had never believed any of the bullshit about how people who committed suicide went to hell but everything she was experiencing was making her question her belief.

Why else would Catrina be showing up in her afterlife?

Lightning flashed from all sides. Blood roared in Isobel's ears. When she focused her energy on Catrina, suddenly she was back in her body and flying toward the bitch.

Actually flying. Her feet barely touched the ground. Her body defied gravity. She was fucking invincible.

And she was going to make Catrina pay. She was a fucking superhero and this bitch was finally going down.

Ding dong, the fucking witch is *dead.*

Isobel crashed into Catrina with every ounce of momentum she'd gained, immediately taking her to the ground. Her hands wrapped around her stepmother's throat.

As soon as she did, though, Catrina's face distorted and her eyes started glowing red. Horns sprouted from her temples on both sides of her head.

"She's the devil!" Isobel shrieked. "It's Satan!"

But then suddenly bands of steel whipped out of nowhere. They wrapped around Isobel from behind and from the left and the right and she was ripped away from her target.

"No!" Isobel screamed. "It's the devil! I have to kill it. It has to die! I have to kill it."

But the monster that had gotten hold of her wouldn't let her go. It had so many arms. She fought and clawed but it has so many arms—

"What the hell is going on here? Isobel?"

Isobel looked toward the door and there was Hunter. He was bathed in golden light.

Hunter.

Sent from heaven. The love she could have had. The future that might have been hers. If it hadn't been stolen by Satan.

She roared and threw off the arms that held her back. Then she barreled forward through all the shields surrounding the devil.

Isobel was already in hell. But she wouldn't go down without taking Satan with her.

Chapter 25
HUNTER

Hunter had no idea what the *hell* was going on. He'd hurried back from the farm call as quickly as he could—the cow had milk fever and had just needed a dose of calcium and magnesium. She was up on her feet in no time.

Then to get back here only to find Liam, Reece, and Jeremiah trying to restrain Isobel, who looked so furious she was about to burst a blood vessel. Not to mention the TV crew and gaggle of reporters that had descended on the bar. They were snapping shot after shot of Isobel like fucking paparazzi.

His eyes went back to Isobel. She did *not* look okay. Her face was red and sweaty and she was snarling that she was going to kill someone. The way she was staring at the woman across the room cowering behind several reporters made it pretty clear who.

Hunter started toward Isobel but all of the sudden, Isobel screeched at the top of her lungs and somehow jerked loose of the guys. She charged at the group of reporters like a raging bull. One of the bastards tried shoving a microphone in her face. "What does it feel like to see your—*oh*!"

Isobel shoved him violently aside, clearly trying to get to the tall, statuesque woman behind him.

Hunter jumped forward as Isobel screamed something that might have been, *Satan!*

What the *fuck* was she on? If one of the guys had given her some goddammed party drug to help her have a 'good time' on her birthday, he swore he'd kill the fucker.

"Bel!" he yelled right as her hands went for the woman's throat. He wrapped his arms around her waist and pulled her backwards. Her legs flew up and she immediately started thrashing wildly.

"Satan! Have to kill Satan!"

He saw how she'd gotten away from the guys earlier. She was using every ounce of strength she had to fight and it was like she didn't care if she hurt herself to do it. The way she was thrashing, she was likely to dislocate her own arm but it wasn't stopping her.

Hunter carried her toward the back wall, all the guys and Mel grouping around him as he went. "Nicholas," he nodded to the largest man, straining to hold on to Isobel who was still fighting like a hellcat.

"Bel. Isobel. It's us. It's Hunter. You need to calm down, honey." Hunter tried to flip her around so she was facing him but she just used the opportunity to thrash out and elbow him in the face.

"Damn." He grabbed his jaw as Nicholas took hold of Isobel from behind. He crossed her arms over her chest and held them down at her sides like a straightjacket and then gripped her in a backwards bear hug.

"What happened?" Hunter asked, looking around from one shocked face to the next.

"I don't know," Liam said, jerking a hand through his hair. "One second she was fine, dancing and partying. The next it was like she was hearing voices. Then when her stepmom and the film crew showed up she just freaked the feck out."

Hunter's head jerked around to look at the woman Isobel had attacked. Her stepmother. Who was currently talking to Marie. The Sheriff. And pointing in their direction.

Shit. "We don't have much time," Hunter said. "Did any of you give her any drugs?"

"Fuck you," Mack said, stepping into Hunter, eyes cold.

Hunter wasn't backing down. He went chest to chest with Mack. "She's high as fuck on *something*."

"None of us gave her anything," the dread-lock twin said.

"Well what has she had to drink since she's been here?" asked his brother. He looked around at the little group. "Someone could have roofied her drink."

"That's no roofie," Mack said darkly. "More like fucking meth or angel dust."

"They handed her some champagne when she came in but I don't think she even drank it," Mel said.

"It could be food too," Hunter said. "Something she ate. We ate at the diner a couple of hours ago but I ate off her plate and I'm fine. Did she eat anything here?"

"Just the pie Nicholas made," Mel said. "A waiter gave her a piece as soon as she walked in the door."

"Did one of you tell him to do that?" Hunter asked.

Everyone in the group looked around at one another. Isobel had quieted down with a zoned out look on her face. Christ. They needed to get her to a doctor and find out what the hell was in her system.

Hunter looked at everyone. "So? Did anyone tell the waiter to give her the pie? Were they walking around giving pie to everyone else?"

"They were handing out champagne to everyone," Mel said, "but not pie."

"You think someone put something in the pie before they gave it to her?" Reece asked, obviously horrified.

"Pie?" Hunter shook his head in confusion. "Why was there pie anyway?"

"It was a family tradition," Jeremiah spoke up. "From when she was a kid. She'd have apple pie for her birthday instead of cake. She told us about it this morning."

"So who else would know she always ate pie on her birthday?" Mack asked, anticipating Hunter's next question. "If that's how they drugged her?"

"We were the only ones there," Mel said, looking around the small circle.

"No. There's someone else who would know." Hunter turned around and looked at Isobel's stepmother. Marie had finished with her and she was apparently so distraught she just *had* to talk to one of the reporters. On fucking video.

"That bitch," Mel whispered.

"We've got to find the plate Iz was eating from," Jeremiah said. "There are probably traces of whatever she was dosed with."

"And find the goddamned waiter, too," Hunter growled.

"On it," Liam said, heading toward the back of the bar.

Marie strode toward them. Though she was petite with short blonde hair that made her look more like a pixie than an officer of the law, she walked with an air of authoritative confidence. She'd earned the respect of almost everyone in town a couple years ago when she singlehandedly solved one of the most brutal homicides the county

246

had seen in a decade. "Sorry guys, but I gotta take her in. Her stepmother is pressing charges."

"The hell you are," Mack said, stepping between Marie and where Nicholas was still holding Isobel. Nicholas hadn't let up on his grip, but Isobel had gone limp.

"She needs a doctor, not a jail cell," Jeremiah pushed Mack aside. "She's been drugged. Just look at her."

Marie frowned. When she stepped forward to look at Isobel, Mack tried to block her again but Jeremiah shoved him back. The two men glared at each other but Marie ignored both of them. She took out a pen flashlight and shined it in Isobel's eyes. Isobel flinched from the light but gave no other reaction.

"She's on something all right," Marie said. She stood up straight and looked around at all the tall, intimidating men around her. She only came up to Jeremiah's chin but she didn't back down. "But she's heading to lockup first. Then she'll receive medical attention."

Mack started to interrupt her but she cut him off. "And if any of you so much as *think* of interfering with an officer of the law, I'll haul your ass in with her." She leveled each one of them with a cold stare that dared them to fuck with her.

Then she turned back to Isobel. "All right, honey. I'm gonna take you in now." She looked up at Nicholas as she pulled out a pair of cuffs. "Let her go, please."

"Are handcuffs really necessary?" Reece asked.

"Standard protocol for a 10-15 call."

"You swear you'll get her checked out first thing?" Hunter demanded.

Marie nodded, looking him straight in the eye. "We've got Dr. Lucero on call and I'll get him on the line as soon as she's in the squad car.

Hunter huffed out a breath, but letting her go with Marie was probably the quickest way to get her medical attention.

As soon as Nicholas let go of Isobel, it was like she came back to life. She flew at Hunter, grabbing his face in her hands. "I would have loved you. But you're not real. Just my beautiful might have been." She looked so devastated as she said it.

247

Hunter grabbed her around the waist. "I'm here. Bel, I'm right here and I'm not going anywhere."

But she just shook her head, a tear sliding down her cheek.

And then Marie was pulling her hands behind her back to put the cuffs on.

"I'll get to the bottom of this," Hunter said fiercely. "I swear." He kissed her even as Marie finished latching the cuffs and started pulling Isobel away.

"I swear I'll fix this!"

Isobel kept looking back at him as Marie led her out of the bar, hand on her shoulder.

He wanted to run after them. But what would that accomplish? He'd promised Isobel he'd fix this and he could do more here. Isobel would be safe at the sheriff's office and the doctor would see to her.

The reporters and cameramen tried to follow Isobel out the door but Marie barked at them. She handed Isobel off to one of her officers at the door and blocked the rest of the squawking reporters.

Damn it, he had to fix this. Fast.

Hunter looked around, then jogged over toward where Liam and Mack were questioning a young guy in a white button up shirt and black slacks. The waiter.

"Talk or I'll smash your fucking face in," Mack said right as Hunter got to them.

The kid's face went white.

Liam rolled his eyes. "Ignore this slap-happy bastard." He pulled out his wallet. "We can be civilized here." He took five one-hundred dollar bills out of his wallet and handed them over to the waiter.

The kid took the money with wide eyes. "That's way more than she gave me."

"Who?" Hunter and the other two asked at the same time.

"Her." The waiter pointed at Catrina. "She just said she wanted everything to be special for the lady's birthday. So I should make sure to give her the piece of pie as soon as she came in the door. Then she gave me the plate of pie and a hundred bucks." He held up his hands. "And she said it was a surprise so not to say who it was from."

"You fucking idiot," Mack muttered.

"The pie was dosed with something," Hunter said. "You helped drug that woman."

The waiter's eyes went wide as saucer's. "I didn't have anything to do with that."

"Then you better go tell the sheriff everything you just told us," Jeremiah said, leading the guy by the arm toward Marie, who was still fending off reporters at the door.

"Sheriff!" the radio at Marie's hip erupted loud enough to be heard across the bar. "Suspect is out of her cuffs. Attempting to apprehend now."

The bar went completely silent for a second.

And then Marie bolted for the door, the reporters and cameramen right on her tail. Hunter was right behind them.

"Get out of my way." He shoved at the people bottlenecked at the door. Shit. He yanked a skinny guy with a huge camera around his neck out of the way and finally made it outside.

Just in time to see Isobel sprinting down the center of Main Street. A fat deputy trailed her, huffing and losing distance with every step. Isobel was screaming words he couldn't make out. He immediately took off after her, noting with disgust that the fucking cameraman had set up his tripod and was recording the whole thing.

Isobel was more than half a block ahead of him and his heart all but stopped when she ran straight to her car.

"No!" he shouted. "No. Bel. Isobel!"

But like a nightmare doomed to repeat itself, he watched the woman he loved get into her car and then—

"Isobel. Stop!"

Her door slammed.

It was supposed to happen in slow motion. That was what he'd always heard about moments like this.

But Christ, no, it was just a blink of an eye and then it was over.

The engine rumbled to life.

Then the car jumped forward like she'd stomped the gas. Maybe thinking it was reverse? But it wasn't. It was in drive.

The car jumped the curb and ran straight into the front of the diner.

Glass shattered. All around, people shouted.

And Hunter ran harder and faster than he ever had in his life.

249

Chapter 26

HUNTER

They'd had to airlift Isobel to the hospital in Casper. Her injuries had been that severe.

In her altered state, she hadn't been clearheaded enough to put on a seatbelt.

PCP. They found fucking PCP in her bloodwork. Not just a little bit, either. Her stepmother had poisoned her. With her birthday apple pie.

And it had fucked Isobel up so much that she'd broken the bones in her left hand to get out of the cuffs without feeling a thing.

Then she'd gotten in her car and—

Hunter fisted both his hands and leaned against the hospital corridor wall. Blood. There'd been blood everywhere when he got to the car. And his Isobel was lying on the hood like a broken doll, her head and half her torso through the front windshield.

There was so much swelling on her brain, they'd had to induce a coma. That was four days ago. Now they were waiting for her to wake up. She should have woken up by now. Why the hell wasn't she waking up?

The door to her hospital room opened and Hunter jerked his head toward it. It was only Reece coming out, his face somber.

Still, Hunter couldn't help asking, "Any change?"

Reece shook his head. But then he closed his eyes and took a deep breath in. With a decisive nod, he opened his eyes. "But Izzy's strong. She'll make it through this."

Hunter didn't reply. Janine had been strong too. Hunter knew all too well that sometimes it didn't matter how strong you were or how much you prayed or how fair it was. Death was going to snatch whoever he wanted, whenever he wanted.

Still, as Hunter walked into Isobel's room, he caught himself praying, "God, not this time. Not this one."

Seeing her so small and pale in her hospital bed hit him straight in the gut just like it always did. It was so *wrong*. She was supposed to be up, standing toe to toe with him, eyes flashing, calling him on his bullshit.

He went to her side and sat down in the chair that was rarely left unoccupied. They all took turns sitting with her. Xavier had the kids at home while the other guys took shifts driving back and forth to be here with Isobel and help with the horses.

Only Hunter and Mel had stayed at the hospital the whole time—though she'd eventually had to get a hotel to sleep at night, what with her being seven months pregnant. She'd offered to get Hunter a room too, but he'd declined. He didn't mind sleeping in uncomfortable hospital waiting room chairs. He needed to be there the second Bel woke up.

Because she *would* wake up. She had to.

"Hey Bel." He reached over and took her hand. "They said we should talk to you. Let you hear our voices. That you might be able to hear us even if you can't respond yet. So I just want you to know I'm here. I'm here and I'm not going anywhere."

He pulled her hand up to his mouth and kissed it. Her skin was so cold. He rubbed her hand between his to try to warm it up.

"Liam just got back from his turn with the horses. Thought you'd like to know that Bright Beauty's doing real well. Her back legs are healed up almost completely. Dean was begging to ride her so Xavier saddled her up. Liam said she seemed excited to have a rider again. Even if his feet could barely reach the stirrups."

Hunter attempted a smile but mostly failed. He kept trying to warm her hand up, then paused and reached over to pull up the blanket that had fallen down to her waist. "Gotta keep warm, honey."

He picked up her hand again after fixing the blanket. It lay so limp in his. His throat got tight.

Just keep talking.

"Things are moving forward in the case against Catrina. Thought you might like to know that too. Marie found another vial of PCP when she searched Catrina's purse." Marie had probable cause because of what the waiter had told her. "That was enough to throw her in lock up. Then Xavier and Mel got their lawyer involved. I guess he specializes in inheritance law. They looked into it with your dad's estate lawyer and it turns out it's true—he did leave all the money to you. But if your stepmom could get you declared mentally unfit—well, then she's still officially your next of kin."

Hunter's jaw clenched. He'd never thought himself capable of violence toward any woman, but he just might make an exception for Catrina Snow. She'd put Isobel through hell. Not just now. Isobel hadn't told him much, but it was clear enough that Catrina was a toxic presence in her life. And after what the attorney's PI had turned up...

Hunter's stomach went queasy at the thought of Isobel having to grow up with such a vicious, vindictive witch.

"When Xavier's lawyer contacted your father's estate attorney, the guy flew out here to confirm it was actually you. I don't know if you remember, but he's actually been in here a couple times. Dan. He and your dad were good friends. Your dad had asked him to look into a few things the last year. Like investigating the psychiatrist you saw throughout your teens."

Hunter had to let go of her hand because he was afraid he might crush it. Every time he thought about this part, he got so furious he wanted to break things. "It turned out there was a lot to know about Dr. Rubenstein. Like how he had a gambling habit. And how on several occasions, he just *happened* to have large sums of money deposited into his account. And how those deposits just *happened* to coincide with extravagant 'trips' your stepmother claimed she was taking a group of girlfriends on."

Hunter's hands balled into fists and he could feel his blood pressure rising. He paused and took several deep breaths. He looked back to Isobel and it killed him knowing she'd been abused by the people who were supposed to be helping her. "I'm so sorry, Bel. I'm so sorry that she had everyone believing her lies. That she even got the therapist involved to gaslight you and make you think you were crazy. Who the fuck does that?"

He took her hand again. "But your Dad knew. He knew in the end what they'd done to you. Dan gave him the report about a week and a half before he died. That's when he changed the will. Dan says he was horrified by it."

Hunter willed her to respond. Watching for any twitch.

Nothing.

"So with all that, the county judge set your stepmom's bail at half a million dollars. Without access to your dad's money, she's broke. She's being charged with attempted manslaughter and with felony possession. And those are just the charges she faces in Wyoming."

Hunter had run out of things to say. "I miss you, Bel. Please… just… please."

He watched her for any sign that she was hearing him.

But she continued lying still like she was frozen under some supernatural spell. Beautiful and perfect and young but forever out of reach.

Hunter looked around and, not seeing anyone, got up from his chair. He leaned over Isobel. He rolled his eyes at himself for being a fucking idiot, but still. He kissed her. He squeezed his eyes shut as he pressed his lips against hers.

Please, Isobel. I'm here. Can't you feel me here? Come back to me. Fight for us.

Her lips were soft as always, but unresponsive.

He pulled away, eyes searching her face for long moments.

Still nothing.

He huffed out a laugh at himself, then ran both his hands through his hair. Jesus, he was losing it. Like a kiss was going to just magically make her wake up.

He scrubbed his hands down his face.

Beep. Beep. Beep. Beep beep beep, beep-beep-beep-beep—

Hunter looked up in alarm to see the machines monitoring Isobel start to go crazy.

Isobel began convulsing.

"Isobel!" He reached for the nurse call button and punched it. "Help, we need help in room 301."

Jesus! Hunter reached out for her but didn't know where to hold her that wouldn't make things worse. "Fuck! Fuck!" He ran for the door. "Doctor!" he yelled.

But a team of doctors and nurses were already headed toward the room. Hunter pulled back to make way. "Her heartrate started going crazy and then she started shaking like—"

"We'll take it from here," said a male nurse, trying to usher Hunter out of the room while the others went to Isobel's side.

"She's going to be okay, right?" Hunter asked, shoving the man aside so he could see what they were doing to Isobel.

"Sir, if you'll just—"

Suddenly the beep-beep-beep of her heartbeat became a loud flat line.

Hunter screamed, "Isobel!"

Chapter 27
ISOBEL

Isobel woke up in a white room. White walls. White bedsheets. White floor tiles.

She sat up and swung her legs over the side of the bed, immediately lifting her hand to her forehead. Whoa. She felt dizzy.

"Hello?"

Where the hell was she?

The room was empty except for a man standing beside a window lit up by bright sunlight. The man was dressed in—of course—all white. They looked like comfortable white scrubs, or maybe a t-shirt and sweatpants.

"Hello?" she said again, standing up. She was struck by another wave of dizziness and had to hold onto the wall beside the bed to steady herself.

Her body felt weird. Oddly… light.

She shook off the feeling. There was something familiar about the man by the window. She took several more steps forward to investigate.

And then her mouth dropped open.

"Daddy?"

The man winced at her words and turned away as she ran forward and grabbed his arm.

It *was* him.

"How…?"

He looked healthy. His skin was flushed a healthy pink and he was on his feet—far from the emaciated man who couldn't even sit up in bed by the end.

"Isobel." Her name was heavy on his lips. His head sank to his chest as he said it and he lifted a hand to his temple like he was in pain. Because of her.

Her elation at seeing him again sputtered. Even in this miracle place where her father was healthy again, he still couldn't stand to be around her. His own daughter.

"I'll go." She backed away from him, her voice thick.

But as she started to turn, her father's hand shot out to stop her.

"No, Isobel." He finally lifted his head and what she saw on his face froze her in her tracks. Tears welled in his eyes.

"I'm so sorry. I don't expect you to ever forgive me. But I'm so, so sorry."

Isobel blinked, struck speechless.

"I failed you for years. Didn't believe you when you said—" He turned his face away from her. "I was too much of a coward to face things and make it right. And then it was too late. I know money can't make up for how I failed you but I just needed you to know—you were everything to me."

"Daddy!" Isobel threw herself into his arms and he wrapped her up in his embrace. She'd never felt such soul-deep warmth in her life.

"I needed you to know that, baby. I love you and I'm so sorry for how I failed you. But now you need to make a choice."

He pulled back from Isobel and pointed behind her.

She turned around and saw her body on a hospital bed, doctors working frantically all around her. And Hunter near the door, an orderly holding him back.

She swung back around to her father. "What? I don't underst—"

"Sure you do," her dad said, putting a gentle hand on her arm. "You're so beautiful." He reached out and touched her cheek. "Just like your mother."

Isobel jerked back from him. "Exactly."

Her heart sank as she looked back at herself on the bed. "I'm too much like her, Dad. This will be hard on Hunter. But," her voice cracked and she had to swallow before going on. "But maybe it's better this way—before I go crazy like mom and screw everything up. Or if we ever had children..." She shuddered at the thought. No, she'd never put a child through what she'd gone through. Better her heart stop beating while she lay on that hospital bed right this second.

Maybe this was what loving Hunter meant. Hurting him now to save him from the far greater hurt she might inflict later on.

"Baby, you aren't your mother," Dad said, his eyebrows furrowed. "All I ever wanted for you was to live your own life. I never wanted that single day to define you. It's why I tried to get you help." He shook his head but then took her hands, entreating her. "You're perfect just the way you are. Whether you come with me now or many, many years from now, please know that. You're perfect."

There was such sincerity in his eyes as he repeated it over and over. That she was perfect and he loved her just as she was.

But then he glanced over her shoulder.

"Not much time now. You've got to make a decision."

Isobel's throat went tight as she turned, looking back and forth from the hospital scene to her father. She didn't know what was the right thing to do.

"What if I can't decide? I mean, this is too big. I can't—"

"Doing nothing is making a choice."

She clutched her dad's hands.

"I'm scared."

"I know."

Her eyes moved from her still form on the bed to Hunter, fighting against the orderly, trying to get back to her.

I want a future with you. I want it all. I want to wake up with you every morning and have babies with you and grow old together.

Was she still running? Even now?

Wasn't Hunter and the life they might have worth facing her worst fears?

It was then that she knew what she had to do. She just hoped she wasn't too late.

"I love you, Daddy." She squeezed his hand.

He smiled and it was full of the morning sunlight. "I know that, too. Love you, baby."

And then she started running.

Toward Hunter.

Toward a future.

Toward life.

Chapter 28
HUNTER

"I've got a pulse!"

"Eye movement."

The orderly holding Hunter back released him and Hunter ran toward the bed.

"Isobel!" he called out. He stayed several feet behind the doctor and nurses, not wanting to get in their way.

Especially when he saw that they were right, Isobel was blinking and coughing and moving her head like she was trying to get her bearings.

"Bel!" he called, laughing and crying at the same time. One of the nurses moved aside and Hunter couldn't help himself. He fit himself into the empty spot at Isobel's side and grabbed her hand that didn't have the IV in it.

"I'm here," he said, lifting her hand and kissing it. "Bel, I'm here."

Isobel's eyes had been flickering wildly around but at his touch and voice, they settled on his face.

Her mouth opened up and it seemed like she was trying to say something.

She winced, dragging her hand to her throat.

"Water," Hunter called out. "We need some water over here."

Hunter had no idea who he was barking orders to or if any second they were going to try to boot him from the room again.

Screw that. His Isobel was alive and awake and nothing was going to drag him away from her side except the goddamned reaper himself.

Apparently someone had been listening, because the next second, he was handed a cup of water with a straw in it. He immediately held it up to Isobel's mouth, settling the straw between her lips.

She took a sip, then coughed a little, then took another sip.

She tried talking again. Her voice was still croaky and Hunter could barely make her out when she said, "Yes. My answer is yes."

"What?" Hunter asked, leaning in to hear her better.

She took another sip of water and then said louder, even though it looked like it was taking all her energy, "Yes, I'll marry you."

Did she really just—

Hunter let out a whoop and almost dumped the water over in his eagerness to kiss her. Then he pulled back and looked at the doctors and nurses still in the room. "Did you hear that? This woman's gonna be my wife!"

Isobel's exhausted giggle was the most beautiful sound he'd ever heard in his life.

Epilogue
LIAM

Liam's leg bounced up and down while the pastor droned on and on and on. For better or worse, for richer or poorer, yada yada. He had to scoff at that last one though. All the people who'd ever loved him had certainly only been in it for the riches.

Hunter had loved Isobel before he knew he was getting a half billion-dollar payday out of the deal, so they might be all right. Liam had tried to get her to write up a prenup but she wouldn't have it. Half a billion was chump change to him but he'd seen people lose their shit over *far* less.

"I do," Isobel said, beaming at Hunter.

"It's just so beautiful," Reece said from beside Liam, wiping his eyes with a handkerchief.

Jeremiah shook his head at his brother but Liam saw him swipe at his eye when he thought no one was looking.

Liam smirked at them. They were a good bunch. Well, except for Mackenzie. That guy was just an asshole. But the others... Liam glanced down the row at the twins and Nicholas. Xavier and Mel were sitting a row ahead of them with their sons—all *three* of them. The baby was napping quietly in Xavier's arms.

Liam had never really had friends like this before. People who were nice to him, just, well, for *him*. The only ones who knew who he was or how much he was worth were the Kents and somehow, Mack. He had no idea how the fucker had found out. He was sure neither Xavier or Mel had told him.

After Mack confronted him one night about his 'hidden identity,' Liam had done his own digging. Which was when he found out Mack had done hard time. An eight year sentence for attempted manslaughter.

Did the Kents know who exactly they had under their roof, hanging around their kids? Apparently they did. Or at least Xavier did. Xavier just waved him off and said not to worry about it when Liam tried to talk to him about it.

"I now pronounce you husband and wife. You may kiss the bride."

Everyone started cheering as Hunter dipped Isobel and planted one on her. It wasn't a quick peck either. Liam had to tug at his collar because damn. It had been too long since he'd had a warm woman wrapped around him. Far too long.

"There's a reception after this, eh?" Liam shouldered Jeremiah.

Jeremiah nodded. "At Bubba's."

"Classy."

Jeremiah punched his shoulder and they both got to their feet as the crowd stood up. Isobel and Hunter clasped hands and walked back down the aisle. Liam clapped along with everyone else. Even his cold, sarcastic little heart had to give it to them—those two crazy kids deserved their happy ending.

Liam thought his dad was a piece of work but he was fucking Gandhi compared to the sociopathic shitshow that was Isobel's stepmom. At least the bitch would be locked up for a while. She made some kind of plea deal so she didn't get the max sentence but when she got out, she'd be broke, alone, and friendless. Meanwhile Isobel had Hunter and the rest of them. And, ya know, half a billion dollars.

What more could you ask for in a happily ever after? You can bet the media ate that shit *up*. Liam had flown in his PR guy from Dublin to handle the spin. He was one of the few people Liam actually trusted from back home. Then again, bullshit was the guy's business, so it was entirely possible he was just better at buttering Liam up than everyone else.

That was the problem with money. You never know who was just begging to be bought. In his experience, everyone had a price.

Everyone.

But he was enjoying this little vacation to the wilds of America to pretend for a little while that they didn't.

And toward that end...

"I call dibs on the hot blonde in the pink dress," Liam said as they joined the sea of people crowding into the aisle to leave the church. He'd only meant for Jeremiah, Reece, and maybe Nicholas to hear.

Mack was several people in front of him but he turned around and glared. "Shut the fuck up. Women aren't meat." More and more

261

people crowded in from the side pews and Liam was forced to pause halfway down the aisle.

So he couldn't do anything but watch on as Mack plunged through the crowd—people had a habit of making way for a six foot giant covered in tattoos of gargoyles and monsters—and approached the woman in the body-hugging pink dress.

Liam's mouth dropped open and his blood spiked. That ruddy bastard—

Mack took the woman's hand and drew it to his lips. She blushed and as soon as Mack released her hand, started toying with her hair.

"Fucker," Liam whispered.

Mack dropped his hand to the small of the woman's back and ushered her out of the church.

"Oh you've done it now, boyo." Liam rubbed his hands together and then shook his arms out like he was getting ready for a jog. "Let the games begin."

Please consider leaving a few words in review at the retailer where you purchased this book.

Want to get news about all upcoming releases and the opportunity to access **FREE** Advanced Reader's Copies of all my future books (no spam, ever!)
www.stasiablack.com

OTHER NOVELS BY STASIA BLACK

Bay Area Bad Boys Series
Crush Me
Please Me
Scarlet (previously Woman Named Red)

Stud Ranch Series
The Virgin and the Beast (prequel)
Hunter
Ducking Ugly (Jan 2018)
Throw Down (Spring 2018)

Other
Daddy's Sweet Girl: A Dark Stepfamily Love Story

ACKNOWLEDGEMENTS

Aimee Bowyer, like always, you are my magical unicorn beta reader and this book was no exception. Thank you for working on crazy timelines even when your own life was upended to get this one back to me on a tight deadline. You always help me shape my stories and characters into deeper, more meaningful places.

Trisha Wolfe—thank you again for reading while you're on insane deadlines. Your feedback helped me with the last touchups to make this thing solid and I SO appreciate you! And I can't wait to read your next book – I need it NOW!

Belinda Donaldson, thank you for your amazing, lightning fast read on this one. I'm always so nervous sending books out to my first few readers and your quick response and encouragement means SO much.

This book would be an ugly mess of miscapitalizations, grammar mistakes, and missing words without the proofreading genius of Maria Pease from The Paisley Editor. She's awesome! Fellow authors, highest recommendations!

And thanks as always to super hubby, love of my life, shine in my star, google in my googolplex. Love you to friggin' pieces.

ABOUT STASIA

Stasia Black is an author who's drawn to romantic stories that don't take the easy way out. She wants to see beneath people's veneer and into their dark places, their twisted motives, and their deepest desires. She likes to toss her characters into the tempest and watch them hurt, fight, bleed, and then find out what, if anything, comes out the other side. Come along for the journey because it's one helluva ride.